THE MISSING WOMAN

The Missing Woman

PROLOGUE

Wilder Residence, The Emerald Pines Luxury Apartments; Downtown Seattle

FOR THE LAST COUPLE OF DAYS, THE SKY OVERHEAD HAS been blanketed in gray. Enough rain has fallen that I'm about ready to start gathering animals and build an Ark. The sky flashes brilliantly, and a moment later a peal of thunder crashes hard enough to rattle the windows. It's a dark, bleak evening, but it seems to match my mood pretty perfectly. Deciding to forgo normal lighting for the night, I lit half a dozen candles or so, leaving most of the apartment dim and gloomy. The soft glow of the candles is more soothing and relaxing than the normal lighting in my place.

I'm sitting on my sofa with my laptop sitting across my thighs, Miles Davis' music issuing softly from the speakers, and a glass of Merlot in hand. I'm waiting for her call. It still feels strange to have something red in my hand. For so many years, it was a color I shunned. A color I couldn't have anywhere around me. But my baby sister Kit, whom I thought long dead, miraculously turned up alive and well. Okay, maybe not entirely well. After hearing what her life was like the eighteen years she was missing, the person she'd been forced to become, and the things she'd been made to do—I know she won't be entirely well for a long, long time. Maybe not ever.

But she's alive. A very well-trained spy and assassin, but alive. It was Kit who did what Dr. Reinhart, my longtime therapist, has never been able to accomplish—get me over my aversion to the color red. The strange feeling about it still lingers, but Kit's return to my life and her assistance in taking down the organization responsible for the murder of our parents has healed me in ways I never expected. I've gone through my entire adult life trying to learn to cope with the tremendous loss of my childhood—my parents and my sister gone in one afternoon.

But in a matter of days of bonding and reconnecting with her, that hole in my heart—in my very soul—had started to heal. I'm not just coping with the pain of my loss anymore. I feel like I'm on the road to becoming whole again. I still have a lot of work to do on myself, but being whole is something I never thought would happen in my lifetime. I've never been so grateful.

The chime sounds on my laptop, informing me of an incoming video call. I punch the button to connect the call and Kit's smiling face fills my screen. I immediately start scanning the background, looking for any clues about her location—but as always, Kit has taken measures to keep her background entirely nondescript.

"Hey," I greet her. "How are you? Are you safe?"

"I'm good. And yes, I'm safe," she says with a patient smile. "And how are you? Catching bad guys?"

"Can't complain. Yeah, we've got a couple of cases we're working," I reply. "Where are you? Generally speaking."

Her smile is soft. "I'm around. You know I can't tell you that," she says. "It's for your safety and for mine."

"Yeah, I know. It'd just be nice if we could..."

I let my voice trail off without finishing the statement and take a swallow of wine instead. She knows what I wanted to say.

After we took down The Thirteen, the organization that had our parents murdered and kidnapped her, Kit had to flee. She double-crossed them to get revenge, but it put a target on her back. Given my position within the Bureau and the modest amount of celebrity I enjoy because of my work, I'm somewhat insulated from reprisals. But Kit isn't, and they're hunting her like a dog. I hate that she's on the run and can't settle down, but I know it's for her safety—and my own. I'm so glad she's alive, but we still can't be a family again. Not yet anyway.

The Thirteen has been broken and their power stripped from them, but there are still elements of it out there. We didn't get all the snakes in the nest, and those who survived the purge are lurking in the shadows just biding their time—including the individual who ordered the hit on our parents. I thought we got him, but Kit informed me otherwise. He's out there and he's hunting for her. And they won't stop until they kill her. As much as I want to say the Bureau can protect her, the truth is, I can't guarantee that. I know we have leaks and moles within the office—agents on the payrolls of some really bad people. It makes me sick, but it doesn't make it any less true.

"So, tell me what you're doing—wherever you are today," I smile.

"You mean besides avoiding men with big guns and bad intentions who are trying to murder me?" she replies with a laugh.

"Very funny," I say. "Honestly, Kit, I don't know how you can be so flippant about all of this. You are in very real danger."

Her face grows serious, and she looks at me through the screen. For all I know, she could be in the apartment next door, or she could be on another continent. But staring at her on a computer screen makes me feel like she's as far away as the moon. I'm her big sister and it's my job to take care of her. But it feels she's the one taking care of me by staying away and keeping the focus of the men pursuing her off me.

"I know I'm in danger—as are you," she reminds me. "But do you remember what Dad used to say about keeping things positive?"

I laugh softly, recalling the many pearls of wisdom our dad liked to dispense. That was always his thing. That, and being upbeat and positive.

"Letting circumstances dictate your mood and attitude only let those circumstances control you," she quotes.

I nod. "Yeah, I remember that one."

"Felt like he had a saying for every situation."

"I'm pretty sure he did," I reply.

We spend the next hour talking and laughing with one another as we reminisce about things we remember about our childhoods. Surprisingly enough, for having had as few years together as we had, we find a lot to talk about. We had a lot of shared memories and good times as children. And then our worlds were both upended.

"Well, I should get out of here. I've got a few things to do," she tells me. "But I'll check in with you in a couple of days."

I nod. "You better."

"I will. Love you, Sis," she says.

"Love you back."

She disconnects the call, leaving me sitting there looking at a blank screen. I swallow the last of my wine and realize I feel a bit lightheaded. Looking at the bottle on the coffee table, a slurred laugh bursts from my throat when I see that I've consumed the entire bottle. That would explain why I feel like I'm floating right now. Strangely enough, I don't feel nearly as drunk as I should be for having had a bottle of wine to myself.

I manage to set my laptop down on the coffee table without dropping it and lean my head back on the sofa cushions, staring up at the ceiling that seems to be swimming. I take a deep breath, close my eyes, and try to get myself back under control.

~

My eyes open slowly, but my vision is hazy and I'm dizzy. The one thing I'm acutely aware of, though, is the stench of smoke. It's thick and suffocating. My entire body aches and there's a sharp throbbing in the back of my head. It's a struggle just to get to my hands and knees. And when I finally manage it, I yelp in pain as the shattered remnants of a wine bottle dig into the palm of my hand.

"Dammit," I growl.

I raise my palm and pluck the shard of glass out of my hand. Blood flows from the wound and I'm transfixed by the crimson droplets spattering on the floor beneath me. Maybe it's because my ears are ringing, I'm wracked with pain, and my head is still fuzzy, that the flames starting to crawl up the walls around me took a back seat in my mind. But now, I look at the war room I'd set up in the spare room and watch as flickering fingers of orange flame crawl up the wall. The pictures and papers curl and turn black as they're consumed and the heat surrounding me is growing more intense by the minute.

I cough harshly. My throat feels like it's been scorched as my eyes water. Tears streak down my face and that lightheaded feeling comes back. I force it away as best I can, knowing I need to get out of here before the smoke overwhelms me. I push through the pain gripping my body and crawl on my hands and knees toward the door. Every time I put my injured hand down on the floor, an electric jolt of pain shoots through my body. But I keep moving, leaving a trail of bloody handprints behind me.

A coughing fit takes over; not even pulling my shirt up over my nose and mouth is helping to cut the smoke filling my lungs. My vision blurs and the dizziness grows stronger. The door still feels like it's a hundred miles away and I feel my strength ebbing. I fall onto my stomach and try to pull my body along the hardwood floor, trying to get to the doorway. But the heat all around me grows and sweat is slicking my body as darkness creeps in at the edge of my vision.

My body is wracked by coughing. My strength is rapidly fading and my field of vision narrows to a pinpoint. I try to hang on. Try to crawl for the door, but slump down. With my cheek pressed to the floor, the last thing I see is the charred and smoking remains of Willem Mangold's photograph drifting to the ground.

And then the darkness takes me.

CHAPTER ONE

Seattle Community Medical Center; Downtown Seattle

TRYING TO WAKE UP AND COME BACK TO MYSELF IS LIKE pushing through layers of something thick and gelatinous that makes it hard to breathe, let alone move. But my eyes eventually flutter, then open, and I find myself staring at the white acoustic tiles on the ceiling above me—and suddenly realize I have no idea where I am.

The light is harsh and sudden and I'm forced to close my eyes again for a moment. I try again, this time more careful to slowly slide my eyelids open so I can take in where I am. Turning my head is an exercise in torture that makes me groan miserably. But I see wires and tubes connected to just about every inch of my body on one end and machines on the other. I'm clearheaded enough to deduce that I'm in a hospital.

I slump back against the pillows, going back to staring at the ceiling because that takes the least amount of effort and causes the least amount of pain. The fluorescents above me are still too bright, though, making me wince. It's too much to deal with right now so I close my eyes again. They're more sensitive than normal, but seem to go hand in hand with the hard pounding inside my skull. If there's an area of my body that doesn't hurt, I don't know what it is. It feels like somebody hung me up like a piñata and invited the neighborhood kids to gleefully beat me with a baseball bat.

I rack my brain, trying to remember how I got here, but my memories are hazy and my brain is covered in fog. There's an opaque wall between my mind and my memories of what happened. I can see the shapes of them, but it's like looking at something through frosted glass. No matter how hard I strain my mind to break through that barrier, I can't. It does nothing but makes my head throb even harder. I gingerly touch the back of my head and feel a lump—and something crusty and moist. And when I look at my fingertips, I see smears of red.

My throat feels raw, and when I lapse into a coughing fit, that hurts too. Good to know my insides hurt as much as my outside. My mouth is gummy and I'm having trouble working up any saliva. I could really go for a glass of water right now. I give thought to getting up and trying to find something to drink, but the low, steady pulsing of pain that throbs throughout my entire body discourages that idea. So it looks like I survived whatever I went through and am now just going to lay here until I die of thirst.

Perfect.

A couple of moments later, the door opens and Amanda Gregory, a nurse who's treated me for my various workplace injuries on several occasions, bustles in. She's in her mid-forties, with dark hair cut in a bob and warm brown eyes. She's got smooth, pale skin, and a nearly ageless face that makes it nearly impossible to tell how old she is. I only know because she told me. But to look at her, you might say early-to-mid thirties. Maybe.

She sees me looking back at her and gives me a warm, genuine smile. "Well, look who's back. You gave us all a pretty good scare, Blake."

"Are you sure I'm not dead? I'm pretty sure this is what being dead feels like."

"And you think this is where the afterlife would drop you off?" she prods.

"Fair," I admit on a painful exhale.

Nurse Gregory steps to the side of my bed, checks all my vitals, and jots some notes down on her tablet. When she's done, she looks up and gives me a smile.

"What did I tell you the last time you came in with an injury?" she ponders aloud. "I mean, aside from telling you that you need to learn to move faster to avoid getting stabbed."

I laugh and immediately regret it as I'm wracked with pain. It's as if the fire still has a few embers lit inside of my lungs. I draw out a long, loud groan. "Don't make me laugh. It hurts."

"Well, what I told you is that pain is a good thing. It tells us we're alive and our bodies are healing," she tells me with a smile.

"Can't they heal without all the pain?"

Nurse Gregory laughs. "Not how it works, kiddo. But maybe if you stopped stepping into freight trains, you might not have to listen to my pearls of wisdom so often."

I give her a smile. "If not for you, I might not have any wisdom at all."

"Judging by how often you're in here, I'm not sure my wisdom is doing you much good anyway," she replies with a laugh. "Are you thirsty?"

"A couple fingers of bourbon?"

"Nice try. Best I can offer are some ice chips."

"Boring. But it'll do, I suppose," I wheeze. "How'd I get here, anyway?"

"Ambulance brought you in," she tells me. "Do you not remember?"

"Not a thing. It's like there's this big blank spot in my head."

She frowns for a moment. "Don't worry about it too much.

You took a pretty good knock on the head. When you have that sort of head trauma, you can sometimes suffer from temporary amnesia," she tells me. "You've got some bumps and bruises, a little smoke inhalation, and there's a good knot on the back of your noggin. Probably got it when you fell, and it opened a bit of a cut. But the good news is your CT scans came back clean and I'm sure your memories will come back in short order."

"I hope so. I hate not being able to remember anything."

The door to my room opens again and Astra steps in with a cup of coffee in hand, looking like she hasn't slept all night. She smiles wide and tries to act casual as she crosses the room, but I can see the look of relief in her eyes. Nurse Gregory gives me a smile and squeezes my hand.

"Your friend here has hardly left your side all night," Nurse Gregory notes.

"Just when I was hoping to get rid of her," I mutter. From the corner of my eyes, I see Astra rolling her own, but her mouth still breaks out into a smile.

"I'll go get those ice chips," she says.

"Thank you. And if you could slip just a little bit of bourbon into the cup, I would be forever grateful."

She laughs as she heads for the door. "Nice try, Agent Wilder."

Astra pulls the chair to the side of the bed the drops into it and takes my hand, giving it a firm squeeze. Even with all the pain in every square inch of me, it's good to feel her friendly touch. The look on her face tells me the situation is more serious than I thought. But she quickly covers it and offers me a sarcastic expression and her trademark smirk.

"How are you feeling?" she asks.

"Like hot, battered garbage."

"So, pretty much how you look."

I nod slowly, trying not to move too much. "Yeah. Pretty much."

"You really will do just about anything to get out of work, won't you?" she comments. "I just never expected you'd try to set yourself on fire. That's some serious commitment, babe."

"Set myself on fire?"

She nods. "Do you—"

I shake my head. "Don't remember anything, no. She said my CTs are clean and to expect that my memories will eventually return but right now, there's just nothing but a big blank spot in my head. How did I get here? Do you know?"

"Your neighbor, I think his name is Charlie—he's gorgeous by the way—"

"Charles. Yeah," I say. "He's SPD. One of the good ones."

"Right. Anyway, he came home from his shift, saw your door was ajar, and smelled smoke. He called it in then got you out of there," she tells me.

"You keep mentioning fire. What happened?"

She shrugs. "Near as anybody can tell at this point is that you were pretty liquored up and knocked over a candle in your war room. The room was damaged and all the evidence you have on your walls is gone, but it's mostly superficial. Charles pulled you out and got the fire out before things got bad. Thank God."

I shake my head and look down at the bandage around my hand. There's a twinge of pain when I flex my fingers, but I can't seem to recall how I injured it to begin with. And no matter how hard I push at that opaque wall of memories, the answer won't come. But then something she said stands out to me and I look at Astra.

"Why does everybody think I was all liquored up?" I ask.

"Because they found the remnants of a broken wine bottle on the ground where he found you," she tells me.

As if out of nowhere, an image flashes into my mind with startling clarity. It's my hand, but it's covered in blood, and the crimson drops on the floor beneath it seem especially vibrant. I look again at the bandage around my hand and frown. Slowly, I begin to recall pulling a shard of glass out of my palm and watching the blood flow from it.

That seems to line up with what Astra is saying. But why was I drinking in my war room? Another question that occurs to me is, why did I have candles in there as well? The war room isn't where I unwind with candles and wine. That's done in either my bathtub or in the living room. My war room is for work. Period. I've never sat back and relaxed in there. Nor do I get so inebriated at home, by myself, that I lose consciousness. Well, not usually. I'm in my thirties now. Astra and I used to get up to some pretty hard partying back in the day, but it's been a long, long time.

"Listen, I see that big brain of yours working and you need to stop. Relax. It was a stupid mistake," she orders me. "You'll heal up and be back on your feet in no time."

"Yeah, but there's so much that doesn't make sense to me."

"I knew you'd do this," Astra says with a grin.

"Do what?"

"Drum up some conspiracy in your head because you can't believe you'd be boneheaded enough to get hammered and knock over a candle," she replies dryly.

"I'm not drumming anything up. I'm just saying, some things don't really make sense to me about this whole scenario."

Astra gives me a patient smile. "You've had a lot on your plate this last year or so. I mean, a lot," she points out. "It's bound to take a toll on you. What you've been through—it's going to cloud your thinking and have you jumping at shadows. I think that's just natural, and you should take it easy on yourself."

I give her a soft smile. "So, what, you're some sort of psychological guru now or something?"

"I watched a few clips on YouTube, so I guess you could say I'm an expert in all things psychological now, yeah."

The pain grips me tightly when I laugh and my body clenches

up. The agony slowly subsides, and I slump back against the pillows feeling entirely wrung out.

"So, moving on to happier topics, why have you never mentioned your neighbor Charles before?" Astra asks.

"I thought you said we were moving on to happier topics."

"Oh, it could be a very happy topic if you let it be," she fires back.

I groan. "Do we have to talk about my love life while I'm still feeling medium-rare on the inside?"

Her eyes gleam in mischief. "Don't you know me, Blake? Of course we do."

"Yeah well, I'm abstaining from anything romantic. In case you haven't noticed, my taste in men is suspect. At best," I tell her. "Or did you forget my last boyfriend was inserted into my life to spy on me and then kill me if necessary?"

"Of course I didn't forget. But I mean, we've all had our fair share of bad exes," she chirps cheerily.

I try to level her with my best attempt to raise an eyebrow, but it hurts too much and I wince. "I think you're simplifying a bit."

"Well, Charles seems like a great guy. He's thoughtful and smart. He already seems to be into you and he's absolutely gorgeous," she tells me. "And he kind of saved your life."

"Which means he's probably got some fatal flaw somewhere and I should just stay away from him."

Astra rolls her eyes and laughs but then her expression grows serious as she looks at me. She leans a little closer and grips my hand tighter.

"Blake, I know how hard things have been for you lately. But even before we found out about what Mark was really up to, I could tell you weren't happy for a while. I just want you to be able to open yourself up instead of losing yourself in work all the time. You deserve that."

The corners of my mouth curl slightly upward as I take in what she's saying but I don't say anything. What is there to say? After what happened with Mark, I honestly don't know that I can trust myself when it comes to men. My entire dating history has been a series of poor decisions. None of them have ever been nearly as bad as Mark, but it's been a seemingly endless string of bad decisions, nonetheless.

I consider myself a naturally intuitive person. I usually know when somebody's lying to me, which is helpful in my line of work. So I don't know what it is that doesn't allow me to see the red flags about a guy until it's too late. It's crazy, but it's been this way my entire life—just a constant string of horrible misses. Mark put me over the top though. To have missed on a guy that badly was embarrassing.

"But anyway, the good news is that you're going to have the next week to get to know Charles. And I want you to take advantage of the time—"

"Wait… what are you talking about?"

"Rosie asked me to deliver the news that you're not to come into the office for the next week," she tells me.

"What? That's ridiculous," I groan, my tone growing hot. "I'll be fine. The doctors already said so. I don't need—"

"Whoa there, girl, let's back that pony up," she cuts me off. "I'm just delivering the message."

"We'll see about that. A week off. That's a load of crap," I grumble. "I'll be in just as soon as I'm discharged."

"Yeah, about that," Astra says with a grimace. "She's already put a flag on your ID. You're not going to be able to get into the office."

I roll my eyes and let out a frustrated sigh. Rosalinda Espinoza—Rosie to most of us—is our boss. She's the top cop in our field office, the Special Agent in Charge, or SAC. Rosie is a good woman, a legendary agent, and one hell of an amazing boss—but also, sometimes, an absolute thorn in my rear end. And when she wants me to take time off, she's gotten into the habit of deactivating my ID—which bars me from entering the field office. She thinks she's clever.

"You can use the time off, boss," Astra insists. "Rest. Relax.

Try to get your head and your body right. And if someone tips off a super-hot cop neighbor of yours to come visit, don't come blaming me."

I laugh softly. "Don't you dare."

"What are you gonna do? Stop me?"

"Maybe I should have stayed in the fire," I grumble. Astra throws her head back in laughter, clearly taking utter delight in torturing me.

"For real, Blake. Relax. R-E-L-A-X. Look it up in the dictionary if you have to."

"I don't want to relax, I want to get back to work."

"Well, too bad, you have no choice," she offers. "I'm actually considering shooting myself in the foot to get a little time off myself."

"How about I save you the trouble and shoot you myself?"

"Well, I can see you're getting back to your normal, cranky self," she grins. "You're right, I think you'll be right as rain pretty quick."

I give her a smile. "Thanks for being here, Astra," I say sincerely. "I'm sure Benjamin would love to have you home."

"Benjamin has me at home every night. He knows what's important."

"He's a good man."

Astra nods. "He is. The best, in fact. But there are more like him out there."

I wince but can't stop my laughter. "You just can't help yourself, can you?"

"Not until I have you all wifed up."

"Stop," I cry. "It hurts too much to laugh."

"They say it's the best medicine."

"I think they lied."

Astra gets to her feet and gives my hand another squeeze. "Rest up and get back on your feet soon," she tells me. "We need you back. I love Rosie but I don't love her running the show."

"Oh, God."

"Exactly."

"I'll be back soon," I tell her.

"I'm counting on it. We all are."

Astra leaves and I close my eyes, feeling absolutely wiped out. I try to hold on until Nurse Gregory comes back with the ice chips, but my grip on consciousness slips, and I plunge back into the darkness of sleep.

CHAPTER TWO

Wilder Residence, The Emerald Pines Luxury Apartments; Downtown Seattle

THE SMELL OF SMOKE IS STILL THICK IN THE AIR, SO I WALK around my apartment, opening every window I have. After two days in the hospital, they finally discharged me—likely because they got tired of listening to me complain about wanting to be discharged. The first second I got out of antiseptic purgatory, I made a beeline for home. I wanted to see just how bad the damage is and see if I can put together what the hell happened the other night.

After getting some air flowing through my place, I stand in the doorway to my war room. It's not as bad as I feared, but that isn't saying it's good either. Three of the walls are blackened, the papers I had tacked to the wall are all gone, a few of the boxes are charred, and most of the others have water damage and can't be salvaged. Everything I'd collected on the Thirteen and that whole investigation has literally gone up in smoke. It's a good thing I have everything backed up and stored at the apartment in Chinatown that Fish is letting me use.

I pace around the room looking at the ruin that's been left

behind. The light slanting in through the window glints off the fragments of glass that are scattered about on the ground. The shards are all dark green—like a wine bottle. And in the corner on the charred remains of a table are the dried and hardened pools of wax studded with jagged pieces of the candle jar. I walk the perimeter of the room and knock on the walls. My hand goes through the drywall in a couple of places, but everything still seems solid. Thankfully.

From all appearances, I can see why the initial assumption is that I got drunk and set the fire. For the millionth time, I strain to try to remember what happened that night but come up empty. If it still wasn't so sore I'd beat my head against the wall to see if anything shakes out. No matter what I do, I can't remember what happened. Frustrated, I kick at the remnants of the bottle on the ground.

"There's that temper I've heard so much about."

I wheel around, my hand automatically going to my hip where I usually keep my weapon holstered. The man standing in the doorway raises his hands to show he's not a threat. But I'm not carrying at the moment, so my holster isn't on my hip, which makes the man chuckle.

"Don't shoot. I come in peace," he announces.

Feeling foolish, I drop my hand when I see it's my neighbor Charles Kragen, one of SPD's finest. Not that that's saying much, but he really is a good guy. He's standing there with a wide grin on his face.

"What are you doing here, Charles?"

He gestures back toward the living room. "The door was open."

"So, you just walk right on in?" I grumble. "A little presumptuous to invite yourself in like that, don't you think?"

He shrugs. "Well, you're not usually careless enough to leave your door open so when I saw it open again, I was concerned," he points out. "I mean, the last time your door was open, and I invited myself in, I kind of saved you from burning to a crisp."

A wry grin touches my lips as I look down at the shards of glass on the ground again. I really can't say much to that because he's right. He did save my life. I run a hand through my hair and give him a sheepish smile.

"Yeah, I guess I kind of owe you," I admit.

He waves me off and flashes me a smile. "All in a day's work."

"And all without a rubber suit and a cape. Impressive."

"It's at the dry cleaner. Blood's pretty tough to get out of a cape."

I laugh and shake my head. In all the time I've lived here, this is probably the longest conversation I've had with Charles. We see each other in passing and greet one another, but that's been about it. He's a handsome man and cuts a striking figure. Six-three, with dark hair, green eyes, a strong jawline, and chiseled features. With broad shoulders, a thick barrel chest, and arms as big around as my thigh, it's obvious that Charles works out. A lot. But he's never come across as one of those douchey gym-bro types. In fact, in the few interactions I've had with him, he's actually been pretty humble for a man as good-looking as he is.

"Well, thank you for pulling me out before I got barbecued," I tell him.

"Not a problem. It's the neighborly thing to do, right?"

"Yeah, but let's hope I don't ever have to return the favor."

"Let's hope not," he says with a grin. "So, what happened in here?"

I shrug. "I guess I had a little too much to drink and knocked over a candle."

"That's what they're saying, yeah. But what really happened?"

I pick up the half of a photo of Willem Mangold that hadn't burned. The edges are blackened and crispy, but half of his face is still visible, and his eye seems to be boring into me. Mangold is a man without conscience or mercy, but he's also a man sitting in prison, where he'll be for a long time. But even behind bars, I know he's still a threat. Especially to Kit. There's a part of me that wishes I had pulled the trigger the night we took him down. But as soon as the thought crosses my mind, I push it aside. That's not me. I know I wouldn't have been able to live with myself if I'd killed him in cold blood like that.

I shake my head. "I honestly don't know. I can't remember anything about that night," I shrug. "Temporary amnesia. The doctors say my memories will return eventually but it might take a little time."

"That's a rough break."

"Tell me about it," I reply.

Charles purses his lips. "I mean, I don't really know you or anything, but you've never struck me as the blackout drunk kind of person."

"That's because I'm not," I tell him. "But I've had a lot on my plate lately. A lot of things going on. So, I'm guessing I just got carried away the other night."

He nods. "That happens once in a while. We all go through things sometimes."

"Yeah, I suppose. But not everybody nearly burns their apartment down."

He laughs softly. "That's true too."

"It's kind of embarrassing, truth be told."

"Don't worry, only half the SPD and a couple of fire companies know about it," he says. "I'm sure word of this won't spread too far."

I roll my eyes. "Great. Thanks. That's very comforting."

"I do my best."

I drop the picture in my hand and walk out of my war room and out to the kitchen. Charles follows me out and leans against the counter as I open the refrigerator and pull out a couple bottles of water and hold one out to him. He accepts it with a word of thanks and we both take a minute to take a drink. I lean back against the counter across from him.

"So, what are you going to do?" he asks.

"Guess I'm going to have to get a contractor in here to fix the room," I say. "Shouldn't be too bad. Thanks to you, the fire didn't burn long enough to do any structural damage."

"Just glad to help," he replies. "Do you have a contractor?"

I shake my head. "I figure I'll do a little research online. Yelp's usually pretty helpful."

"Oh God, no. Don't do that," he says. "People on Yelp don't know what they're talking about. You're more likely going to get somebody who will end up doing the structural damage you just avoided."

I laugh. "Well, I'm no good with a hammer. Construction really isn't my forte."

"Don't worry. I've got a guy. My brother-in-law, actually, but he does good work," he says. "I'll get you his name and number."

"Thank you," I reply. "Seems like I owe you more than one."

"Well, I'd be willing to let you take me out for a drink to repay my kindness."

My smile is weak and faltering and I look down at the floor. I hoped it would be otherwise, but I had a feeling things were going this way, and now that we're here, I feel uncertain. Charles really does seem like a great guy—which means there's probably some red flag waving somewhere that I'm missing. I give him a small smile and judging by the look on his face, he knows I'm about to turn him down.

"Remember when I said I had a lot on my plate lately?"

He nods. "Yeah."

"Had a really bad end to a relationship," I tell him. "I mean really bad."

"Like, move to another state, scary stalker ex kind of bad?"

I frown, knowing I can't tell him much. I don't even know him. But I opened the door to the question, so I need to say something or it's going to seem like I'm just brushing him off and he deserves better than that.

"No, he—he was murdered," I say. It's not the whole truth, but it is the truth.

Charles can't hide the surprise on his face but he's able to quickly cover it. He clears his throat and looks down at the floor, clearly a little uncomfortable with the unexpected turn the conversation took. But he looks up at me and I see understanding in his eyes.

"I get it," he says. "That's really rough."

"Yeah, it's not easy. And you seem like a really nice guy, Charles," I tell him. "To be honest, I'm a mess and wouldn't want to inflict myself on you right now. Not until I get my head sorted out anyway."

"That's fair," he says. "And hey, if you get your head sorted out, give me a call. That offer of a drink is good anytime."

"I'll keep that in mind."

He raises his bottle of water to me and smiles before turning and walking toward the front door.

"Don't forget to close and lock your door," he calls over his shoulder.

I smile and follow him out, closing and locking the door behind him. That done, I head back into the kitchen and grab another bottle of water from the refrigerator. I drain the last of my first bottle then drink down half of the second. Setting the bottle down on the counter, I start to pace around my apartment, feeling restless. It's been an hour and I feel like the walls are closing in on me already.

I know I should be taking it easy and resting. But I can't quiet my brain or settle my body down enough to do that. So, I do the only thing I can think of right now. I get changed into some grubby clothes then head into my war room are start picking up the disaster area it is. The least I can do is make sure it's clean and debris-free for when the contractor comes.

"Dear God, I'm not going to survive a week of this," I mutter to myself.

CHAPTER THREE

SSA Wilder's Office, Criminal Data Analysis Unit; Seattle Field Office

"SORRY I'M ONLY JUST NOW ABLE TO GET IN TOUCH WITH you. I was out of touch for a bit," Kit says. "But are you all right? I heard what happened."

"How in the world did you hear what happened?"

She shrugs. "Do you really think I don't know how to keep track of what's going on in my big sister's life?"

I laugh. "I suppose not."

I lean back in my chair and look at Kit's face on the computer screen. I'd gotten in the building before everybody just so I could go through everything and get myself up to speed before the official start of the day. I called Rosie last night just to be sure she cleared my ID so I could get into the building. Thankfully, it worked. I honestly half-expected her to keep me on the bench a little while longer.

Within five minutes of me getting into my office, though, Kit sent me a video conference request. Which is kind of sweet, but kind of creepy at the same time. As usual, the background of her video call is wholly generic. This time it's just a blank white wall that could be literally anywhere in the world. There is absolutely no way I can tell where she is. There are no hints and no clues that might tip me off to where she is.

Kit obviously has a way of keeping tabs on me though. But for the life of me, I can't figure out what it is or how she's doing it. And she's certainly not telling me. I kind of think she enjoys playing the mysterious superspy and keeping me on my toes. It's just as blank as my memories from the night of the fire.

"So? What happened?" she presses.

"I don't know. I guess I had a few too many and I passed out. I must have knocked over a candle or something because my war room went up in flames."

"Well, I wasn't going to say anything, but you did seem to be hitting the wine pretty hard that night," she tells me.

I cock my head. "Wait, what? We talked that night?"

"You don't remember?"

I shake my head. "No. The whole night is a blank," I tell her. "The doctors told me it's temporary and my memories will come back, but right now it's just a big blank spot."

"Wow," she comments, sounding worried. "They ran a CT and all that?"

"Yeah, they ran every test. Twice."

"That's scary, Sis," she sighs. "But yeah, we talked for a while that night. I just noticed that you were drinking a little more wine than usual. I didn't think anything of it or I would have said something."

"Huh. Well, that's one piece of the puzzle," I reply. "But anyway, I'm fine. I've been cleared, I'm back at work, it's all good."

"Well, it's not all good until your memories come back."

"Near enough then," I tell her. "Where are you, Kit?"

"Narnia," she replies without missing a beat.

I laugh. "Funny."

"I try," she chirps. "You promise you're all right?"

"Swear it."

"Good. That's a relief," she tells me. "Do me a favor and stop doing stupid stuff. I don't want to have to keep worrying about you."

"I'll do my best, Kit."

She purses her lips and looks at me. "I guess that'll have to do," she says. "Anyway, I'm sorry but I have to run. I just wanted to check in on you."

"Thanks, Kit. I appreciate it."

"I'll get in touch with you soon."

"You better."

"Love you, Blake."

"Love you back."

She smiles and then the screen goes dark as she disconnects the call. I think about it for a moment and try once again to cut through the haze of my memory with the new information about talking to Kit that night added into the mix. I still come up with nothing, though. I'd hoped that nugget of information would open to door to remembering what happened that night. But it does absolutely nothing to jump-start my brain. Trying not to dwell on it too much, I mutter a curse as I open my email. And then mutter another curse as I start going through my correspondence for the last week.

"It's going to take me a week just to get through all this garbage," I mutter.

But this is why I came in early—to get some things done. So, I spent the next hour replying to some of the most pressing emails, flagging others to be dealt with later, and deleting a bunch of garbage emails. The amount of stupid, sexist jokes people pass around is alarming. HR would have a field day with some of this crap.

Just when I feel like I'm about to go cross-eyed and then blind from reading all these stinking emails, I see Rick walk through the doors to the CDAU. It's all I can do to keep from jumping up and rushing out there to whoop it up with him. But I vowed to maintain my dignity, and so I wait. Rick gives me a wave as he walks to his workstation, so I return it, trying to look as casual and not as excited to be here as I can. It's just another day in the shop. There really is nothing to be too excited about. Except for the fact that this is my first time in the shop in over a week and I'm glad to be back. Sitting around doing nothing all day has been killing me; I'm itching to get back to it. But I'm going to wait until everybody's in before I go rushing out there to make a fool of myself.

Astra and Mo saunter in about twenty minutes later and I give them a moment to settle in before I get up and walk out of my office. I casually go to the small kitchen area set off to the side of the room and pour myself a cup of coffee before walking back over to them. Astra is giving me a grin, looking like the cat that ate the canary. Mo and Rick are pointedly trying to avoid looking at me, which immediately tells me something's up.

"What?" I ask suspiciously.

"We all chipped in and got you a gift to welcome you back," Astra chirps.

She slips an envelope out of her bag and hands it over to me. Still eyeballing them closely, I set down my coffee mug and open the envelope. And inside, I find a fifty-dollar gift certificate to a local boutique candle shop.

"We thought you might want to get some new candles since you burned up all your other ones," she says, snorting as she laughs.

"I'll have you know I voted for new smoke detectors. Safety first and all," Rick calls. "But I was voted down."

"They've also got safety sconces that prevent the candles from setting anything on fire if you knock them over," Mo adds.

"Et tu, Mo?" I ask. "I would have expected this from those two, but you?"

She tries to speak, but it devolves into a fit of laughter. I can't help but join them. These guys are clowns, but they've become like a second family to me. And ragging on each other is just one of those sacred family traditions that we all observe.

"Well, I'm glad you guys can have a good laugh about my traumatic, near-death experience," I say. "I'll keep it in mind during performance reviews."

"But it was only near-death. You're alive and standing here in front of us," Astra counters. "Therefore, we are allowed to have a laugh about it. Don't blame me, it's in the rules."

"You're such a jerk," I reply with a smile.

"I think it's important that we laugh at life's tragedies—and near tragedies," Mo says.

"Exactly right," Astra nods. "It's why Rick's mom laughed at him so much growing up."

"To be fair, it wasn't just when I was growing up," he chimes in. "She still laughs at me."

"See?" Astra asks with a wide grin.

The laughter filling the room tapers off as the doors to the CDAU slide open with a pneumatic hiss. I turn to see Rosie step in. She's walking with a purpose and carrying a folder in her hand, which tells me she's not here to deliver another gift certificate for candles.

"Blake, welcome back," she greets me.

"Thanks for reactivating my ID badge," I reply.

"It would be nice if I didn't have to take the measures I do just to ensure you're taking care of yourself," she remarks pointedly.

I grimace but hide it with a laugh, feeling like I've just been chastised by the principal. "And here I'd think you'd want dedicated agents who love their work."

"Oh, I do. I just don't like having them drop dead while on duty. That makes me look bad," she says, then turns to the room. "Well, it sounds like everybody's having a good time."

"Just welcoming back our fearless leader," Astra says.

"Funny, so am I," Rosie responds and thrusts the folder into my hands.

I give Rosie a grin and open the file. There are only a few pages in it, which tell me this case is fresh and all we have is the police report to work with. I scan the page and take in the scant details we have.

"Valerie Osweiler, forty-three years old. She's been missing for two days," I read aloud. "Labor attorney, resides in the Windermere neighborhood."

"Oh, she's one of the fancy folk," Astra whistles. "No wonder you walked that down here personally, Rosie."

Rosie has mastered the art of being able to give looks so scorching they can curdle milk. And when she turns, delivering one of her patented milk-curdling glares, Astra blanches before my very eyes.

"Valerie is a prominent labor attorney here in Seattle and her husband is an Assistant District Attorney," Rosie explains. "She was supposed to appear in DC but never showed. Turns out she never got on her plane, which has plenty of people worried, as you can imagine."

"No wonder they're pulling out all the stops," I reply.

"Big-time labor lawyer and an ADA," Astra says. "Talk about a power couple,"

"They are," Rosie nods. "She's won some big cases against some big companies—"

"And probably made some big enemies in the process," I muse.

Rosie nods. "Yeah, more than likely. Anyway, she was being vetted for a spot in the DOJ, so she's a high-profile personality," she goes on. "The Director wants my best team on it. But since Murphy and his guys are busy on another case, I'm giving it to you."

Astra, Mo, Rick, and I all turn to her in unison, matching expressions of shock on our faces. Rosie turns to each of us, her face completely deadpan, but then she can't help herself and bursts into laughter. Astra and I exchange a glance and we both roll our eyes, which makes Rosie laugh even harder.

"Your faces—priceless," Rosie says. "Just priceless."

"Boss-lady's got jokes today," Astra responds with a grin.

My team and I pride ourselves on being the best-specialized unit not just in the Seattle field office, but in the entire Bureau. We take on big cases, work hard, and get results. We take what we do seriously and we're proud of our track record, so we don't really like it when our status as the best is questioned. Still, we probably should learn to lighten up a bit.

Rosie finally gets herself back under control and wipes away the tears of mirth that had spilled down her cheeks. She takes a breath and lets it out, calm once again, though she still looks amused and pretty proud of herself. I don't think I've ever seen her laugh that hard.

"Anyway," she says. "There are a lot of eyes on this one so it's the priority in your caseload right now. Find this woman, and"—she cuts another milk-curdling glare over to me—"for God's sake, play by the rules."

I look at Rosie, an expression of faux offense on my face. "When have you ever known us to not play by the rules?"

She doubles down, somehow managing to make her expression even more withering. "By the book, Wilder. I mean it."

I snap her a salute. "Ma'am, yes, ma'am."

Rosie turns and leaves the CDAU so we can get started. I read over the file once more just to see if there's anything pertinent I need to know nestled in among the information we have, paltry though it is. I close the file and look up.

"All right. Let's get started. Mo, I want you to do a full workup on Mrs. Osweiler. I want any and all financial transactions and cell phone records," I tell her.

"On it," Mo responds.

"Rick, I want a trace on all her electronic devices—phone, tablets, vehicle GPS—the works," I say. "I want to know everywhere she's been over the last—let's start with the past week. We'll work back from there if necessary."

"Roger that."

"And Astra, you're with me," I say. "We're going to go have a chat with Mr. Osweiler."

"Let's go," she responds as she jumps to her feet.

CHAPTER FOUR

Osweiler Residence; Windermere District, Seattle

"I'M TELLING YOU RIGHT NOW, THE HUSBAND DID IT," ASTRA comments as I pull the car to a stop at the curb in front of the Osweiler home.

I turn off the engine, then look at her sitting there on the passenger's seat looking for all the world like she's already cracked this case. I grin and shake my head.

"What makes you say that?" I ask.

"The husband always does it. Don't you ever watch Dateline?"

I laugh. "That's not even remotely close to being true."

"Fine. The husband often does it or is somehow involved," she amends her statement.

"You shouldn't be pre-judging the case."

"I'll bet you fifty bucks that Mr. Scott Osweiler has played a role in Mrs. Valerie Osweiler's disappearance."

"You're on," I grin.

We shake hands and climb out of the car. I probably shouldn't be encouraging Astra to gamble on the outcome of our cases, but she's a talented investigator and a person who isn't afraid to say she's wrong. I admire that about her. There are too many people who will never admit they're wrong or that they made a mistake. Instead, some of them double down on it and get straight up belligerent if you call them out. Not Astra, though. She's usually the first to admit that she screwed up.

Standing on the sidewalk, I look around and notice that the neighborhood is filled with large homes that while not necessarily opulent are obviously upper-class. Windermere may not have the fancy mansions and sprawling estates you'd find in a place like Laurelhurst or Denny-Blaine, but there is a lot of money here. You can practically smell it. Last I checked, the median household income is around one million annually—a fact reflected by the number of Beemers, Mercedes, Porsches, Jaguars, and other high-end cars in the driveways and on the street.

The street itself is lined with large oak trees that have wide, thick trunks. The trees are so old their boughs are growing into one another, forming a natural tunnel of greenery overhead. The street is quiet. The only sound I can hear is from a couple of dogs barking in the distance and the rumbling of a gardener's lawnmower.

The Osweiler house is a large, two-story Mediterranean-style job that's got the classic stucco, red clay tile roof, with wrought iron fencing and grills on the large windows on both floors. The front façade has three wide, ornate archways with the front door positioned in the middle and is flanked by a pair of potted Mediterranean fan palms.

"Gorgeous place," Astra says.

I nod. "It really is."

We climb the stairs that lead us to the porch. The front door is mostly glass and wrought iron, allowing us to see straight into the round foyer that looks made of some marble that probably costs more than I'll make in a lifetime. A large round wooden table stands in the center of the foyer with a crystal chandelier hanging above it. Behind the table is a wide marble staircase, and to either side of the foyer is a door. I reach over and ring the bell.

A few moments later, a frazzled-looking man wearing sweatpants and a faded blue Seahawks t-shirt opens the door. He's tall—six-one, trim and muscular, with dark hair that's flecked with gray, a few days' worth of stubble on his chin, and green eyes that are bloodshot and filled with worry. There are dark circles beneath his eyes, his hair is standing up in a thousand different directions, and he's got a haunted expression on his face. He looks like a man who hasn't slept in days. He probably hasn't.

The fear radiating from him is palpable. It's making the air around us feel heavy and tense, which is understandable, given what's happening. He's looking at us like we're here to tell him that his wife is dead which, is also understandable.

"Mr. Osweiler?" I ask.

"Yes," he responds. "And you are?"

We both badge him. "SSA Wilder, Special Agent Russo. May we come in?"

He looks at us both for a long moment in silence. I can see him calculating the odds that we're here to give him the death notification versus us being here for any other reason. Osweiler apparently decides the odds are better that we're here for some other reason because he finally lets out a long breath and opens the door, waving us in.

"Yeah, sure. Come in," he says.

He walks off without waiting for us, so Astra closes the door behind us, and we follow him through a doorway to our left. We pass what looks like a formal sitting room and continue down a hallway lined with exquisite pieces of artwork. Whoever decorated the house has fantastic taste, I'll give them that. The décor is understated, rather than opulent and gaudy. The Osweilers obviously aren't the kind who need to display their wealth by gold-plating everything like some people I've seen.

The hallway opens up to the back of the house, which has a wide-open floor plan. To our right, a plush sectional sofa with a chaise lounge sits across from a matching loveseat, separated by an elegant wood and glass coffee table. A massive high-def television hangs on the wall above a fireplace and is currently tuned to SportsCenter with the sound muted. Rumpled pillows and blankets are piled up on the sofa, telling me Mr. Osweiler is sleeping down here—or rather, is watching TV all night down here.

To our left is a large kitchen with an enormous island in the center. Bar stools line one side of it and there is a sink on the right-hand side of the island. It looks like it would be fantastic for entertaining. The kitchen is filled with state-of-the-art appliances that are all very sleek and clean. Unlike the homes of many other wealthy people I've been in, this one actually looks like it gets some use.

The flooring is all lightly colored Saltillo tile that's gorgeous. Large area rugs, all loudly colorful but tasteful, cover the floors beneath the sofa and a dining area on the other side of the room that contains a table big enough to hold six. The entire back wall is made up of sliding glass doors that open to a covered outdoor living room that has sets of sofas, another television like the one inside, and another table big enough to hold twelve. There's also a kitchen on the far side that looks like a smaller version of the one inside. This must be where they entertain in the warmer months.

Osweiler opens the back doors to let a little fresh air in and invites us outside. The air inside is a little stale and musty, and I have no trouble picturing him sitting here on the sofa, watching the TV without really seeing it, desperately hoping for word about his wife—and at the same time, fearing the word he'll get. Those are feelings I can understand and relate to. He turns and gestures to one of the outdoor sofas.

"Please," he says. "Have a seat."

"Thank you, Mr. Osweiler," I reply.

We sit down on the sofa, which is a lot softer than I imagined.

It's a really nice couch. Astra must be thinking the same thing because she's looking down at it with a crooked grin on her face. But then she looks at me and quickly gathers herself. She's all business again. Mr. Osweiler sits on the sofa across from us and folds his hands in his lap. He's nervous and plucks at some bit of invisible lint on his pants. He takes a beat then looks up at us.

"You have a beautiful home, Mr. Osweiler," Astra starts.

"Thank you," he replies. "Valerie has good taste. Always has."

He looks down at his hands, which he's wringing furiously in his lap. I'm quick to note that he's speaking of Valerie in the present tense. It's not definitive of course, but sometimes people will slip up and refer to somebody they've killed or had a hand in killing in the past tense. It's an unconscious thing, a slip of the tongue, but it can sometimes be telling. Like I said though, it's not definitive, because somebody aware of that tell can modify their speech. And I'd guess that an Assistant District Attorney would be aware of that.

"So, Mr. Osweiler, we'd like to ask you some questions," I start.

"Please, call me Scott," he says. "And I already went over everything with the police—"

"I understand, Mr.—Scott," I say. "But we'll be handling your wife's case from here on out. Given your wife's profile and the fact that she is being vetted for a position in the DOJ, the Director of the Bureau himself asked us to look into her disappearance."

At the word 'disappearance', Scott chokes up and his eyes well with tears. He holds a hand over his mouth and tries to stifle a sob. I watch him closely, looking for his tells. For any sign that this is just performative. But as I study him, my initial take is that this is genuine. I don't see any sign of deception, no hint that his emotions are an act for our benefit. To me, this looks like a man in unadulterated pain.

"We're sorry to have to put you through all of this again," Astra tells him. "But we just need a little background to get us caught up with the case. Again, we're sorry but it is necessary that we get as much information as we can."

Osweiler takes a moment and composes himself. He scrubs away the tears that had rolled down his cheeks and sniffs loudly, then runs a hand through his hair and finally turns his gaze back to us, looking like he's aged ten years in the past ten minutes.

"It's all right. It's fine. Ask your questions," he states firmly. "I'll do whatever I have to do and talk to whoever I need to talk to if it means getting Valerie back."

"Good. Thank you," I say. "And am I correct in assuming you haven't received any ransom demands?"

He shakes his head. "No. Nothing. It's just been radio silence."

"And when did you last speak with her?" Astra asks.

"The morning she left for the airport," he tells us. "She was catching an early flight to DC that day."

"And you didn't take her to the airport?" Astra asks.

"No, I had a deposition that morning," he says. "She called an Uber to take her."

I shift on my seat and look down, an awkward silence stretching out between us for a moment. I finally clear my throat and raise my gaze to his.

"Mr. Osweiler, I'm sorry I have to ask—"

"Scott," he reminds me. "And no, we weren't having any marital troubles. Our marriage was good. Strong. We weren't having any issues."

I laugh softly and nod. "I suppose you're used to these sorts of interviews."

"Yeah. Just not on from this side of the table. And before you ask, no, neither one of us was having an affair," he states.

There's a momentary flicker in his eyes and a tightness in his tone that makes me think he might not be so sure about that. Osweiler licks his lips nervously and then the expression is gone from his face as though it had never been there. It's quick enough that I think I may have imagined the expression, but I can't confidently say one way or the other. I glance at Astra to see if she picked up on it, but her face is blank. Expressionless. It makes me think I might have imagined it.

I clear my thoughts and purse my lips. It's hard to ask questions designed to give us a chance to gauge a person's response if they know what questions are coming and beat you to the punch. Osweiler is most definitely familiar with all the tricks and traps investigators use, which makes my note about him using the proper tense when speaking about her earlier completely irrelevant. Astra glances at me and I can see she seems to be thinking along similar lines.

"Given what she does for a living, I'm sure she's made some enemies along the way," I say. "Are there any that stand out in your mind?"

He shakes his head. "She's had some run-ins with the Armenian mob. She's won a few cases against companies run by the Yakuza and the Chinese Triads. None of those made her a very popular figure. But I can't say any one of them were making a real run at her."

"She really knows how to pick her battles," Astra muses.

"She really does," he replies.

"Did she ever receive threats?" I ask. "Phone calls, emails, letters—anything like that?"

"Oh, she got plenty of each. She recorded her calls and saved all the written correspondence," he tells us. "I'll make sure I put together copies of everything for you."

"I appreciate that, Mr.—Scott," I say. "Tell me, is there anybody from your own caseload you think might want to hurt you by taking Valerie?"

"My caseload?"

Astra nods and picks up on my train of thought. "Being an ADA, I'm sure you've dealt with your share of unsavory characters," she says. "Do any of them stand out? Are there any you can think of who might want to hurt you personally?"

He scoffs. "I'm sure most of them want to hurt me personally. But there are very few who have the stomach to actually do anything," he replies. "Most of them are gutless turds who talk a bit game but rarely have the stones to follow through with their threats."

"Even still, it's an avenue we need to explore," I tell him. "So if you have any correspondence or messages from your own work, we'd like copies of those too."

"Sure, of course. I don't think you're going to find anything in them though," he says, his voice growing strained and a little impatient. "I never handled anything too controversial. I think it might be a waste of time—time my wife doesn't have."

"I understand, Mr. Osweiler," I say. "But we need to be diligent and thorough."

He grits his teeth and looks like he's on the verge of arguing with me, but he bites it back and lets out a deep breath. Osweiler finally nods.

"Yeah, of course. Whatever it takes. I'll get them over to you ASAP," he relents. "I just want my wife back."

"We're going to do everything we can, Mr. Osweiler. I promise you that."

"I appreciate that. And if I can ask, please keep me in the loop."

"We will."

We spend another half an hour peppering him with questions, most of them designed to get a reaction from him. As much as I hate to agree with Astra, she is right. The vast majority of women who go missing or turn up dead end up being killed by their spouse or significant other. There's a reason people say the first person you look at is the husband or boyfriend. It's unfortunately not entirely inaccurate.

After getting all, we can out of him—at least for now—Astra

and I take our leave. He escorts us to the door and sends us off with another plea to find his wife. I look over at her as we walk to the car.

"So? Still think he's involved?" I ask.

She shrugs. "I don't think we can rule him out just yet. Familiar with our line of questioning or not, he sure did offer up some personal information pretty fast," she notes. "Call me a cynic, but telling us that things were great in his marriage and that neither of them were having an affair as quick as he did set a couple of red flags waving in my head."

I nod as we get into the car. She's not wrong. That he offered up that information as quickly as he did pinged me pretty hard too. It could simply be Osweiler expediting the questions he knew would be coming to save time. I mean, he's not wrong about Valerie being on borrowed time either. But she's been missing for three days already, and part of me fears her clock has already run out.

CHAPTER FIVE

Criminal Data Analysis Unit; Seattle Field Office

"So? How'd things go with the husband?" Mo asks as we walk back into the office.

"Inconclusive," I reply. "Still too early to speculate."

"That's her way of saying she doesn't want to admit that I could be right about the husband being involved," Astra snarks.

"I'm not saying you're wrong about that," I say. "But I'm not saying you're right either."

"So, what are you saying then?" Mo asks with a smirk.

"I'm saying it's too early to say anything one way or the other," I reply.

Astra sits down at her workstation and I perch on the edge of her desk, replaying our conversation with Osweiler over and over in my head. A long moment of silence stretches out over the office as I think about it. Inconclusive is the only word I can use to describe it. There's nothing in what he said that either rules him in or out.

"I don't know about you," Astra finally speaks up. "But I got the feeling there was something he wasn't telling us. Something about his relationship with his wife."

"Like what?" Mo asks.

Astra shakes her head. "I don't know yet. But there's something there. There's something he's not telling us," she explains. "I don't know what it has to do with but he's hiding something."

"Are you sure it's not just you wanting to be right about him that's making you think that?" Rick chimes in. "I mean, I assume y'all have some money on the line and you don't want to be wrong about the guy."

Astra looks over at him. "What makes you think there's money on the line?

He chuckles. "Because y'all are kind of morbid like that."

Astra and I share a laugh then I turn to Rick. "It's more of a test. It pushes us to be better investigators," I shrug. "A little competition keeps us sharp. And sharp investigators always breed better results."

"I think Astra's going to need a lot more competition then," he says. "I mean, I'm talking a whole lot more."

Astra laughs and shoots him an obscene gesture, which gets the rest of us laughing. Those two bicker and rag on each other like brother and sister. That's the sort of camaraderie we have built on the team, and I absolutely love it. To think that we started as a group of disparate parts and ill-fitting strangers and have ended up here, tight-knit like family and one of the most highly effective units in the entire Bureau, makes me prouder than anything else I've done in my entire life.

Astra turns to me. "What did you think? What kind of a vibe did you get off Osweiler?"

I shrug. "I don't think his emotions were performative. I think he is genuinely torn up about his wife going missing," I admit. "But whether he had anything to do with her disappearance, I can't say. It's just too soon to tell one way or the other."

"But did you get the sense he was hiding anything?" Astra presses.

"It's possible. There was a moment I thought I saw something in his eyes, but I could have been misreading him," I reply. "It was when he told us his wife wasn't having an affair—he didn't seem entirely certain. I can't say for sure that he was hiding something."

"But you can't say he wasn't," Astra says.

"Even if he was, though," Mo offers, "that doesn't necessarily mean he had anything to do with her disappearance."

I nod. "Right. But I don't think he was putting on an act. I think his emotions were genuine," I add. "I mean, for all we know, they had an open marriage, and he just didn't want to say anything for fear of what it would look like."

"Okay, that's fair," Astra says.

"I know if I had an open marriage, I wouldn't say anything," Rick chimes in.

Astra turns to him. "I wish you wouldn't tell us half of the things you do."

That sets us all laughing again, and Rick hurls a pen at Astra—missing by a country mile—which only makes us laugh harder. It eventually ebbs and the room settles down.

"All right, it's time to get serious here," I say. "Mo, have you been able to find anything in her financials? Any major withdrawals? Any unusual activity at all?"

"Negative. There's nothing out of the ordinary I can see," she reports. "No big deposits, no big withdrawals. No nothing really."

I frown but nod. "Rick? How about you? Find anything we need to know about?"

"Not yet. She's got a couple of email addresses I'm still working on cracking," he says. "But her phone was shut off the day she went missing, so there's no trace to be had that way. And of course, her car is at home, so the GPS is a bust too."

"Great," Astra mutters. "So, we've got nothing."

"Not exactly nothing," I say and turn to Mo. "We've got the Uber driver."

Astra brightens up and nods. "You're right. It's a place to start."

I turn to Mo. "Can you figure out who her driver was based on the Uber charge the day she went missing?"

"I don't think I can, but Rick might be able to work some of his magic and figure that out," she replies.

"Give me just a second," he says.

We all watch as Rick bangs away on his keyboard. When Rick first got here, despite his jokey demeanor, he was as straight an arrow as there was. He would never even consider going outside the lines and bending the laws. But since he's grown into his roles here, he's grown more comfortable pushing the boundaries a bit. He still won't push them as far as Paxton's friend Brody—though to be fair, Brody never acknowledges boundaries at all—but Rick has started feeling more comfortable coloring outside the lines a little more.

Rick is thankfully starting to loosen up a bit, which makes it easier to get things moving in the right direction in a case. Instead of having to wait around trying to get enough evidence to justify a warrant, turning Rick loose on the problem has proven to be a good way to expedite the issue. For instance, we would likely need to go through Uber's formal request process, and they'd ask for a warrant to access the information Rick is attempting to get right now. Truthfully, we probably don't have enough to justify it. I doubt we'd find a judge willing to sign off on it.

But we don't need all that to find him. All we need is a shot of the license plate and we can work backward from there. I just want to have a conversation with him and see how that shakes out. If I get a feeling he might know what happened to Valerie, we'll find something to justify building a case out from there. But if not, he might still have information that can point us in the right direction. Either way, we need to get that name just to see what we have because right now we're not even far enough along to say we're at square one.

"What time did he say she left that morning?" he calls back as his fingers fly across the keyboard.

"Flight was at ten fifty-eight," I tell him. "He said she called up the Uber at seven thirty-five just as he was leaving."

"Kind of early to head to the airport, don't you think?" comments Astra.

"I don't know," Mo tells her. "I like to get there with more than enough time to get through without having to rush. If I have an early flight, sometimes I just come to the airport the night before and sleep there so I'm ready."

"You couldn't pay me enough," says Rick. He cuts a glance over at me. "And you don't, by the way."

"Focus, Rick," I admonish him.

He grumbles, but redoubles his efforts. "Alright, if she left her house about seven forty, that means she probably got on Sand Point Way a few minutes later. Checking the street cameras… here." He turns his screen around to reveal a freeze-frame of the traffic cameras and points at a small white Toyota Prius. Sure enough, it's turning off of the Osweilers' street toward the major street and has an Uber sticker on the dashboard. If I squint, I can just make out the silhouette of Valerie in the backseat.

"2018 Toyota Prius, white, plate number AZG-2201," he reads off. He clicks over to his second screen and hammers away to type in the information. "All right, it looks like the car is registered to a Stan Horn."

I let out a whistle. "Nice work."

"Yeah, I know."

"Stan Horn, age fifty-three," Mo calls up from her computer. "Single. Once divorced, the former lucky woman's name is Sandra Lehman. No children. Lives alone in an apartment in Sand Point and it looks like he has a regular job at Murray's Auto Repair. He must drive for Uber to supplement his income."

Not to be outdone, Rick speaks up again, his fingers moving in a rapid flurry on the keyboard. "It looks like Horn has a record. He was arrested twice for domestic violence, once for aggravated assault, and once for attempted rape," he says. "He's done a grand total of seven years over various stints at Clallam Bay. He is currently on parole for the attempted rape, by the way."

"Excellent," I say. "That makes it easier."

"That makes it fun," Astra adds.

I flash her a grin then turn back to Rick and Mo. "Okay, tomorrow morning, Astra and I are going to go rattle his cage and see if we can shake anything loose," I say. "I want you guys to hit Valerie's social media accounts. See if you can find anything weird or out of place—"

"And I assume by out of place, you mean dudes she seems unusually close to?" Rick asks. "Dudes who aren't her husband I mean."

"Exactly that," I confirm. "Also pay attention to the comment sections. Check to see if you can find anything threatening or anybody who seems like they want to do Valerie harm."

"Copy that," Mo says.

"All right then. Good," I reply.

By the time we head out for the night, I feel slightly better. We still have a long way to go—a very long way to go—but at least we've got a plan to get the ball rolling. Hopefully from there, we can start building some momentum.

CHAPTER SIX

Grayson's Fish Market; Downtown Seattle

“WELL, IT WOULD HAVE BEEN NICE IF YOU’D TOLD ME what happened,” Annie sniffs.

“I’m telling you now.”

“More than a week after the fact.”

“It’s honestly not that big of a deal,” I protest.

“Nearly killing yourself in a fire? I’d say that’s a fairly big deal.”

“But I’m fine—”

“You might not have been,” she argues. “And I’d say the fact that you’re still suffering from amnesia would is proof enough that you’re not fine.”

“The doctors are sure it’s temporary,” I reply.

“I still don’t know why you won’t come stay with me. Your place must stink of smoke,” she says.

“It doesn’t. I’ve aired the place out,” I tell her. “And it’s already being worked on. If it smells like anything, it’s drywall, paint, and my contractor’s body odor—which is only compounded by the amount of Axe body spray he uses.”

She gives me a look and a frown of disapproval, obviously not finding any humor in my joke. She usually doesn't though.

"It's fine, Annie. Really. My place will be repaired in a couple of days because it wasn't that big of a deal to begin with," I tell her. "Where is Maisey tonight anyway?"

"Out with that boyfriend of hers, of course," she replies stiffly.

I give her a look. "Come on now, Annie. You know that Marco is good for her. He's a great guy."

"Oh, I know," she admits. "It's just... an adjustment."

"I know for a fact she was with you just a couple of nights ago," I say.

Between this and the conversation about the fire, I'm suddenly regretting asking Annie to dinner tonight. But it's been a couple of weeks since I last saw her and I knew if I waited too much longer, Annie would have held it against me for months. She's sensitive like that.

I shouldn't be too hard on her though. Annie just puts a high value on family, and with my cousin Maisey having finally moved out of the house, my aunt is feeling a little more alone these days and puts a lot of importance on these family get-togethers. Knowing that, I've been making a more concerted effort to spend time with her.

"She's a grown woman, Annie. She's in love. You should be happy for her," I press. "I know it would mean the world to her if you'd support her."

She sighs. "I do support her. And yes, Marco is a very good man," she says softly. "This is all just so new to me."

I came to live with my aunt here in Seattle after my parents were murdered. Maisey and I grew up together and she quickly became just like another sister to me. When we were young, we bonded over our frustrations with Annie's overbearing ways and that's a bond that has endured well into adulthood. It's a bond that's grown and matured as we have.

It wasn't all bad. Annie is in many ways a second mother to

me and I love her to death. She's just… a little set in her ways. And once Maisey and I grew up, it was like she regressed even further somehow.

It's only recently, though, that Maisey was able to break free of her mother's hold on her. My cousin had been on a path that would have seen her living the spinster life like Annie. I knew she secretly wanted more than that but didn't have the strength to break free and chart her own path. So I helped her find the strength inside herself.

Now, Maisey has finally moved out of Annie's house, has a boyfriend who adores her, and is off living her best life. I couldn't be prouder of my cousin, but I know Annie is still trying to adjust to life on her own. It's probably the biggest reason I make such an effort to get together with my aunt as often as I can. I want to make sure Annie knows she's not alone. Not that Maisey has abandoned her or anything. It's just that Annie hasn't lived by herself in a really long time, and I know that can take some getting used to.

I've been encouraging Annie to get out on her own and make some friends. Build a social life. I mean, all she does is sit at home night after night, fretting over the local news, which only adds to her multitude of issues. I've told her that having friends she can go spend time with will take the edge off her loneliness and maybe even help her start to trust people again. But she's a very shy, socially awkward woman who has spent her entire adult life pouring herself into her daughter—and me—and now that we're both grown and gone, Annie has no idea what to do with herself.

Annie lacks a sense of self, and although I'm no psychologist, I'd say that's the biggest reason she clings so hard to Maisey and me. Why she can be so overbearing. On some level, Annie thinks she should be as involved in our lives now as she was when we were kids because that's all she knew for so long. She thinks her issues should be our issues and doesn't understand that we're grown up and making our own decisions—which include not taking on any of her issues.

But I will say she's been working on it. Working on herself. Credit where credit is due, Annie has been making a lot of strides in her personal life. She's doing a lot of things for herself these days, which is good to see. That's not to say we don't sometimes slide back into old habits where she slips back into her old ways—like right now—but I'm happy to see the progress she's making toward living a better, healthier life for herself.

"So, what are you going to have?" I ask. "I've had the scallops here and they are amazing."

"I'm not much of a fan of scallops," she replies. "I think I'll just have a salad."

"A salad? Annie, this is one of the best seafood spots in all of Seattle. Live a little. Try something—"

"Everything is just so expensive."

"I invited you out," I insist. "It's my treat. Get whatever you'd like. Honestly."

Annie gives me a small smile, still clearly uncomfortable with the idea of ordering what she really wants. I'm not saying my aunt is a skinflint—no wait, that's exactly what I'm saying. The woman does not splurge on herself for anything. She's had the sweater she's wearing right now for at least twenty years. Granted, she takes good care of it and you'd never know unless you grew up with herm but she's had it long enough that it's gone out of style—and then came back into style again.

The waitress comes by and takes our order. I'm glad to see Annie order something nice and something she wanted, rather than the cheapest thing on the menu for a change. Our glasses of wine are dropped off and we make small talk for a little while. She catches me up on her life and what she's been doing, which is shockingly quite a bit.

"So, wait, your book club—you all are going on a cruise?" I ask.

She nods and I can see the excitement in her eyes. "Just a little trip up to Alaska. It's a seven-day cruise so we won't get to see most of the state, but we'll get to see some of the southernmost portion," she tells me. "But it's the first time I've ever done something like this before. I'm really looking forward to it."

I reach across the table and take her hand, giving it a soft squeeze. "Annie, I'm thrilled for you. Seriously, that is amazing. I'm really happy for you."

Annie looks down again and I can tell there's something she's not telling me. There's a certain gleam in her eye that piques my interest. I look at her closely and see the small smile curling the corners of his lips as her cheeks color.

"Oh my God, Annie," I gasp. "You have a man in your life."

Her cheeks burn bright red, and her eyes are sparkling in a way I've never seen in her before. I've only ever known the bitter, almost man-hating version of Annie. Never in a million years would I have thought that Annie would have a man in her life. But seeing that soft smile that that glitter in her eye makes me happy. Annie deserves to be happy.

"He's not really in my life. Not in the way Marco is in Maisey's life," she waves me off, almost stammering from embarrassment.

"Not yet."

She giggles—actually giggles!—and it makes me laugh along with her. In all the years I've known Annie, I've never heard her giggle like a schoolgirl before and I think it's adorable.

"So? Tell me who this mystery man is, Annie."

"His name is Marlon and he's part of my book club," she tells me. "He's a high school teacher, and surprisingly, we have a lot of things in common. He's a nice man."

"That is fantastic. I am thrilled for you."

"Well, nothing is official or anything. We've just been to dinner a few times," she says. "That's hardly a relationship."

"But you're heading that way. And I take it he's going to be on this cruise?"

She gives me a sheepish smile. "He's the one who convinced me to go in the first place."

"That is really fantastic, Annie. This is going to be wonderful for you."

"I hope so. I honestly don't know what I'm getting myself into."

I give her a smile. "You're allowing yourself a shot at the happiness you deserve. Just like Maisey did."

She returns my smile. "Well then, I guess if Maisey and I have both put ourselves out there, I'd say it's your turn."

A laugh bursts from my mouth. "Yeah, my track record isn't the best. I don't think I'm really in a position where I should be dating anybody right now. You know all about what happened with Mark."

She purses her lips and nods. "I do. But even you have to admit, the odds of you finding a wonderful man are far higher than those of finding another Mark," she offers. "Don't argue with me, I work with numbers for a living."

"Look at you. You've become all pro-relationship now," I marvel. "It's like I've stumbled into an alternate universe or something. You're like a completely different person. I'm not gonna lie, this is totally freaking me out."

Annie takes a sip of her wine and sets her glass down. She pauses and seems to be thinking about what she's going to say next. After a couple of beats, she looks up.

"I know it's taken a long time to get through my head, but if there's one thing I've learned from you girls it's that life is short and there's no sense in spending the time we have alone. Or spending it being miserable," Annie says. "It's scary. Believe me, it's scary. When you've been burned the way I have—the way you have—it leaves scars. But battling through those old pains and finding yourself with something—with somebody—better who can help take those hurts away, can be very well worth it."

I give her a soft smile. "Is that what Marlon does for you? Soothes your old pains?'

She nods. "He really does. He's unlike anybody I've ever met before."

"I'm happy for you, Annie."

"And I want to be happy for you," she says, pointing a finger at me with a gleam in her eye. "So don't let me hear after all this that you're the one all alone."

I flash her a grin. "I mentioned this new Annie is freaking me out, right?"

"I just feel… I feel *alive*, Blake. I feel like now that I'm finally allowing myself to live, I can't stop. For the first time in too long, I feel like I can breathe. I didn't know what I was missing before. But now I feel young again. I feel like Maisey. And I want you to feel that way too."

"Honestly, Annie, I appreciate it, but I still need some time. I'm not exactly chomping at the bit to go trawl Tinder right now or anything."

"You mean to tell me there's nobody in your life you find interesting?"

My mind immediately flashes to Charles and I just as quickly shut that down. I have no idea where that rogue thought came from but it's totally not appropriate and I don't need to be thinking about him that way.

I shake my head. "No. There's really not."

"Well. Just promise me that you won't get to be my age and realize you're making the same mistakes I made."

I give her a gentle smile. "I promise, Annie."

"Good girl."

The waitress arrives with our food, and we chat amiably as we eat. The changes in both my aunt and cousin are profound. These two women are not the same they were just a year ago. They've overcome a lot and have changed. For the better. Maybe it's time I learn from them the way they both say they've learned from me. Maybe.

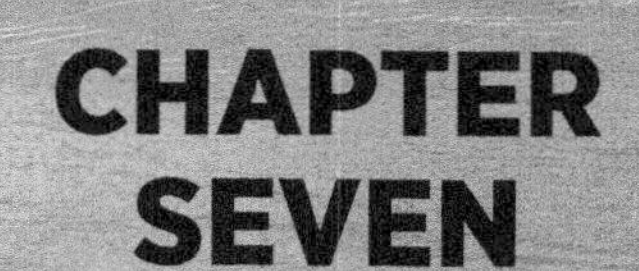

CHAPTER SEVEN

Emerald Garden Apartments; Sand Point District, Seattle

"THIS IS THE MOST DEPRESSING PLACE I'VE EVER SEEN," Astra mutters. "And we've seen some depressing places in our time."

I nod. "Yeah. It really is."

We stand in front of an apartment building that looks like it should have been condemned years ago. The Sand Point neighborhood is an economically depressed section of Seattle anyway, but the Emerald Garden Apartments look worse than most of the buildings around us. Decrepit might not even be an accurate enough description of the place. The roof on the building is sagging in spots and missing most of its shingles. The paint is faded in some spots and cracked and peeling in others, and the second-floor walkway has a definite cant to it.

The front of the building probably used to be lush and green, but now it's mostly dirt and dead plants. There's trash all around, a sofa sitting half on the curb, half in the street, and an old refrigerator laying on its side next to the ground floor walkway. The Emerald

Garden is an eyesore in a neighborhood already filled with run-down, shabby houses and apartment buildings.

"You're up to date with your tetanus shots and all, right?" Astra asks.

"I sure hope so."

She gives me a grin and we head up the walkway. Stan Horn is listed as the resident in apartment three, according to his parole records. There are only eight total units in the building and unit three is on the ground floor and backs up to the parking lot behind the building. In one of the carports, I catch sight of a white Prius. The plate matches the one Rick found.

"Looks like he's home," I note.

"Well good. Hopefully, he can give us some information we can use."

"That would be nice. But you know things are never that easy for us."

"I think it's you. You're like this vortex of bad juju or something," she says.

To the left of the door sits a beat-up plastic chair that's surrounded by beer bottles, cigarette butts, and candy wrappers. Mr. Horn is apparently fond of Snickers bars.

"Charming," Astra says.

I give a firm knock on the door and take a step back. Movement in my peripheral vision draws my attention and I see a little kid, no more than nine or ten standing there staring at us. He's thin and a little on the small side with a head full of curly brown hair, brown eyes, and rich, golden skin.

"He won't answer," the boy tells us. "He don't like the police."

"We're not the police," I say.

He pulls a face and laughs. "Yeah, you are. You can't fool me."

"We're Feds, kid," Astra says. "There's a difference."

"If you say so."

He turns and walks off and I share a look with Astra. "How'd he know?"

"You look like a cop," she shrugs. "You also knock on doors like a cop."

"I do not."

"Yeah, you really do."

I laugh. "Shut up," I say and turn back to the door, pounding on it again. "Stan Horn. FBI. Open the door. Now."

"What'd I say," she snarks under her breath, but I nudge her with my elbow to shut her up.

We wait another couple of moments and when I raise my hand to knock again, I finally hear the door being unlocked. It opens a bit and a man presses his eye to the crack.

"Who the hell are you?" he grumbles.

I hold up my badge. "FBI," I tell him. "Open the door."

"You got a warrant?" he sneers. "I know my rights."

"But you apparently don't know the terms of your parole," I fire back.

"You're on parole, genius," Astra snaps. "We don't need a warrant."

"You still need probable cause—"

"Actually, we don't. Not if you're on parole, moron," Astra cuts him off.

"But if you want cause, we're looking for a missing woman and you are the last person to see her. How does that grab you?" I ask.

"That's crap. I'm not gonna let you frame me for somethin' I didn't do—"

Tired of this game, I step forward and give the door a hard two-handed shove. Horn grunts as the door hits him and he stumbles backward, covering his nose with his hands. The door rebounds off his head but I catch it before it slams shut in our faces and push it open as I step inside. Astra is right behind me and Horn is sitting on his behind looking up at us with wide eyes. His face is flushed red either from embarrassment or rage. I have no idea, and honestly, don't really care.

"Get up," I say.

He lowers his hands and I see a thin rivulet of blood trickling from his nose. He looks at the scarlet smears on his hands then turns his gaze back to me and his face contorts into an unmistakable mask of rage.

"I'll have your badges," he growls. "I'll have you arrested for assault, you bi—"

"When you call in the complaint, be sure to tell them you are a parolee who was resisting a direct order from a law enforcement officer," I say simply. "We wouldn't want to leave out the critical facts now, would we?"

"You can't do that. I wasn't resisting—"

"You were absolutely resisting. I am a witness to everything," Astra interjects. "And who do you think the courts will believe? A man who's got a jacket as long as my arm? Or two decorated, well-respected FBI agents?"

"Now, get up and sit down," I repeat.

A scowl on his face, Horn stands and walks over to the couch. He sits down heavily and uses the sleeve of his shirt to wipe away the blood on his face and glares at us. Horn lives in a one-room apartment that looks as run down as the rest of the building. It's spartanly furnished, and what furniture he does have is battered and worn. Everything looks second, third, and fourth-hand, and not so gently used. If I had to guess, I'd say that a lot of the stuff I see was left here by the former tenants when they bailed out of the Emerald Garden Apartments.

Horn himself is a reflection of his apartment. He's only fifty-three, but it looks like he's lived a hard fifty-three years. He's tall, but gaunt, with sallow skin, a few days' worth of stubble on his chin, and sunken hollows beneath his eyes. Horn is wearing boxers and a tank top that's stained, frayed, and has seen better days. It used to be white but is now a dingy gray color. Still, given his rap sheet, I can't really muster up a lot of sympathy for the guy. As far as I'm concerned, he's a predator and deserves the misery life has quite obviously heaped on him. Frankly, I'm not sure why or how he managed to qualify to become an Uber driver, either.

Astra and I look around his place and the first thing I notice is just how disgusting his place is. Empty pizza boxes and beer bottles are littered all over a round table that's nicked and scarred all over. In fact, empty beer bottles cover almost every surface in the place. The carpets are stained and matted, the sofa is threadbare and ragged, and the entire apartment is covered in filth. It's only because the place is such a pigsty that I belatedly see the bag of weed and bong sitting on a table in the corner. I walk over and pick up the baggie and turn back to Horn. He blanches and stares at the baggie of weed in my hand. I can see his mind spinning.

"Well, well, well," I comment. "Special Agent Russo, does this look like a violation of Mr. Horn's parole to you?"

"Why yes, SSA Wilder, that would most certainly violate him and send him back to prison for a very long time, in fact," Astra confirms.

"What in the hell do you two want?" Horn roars.

"Well, to be honest, I don't really care about the weed," I shrug. "What I do care about is a fare you had yesterday. It was a run to Sea-Tac in the morning. Give us some answers—some honest to God truthful answers—and we'll forget we ever saw the weed."

"But lie to us and we'll have you violated right here and now," Astra warns.

Horn shifts on his seat and keeps glaring at us. I can see him doing the calculus in his head. He's trying to decide if I'm lying to him about forgetting the weed, or if I'll really do it and bring his parole officer into this. And judging by the way he pales in front of me, I get the feeling he's more afraid of going back to prison than anything.

"Fine. Ask your questions," he spits. "What do you want from me?"

"Like I said, you had a fare yesterday. It was in the morning, and you took Valerie Osweiler to the airport," I start.

"I got no idea who that is."

I sigh. "How many runs to Sea-Tac did you make yesterday?"

Horn looks off and screws up his face as if trying to recall exactly. I don't know if he's being deliberately obtuse because he hates cops and is trying to make our job harder or if because all the weed he smokes has muddled his mind.

"Three or four I think," he finally says.

"All right, and of those three or four, how many of them were women?" I ask.

"Two, I think," he replies. "Yeah, two."

Astra calls up a picture of Valerie on her phone and shows it to him. Horn leans closer and takes a look at the photo.

"And of those two, do you remember her?" she asks.

He thinks for another moment and smiles. "Oh yeah. I remember her. Nice lady."

"Okay, that's good. Now, when you dropped her off, did you happen to see anybody suspicious watching her? Anybody who seemed—off?"

He shook his head. "Nah. Nothin' like that."

"So, you didn't see anything out of the ordinary when you dropped her off at the airport?" Astra presses.

"Oh, I didn't drop her off at the airport," he states.

Astra and I exchange a glance then turn back to him. "You didn't take her to the airport? But that was the ride she'd booked on the app with you." I ask.

"Yeah, I know. But when we got to the airport, she gave me fifty bucks to run her somewhere else instead. Off-book, of course," he tells us. "That's why I remember her."

"Okay, so if not the airport, where did you take her?" Astra asks.

"The Churchill," he replies.

"The hotel?" I ask.

Horn nods. "Yeah," he says. "I didn't have another fare at the time, so I figured why not earn a quick fifty? It ain't that far from Sea-Tac."

I feel a hot bolt of adrenaline shoot through me as I absorb this piece of information. Knowing she didn't go to the airport but to a hotel instead feels like a really big piece of the puzzle. I motion for Astra to show him the picture again.

"And you're sure it was this woman," I say.

"Yeah. Ain't a lot of people who'd give me a fifty for a ten-minute drive," he replies. "Those kinda people tend to stick out in my head."

"All right, so did you see anybody waiting for her?" Astra asks. "Or did she happen to say who she was meeting at the Churchill?"

He shakes his head. "Nah. She didn't offer and I didn't ask. Ain't none of my business who she meets or what she does. Or who she does," he adds with a salacious grin.

"Charming," Astra rolls her eyes.

It's a bit of a relief that this trip wasn't a wasted one. We actually have some solid intel to follow up on. And personally, I'd love to get out of here and follow up on it—emphasis on getting out of this foul-smelling cesspool.

"So, we're cool, right?" he asks. "You're not gonna turn me in, are ya?"

I look from him to the weed and back again. I know I should turn him in, but he gave us some actionable intel and to me, that trumps something legal in the state—except for guys like Horn who are on parole for doing bad things.

"Turn you in for what?" I ask, exaggerated confusion written on my face. I turn to Astra. "Do you have any idea what he's talking about?"

She shrugs at me and looks back at Horn. "You know, it's funny.

I can't say. If anyone asks, we'll have to pass along that Mr. Horn was a delightful host and a very helpful witness."

Horn lets out a heavy sigh, obviously relieved, but we don't stick around long enough for him to thank us.

"Let's roll."

"Gladly."

I laugh as we leave his apartment and head for the car. It's still not much, but it's more than we had when we got here, and I'm anxious to start digging.

CHAPTER EIGHT

The Churchill Hotel; Downtown Seattle

The Churchill is a boutique hotel that is, as Horn said, about ten minutes from the airport. It's nestled into an area filled with other small businesses and sits on a street behind a lot of the kitschy Mom and Pop shops, that's not traveled heavily as some of the main thoroughfares downtown. It pretty much fades into the background and unless you're looking for it, you might not even know it's there. Which is why it's such a popular place in some circles.

The Churchill is a small, exclusive hotel that has about a hundred rooms and caters to a wealthier clientele. It's known to be a playground for wealthy men and women who want a discreet place to meet their paramours for a little romp. The hotel's reputation started as something of an open secret. But as that secret became more widely known, the Churchill capitalized on it with a lot of their advertising being a not-so-subtle nod to it. They've pretty much embraced their moniker, the "Cheatin' Churchill." Hey, if you can't beat it, monetize it, I guess. Frankly, I'm surprised more unfaithful spouses haven't met their ends in the hotel at the hands of their jilted spouses.

The exterior is dominated by brick pillars that run along the entire front façade with smoked glass in between each column. The lower two floors are made up primarily of red brick and the upper three are made from some lighter stone that accents it. A long, covered portico extends out into the hotel's circular drive and features the Churchill's logo on the front-facing section of the awning. To our left is a parking structure made of the same red brick and light stone combination as the hotel itself and classical music drifts from speakers discreetly hidden along the frame of the portico. The place is quaint, classy, and has a definite upscale vibe. Which is funny, given its reputation.

The smoked glass doors silently slide aside as Astra and I enter the building and proceed across the marble-tiled lobby. The air in the lobby is hushed, almost like a library, save for the classical music. The front desk is about twelve feet long with the bottom half made of the same marble tile as the floor and the top a long, polished dark wood counter. There are two workstations at the counter, but only one is occupied at the moment, so we veer over to the right and stop in front of a pretty twenty-something with dark hair and light green eyes.

"Welcome to the Churchill," she greets us. "Check-in isn't for another few hours yet, but I think I might be able to—"

"We're not looking for a room, actually," I tell her. "We actually need to speak to your manager on duty."

"Oh, uh, sure," she stammers. "Can I tell her what this is about?"

I flash her my credentials. "Please just tell her we need to speak with her."

The girl's eyes widen and she looks uncertain. But she gives us a nod, then turns and walks through a door behind the counter, closing it softly behind her. A couple of moments later, the door opens and a woman in a blue pantsuit steps out. Her blonde hair is up, and she's got blue eyes behind a pair of rimless round spectacles. She's tall, thin, elegant, and gives us a wide, well-practiced smile that doesn't quite reach her eyes. The woman we spoke with first slips out of the back room and takes her position, doing her best to make it seem like she's not listening in—and failing miserably.

"Hello, I'm Sandy Inman, the general manager of the Churchill," she introduces herself.

"SSA Blake Wilder. This is Special Agent Astra Russo," I say as we flash our credentials to Sandy. "Is there somewhere we can speak privately?"

"Yes. Yes, of course," she replies.

Astra and I fall into step behind her as Inman pushes through a waist-high swinging half-door at the end of the counter and leads us down a corridor. Inman has a smooth gait that makes it seem more like she's gliding rather than walking, which, for whatever reason, makes me think she's had some experience on a catwalk. She turns down a hallway on our left and opens a glass door and holds it for us. When we step in, Inman lets it close and takes her seat behind a large desk, then motions for us to sit. We take the pair of chairs in front of the desk.

I look around and see that the office is perfectly neat and orderly. Everything has a place and everything's in its place. There's a flatscreen computer monitor on the corner of the desk, a felt blotter, a smooth, rectangular piece of granite affixed with a brass plate that bears her name and title, a pen cup, and a phone. Other than that, there's not much else in the entire office. There are no personal accents—no pictures, knickknacks, or anything that gives any hint as to what her personality is like. Inman comes across like her office: cold, sterile, and entirely functional.

"Now, can you tell me what this is about, Agents Wilder and Russo?" she asks.

"It's about a missing woman," I start. "She was last seen here at your hotel."

If she is surprised or has any emotional reaction to my statement, I see no trace of it. Not even a slight widening of her eyes. Inman perfectly maintains her cool composure. I've honestly seen more emotional depth from my Roomba.

"That's quite unfortunate," she replies. "I haven't received reports of anybody missing or anything amiss at all."

"Of course not," Astra says. "I don't think the person who abducted the woman we're looking for would announce it."

"Fair enough," Inman replies. "But what is it I can do for you?"

"We need the security footage for the last five days. All floors," I tell her. "We need to know what room she was staying in and who—"

"I'm sorry, but I'm afraid our security cameras have had a problem. Our entire server has been deleted and the footage from the last week is gone," she interrupts. "We only just discovered the issue and have somebody coming out to fix it."

"Well, that's convenient," Astra grouses.

Inman turns her eyes, cold and hard, onto Astra. "Technology breaks down. It happens," she responds, her voice as icy as her gaze. "I assure you there is nothing nefarious going on here. Who is this woman you're looking for anyway?"

"Her name is Valerie Osweiler," I say evenly. "We know she was here the morning she disappeared. Can you check your computer to see if she booked a room within the last five days, please?"

Inman hesitates, her eyes still boring into Astra's, apparently thinking she can intimidate her. But Astra is not a woman easily intimidated. She's staring right back at the manager, her eyes just as hard and a fierce little smirk on her lips. Inman purses her lips, then turns to her computer and taps away at her keys a bit harder than is probably necessary.

"Unfortunately, I'm not finding a Valerie Osweiler in our records," she says curtly. "I'm sorry, but she wasn't a registered guest here."

"Are you sure you're spelling the name correctly?" Astra asks, then proceeds to spell out Valerie's last name.

Inman says nothing for a moment but she's bristling. I have no idea what's put her on the defensive so quickly or strongly, but she is most definitely not pleased with us being here.

"Yes, that's how I spelled it, and there are no records for Mrs. Osweiler," she says.

I let out a breath and frown. This is like beating my head against a brick wall. We're getting nowhere. We've got no video, no record of her being here, no nothing. I refuse to believe this a dry well, though. She was here and then she disappeared. There has got to be a bread crumb or two here somewhere. If only we knew where to look.

"All right," I say. "If she wasn't a registered guest, she was here to meet with somebody."

"Unfortunately, I'm not a clairvoyant, so I can't magically discern who that might be," Sandy snaps sarcastically.

"That's fine. I don't need you to be clairvoyant," I reply. "All I need is for you to give me the names of all your registered guests for the last five days."

She laughs as if my statement amuses her. "I'm afraid I can't do that."

"No?" Astra raises an eyebrow. "And why is that?"

Iman folds her hands together on top of her desk and looks at us as if we're dim little simpletons that she has no time for. She is really rubbing me the wrong way. The more time I spend with her, the more I don't like this woman.

"Our guests expect a certain amount of discretion and privacy," she says. "I'm afraid I can't just turn the names of everybody who's stayed here for the last five days."

"Ms. Inman, there is a woman's life at stake here," Astra growls.

"I understand that, Agent Russo. And I would truly like to help you, but there is nothing I can do. My hands are tied," she says.

"Your hands aren't tied. You're choosing to let this happen," Astra presses.

"I'm not. In the absence of a court order, I cannot turn the records over to you," she responds with a smug grin on her face. "Our legal department has been more than clear about that in the past."

Great. I half-expected that reply when I asked for the records, but I was hoping she'd be more cooperative. I should have known better; she's been on the defensive from the jump. All we have is Stan Horn's word that he dropped her off here, which doesn't come close to meeting the threshold for getting a warrant. No judge in their right mind would give us an order for those records. Even worse is the fact that she seems to know it. The only cards I have to play are manipulation and pressure.

"I understand your need to protect the hotel, Ms. Inman," I start. "After all, the Churchill's reputation could be on the line if you just started handing over guest records all willy-nilly."

She nods. "I'm glad you understand, Agent Wilder."

"But what we're asking for is a little help," I tell her. "The scope of our investigation is narrow and we're not looking to publicize any of our findings. You can trust our discretion."

"You'll have to forgive me, but my experience with law enforcement hasn't been… ideal," she says. "Those I've dealt with have lacked the very discretion you're promising me."

"Well, we're not those people," Astra counters. "We're trying to save a woman's life, Ms. Inman. We couldn't care less about what else happens in your hotel."

"And I'm not unsympathetic to her plight. But without a court order, our legal team has been very clear," she states. "My job is to protect the Churchill. And that includes the privacy of everybody who stays here. Now, I've already crossed a line by telling you Mrs. Osweiler wasn't a guest here. But I'm not going to risk my job by crossing another line."

I frown and nod. "That's fine. I understand," I say. "But while we're trying to obtain a warrant for those records, I can't guarantee that somebody isn't going to tip off the press that the Churchill is withholding information that could very well help save the life of a very prominent figure in this city."

For the first time since we met her, Inman shows a flash of emotion. She licks her lips nervously and sits up straighter, the mask of cool indifference slipping into place once more.

"You wouldn't—you couldn't," she says, though her voice wavers.

"I never said I would do it. But once you're in a courthouse applying for a warrant, these things tend to get out. Courthouses tend to leak like a sieve. Nothing I can do about that," I comment with a shrug.

"You will destroy our reputation," she hisses. "The negative publicity a story like that—the damage would be incalculable."

"All I'm asking for is a little help, Ms. Inman. I'm trying to save a woman's life," I growl. "I've promised you my discretion and to keep the scope of our investigation narrow. We will not cause any undue burden to your guests. We just need to find Mrs. Osweiler."

Inman gnaws on her bottom lip and looks away. I can see her mind working as she tries to reconcile my request with her duty and loyalty to the hotel. I know I'm putting her in a bad spot, but I have no other choice. I have no other leads and no other direction. Unless she gives me something, Valerie Osweiler may very well never be found.

"I need you to think about what you would do and how many strings you would pull if somebody you loved was missing," I press. "I'm not asking for the moon and the stars. I'm asking you to be a decent human being."

Inman looks down at her hands for a beat then raises her gaze to me. "Let me see what I can do," she says. "Leave your card and I'll be in touch soon."

I pull a card out and put it on her desk. “Please be in touch sooner rather than later. We’re on a clock—or rather, Mrs. Osweiler is on a clock.”

Astra and I leave the hotel, both of us frustrated. We didn’t get what we wanted or what we needed, but I have hope that Inman will do the right thing. And because there’s no way in hell I’ll get a warrant with what we have—or rather, don’t have—all I can do now is pray that my hope isn’t unfounded.

CHAPTER NINE

Criminal Data Analysis Unit; Seattle Field Office

"I COULD GO BEAT THE LIST OUT OF HER," MO OFFERS.

Astra flashes me a grin. "She's becoming so hardcore," she says. "I remember when she would have been appalled if any of us had thought something so draconian."

"You're all rubbing off on me," Mo replies with a shrug.

"We are nothing if not a good influence," Astra says.

"I'm not sure a good influence is the right word for what you are," Rick chimes in.

"Stuff it, hipster boy," she fires back. "Nobody asked for your input."

"Children, do I need to put you both in a time out?" I ask.

"He started it," Astra protests with a grin.

I laugh and shake my head then turn to Rick. "Can you do that camera trick again? If there are any street cameras around the Churchill?"

Rick taps away on his keyboard, bobbing his head to some internal music. It takes a moment, but he looks up at me and nods.

"On the big screens now," he announces.

I turn and step to the side as the flatscreens mounted to the wall at the front of the room. They come to life as Rick plays the images he'd pulled up.

"Looks like there are two traffic cameras that have a view of the front of the Churchill," he says. "But they're not a really great view."

"Better than nothing," I say. "Can you pull up the footage from the day she went missing?"

"Give me a minute," he murmurs.

On the screen, I watch the grainy footage as Rick speeds through time. Everyone falls completely silent as we watch and wait. The footage is blurry and it's hard to make out much of anything, which is going to make this a lot of fun.

"You'd think with technology being what it is, they'd have better quality traffic cameras," Astra mutters.

"The city obviously has better things to spend money on than improving the safety of their citizens," I reply. "Like building a new hockey arena."

"Hey now," Mo pipes up. "The arena's going to provide a lot of jobs and bring a lot of money into the city. It'll pay for the investment made within ten years."

"Oh great, maybe in a decade, we'll have the money to upgrade the traffic cameras," Astra cracks. "Until then, people will keep dying and we'll just muddle by with these Mickey Mouse pieces of garbage."

"Spoken like somebody who doesn't appreciate sports," Mo huffs.

"You got me. Guilty as charged," Astra responds.

"Okay, got it," Rick calls over the din.

On the screens, the footage from the traffic cameras runs on the date she went missing. We all wait in silence as Rick runs the playback, fast-forwarding until the white Prius enters the screen. Rick stops and lets it run full speed. We watch Mrs. Osweiler get out of the back seat and stand there as Horn pulls her bags out and sets them down on the sidewalk next to her. Mrs. Osweiler fishes some money out of her bag and hands it to him. They speak for a moment before she pulls the handle up on her rolling bag. Mrs. Osweiler takes the straps of her other two bags and hangs them on her shoulder, then grabs the handle of her rolling suitcase and turns. She strides to the front doors then disappears and is lost from view.

'Well, that was enlightening," Astra mutters.

"Rick, can you run that back?" I ask.

He does and I watch her again, looking to see if she reacts to anybody. There are several people in the frame, but she doesn't seem to be bothered or threatened by any of them. She simply walks into the hotel, passing them by like they didn't exist.

"Again, please."

Rick rolls it back and hits play. I scan the frame again, looking for anything out of the ordinary. For anybody who stands out. And then I see him.

"Stop," I say. "Freeze the frame."

Rick does. "What do you see, boss?"

"Yeah, that's my question," Astra says.

I step forward and point to the guy who caught my eye. "The guy in the ballcap sitting on the planter. Can you blow him up?"

Rick bangs away on his keyboard and it zooms in on the man's face. It's grainy and a little blurry, so I can't make out his finer features. It's just not clear enough.

"What about that guy caught your attention?" Mo asks.

"He's watching her," I explain. "Closely."

"He is?" Mo asks.

I nod. "Rick, go back to normal view then run it from the start again."

"On it," he replies.

The footage starts again just before Horn's Prius pulls up. It enters the frame and Mrs. Osweiler gets out, but my gaze is laser-focused on the guy in the ballcap. He's sitting on the bench surrounding one of the planters outside the door, and when Mrs. Osweiler gets out of the car, he seems to zero in on her.

The guy looks away, perhaps trying to avoid being too obvious about it, but as he takes a drag on his cigarette, I watch as his head turns in her direction again. It's subtler this time, but to me, it looks like he's still watching her. And when she disappears inside, the man drops his butt on the ground, steps on it, then follows her into the lobby.

After he goes through the doors, we lose him. It's thin, I admit. He may have simply been a guest there just out copping a smoke and just thought Mrs. Osweiler was an attractive distraction for a few moments as he finished his cigarette. I look over at Astra and can see she's not convinced. Turning, I see that Mo has the same sort of skeptical expression on her face too. She looks back and offers me a weak smile.

"Maybe?" she shrugs.

"I know. I might be grasping at straws here. But it wouldn't hurt to track this guy down and ask him a few questions," I offer. "I mean, it's not like we've got much else to go on at the moment."

Astra shrugs. "That's fair."

"Did either of you guys find anything in her socials?" I ask Rick and Mo.

She shakes her head. "Not yet. But we're still looking," she says. "For being such a busy, important woman, she certainly was a social media butterfly."

The doors to the CDAU slide open and a young guy I've seen around the FO before walks in pushing a cart. He's in his early twenties, tall and lean, with sandy blonde hair, dark eyes, and that warm golden skin you usually see on surfers and guys who spend their days working outdoors. And since he spends his days working here, I've always figured that he spent a lot of his free time in the water.

He's kind of a quiet, unassuming kid who, according to Rick, is incredibly adept with computers. Rick has kind of taken him under his wing and is helping shepherd him through the process of being a computer analyst like him. He's a good kid and my hope is that when I finally get the green light to expand my team—something I think should have happened already—that we can scoop him up. Having two analysts would be best, as it would allow me to deploy Mo into the field more often. If we could do that, we could take on twice the workload and be twice as effective.

Unfortunately, those kinds of decisions are above my pay grade. That doesn't stop me from making a lot of noise down here, though. Eventually, they're going to get sick of listening to me and give me what I want just to shut me up.

"Kyle," I greet him. "How are you today?"

"Great, Agent Wilder," he replies. "Thanks for asking. And how about yourself? I heard about what happened and I'm glad you're okay."

"Thanks. So am I," I reply with a smile. "And I keep telling you, call me Blake."

He shrugs. "Maybe one of these days I'll get it right."

I know he won't, though. Kyle is a very respectful kid and seems to be a pretty straight arrow. But then, so was Mo, and now we've gotten her talking about beating evidence out of people, so I'm sure we can work our magic on him too. Astra thinks he's got a crush on me and keeps encouraging me to ask him out, which always earns her a roll of the eyes and an unladylike gesture or two from me. He's a nice kid, but I swear, he looks like he spends all his time on TikTok. And as he crosses the room, she gives me a look and a wicked grin. I give her the eye roll now but save the gestures for later.

Kyle currently works in the mailroom and he's pushing a cart with three large bank boxes sitting on top, which piques my curiosity.

"And what are you bringing us today?" I ask.

"The boxes came by delivery service from a Scott Osweiler," he says, reading off the clipboard. "They've already been scanned and checked. They're hazard-free and good to go."

Kyle takes the boxes off the cart and sets them down on an empty desk. When he's done, he turns to look at me, the expression on his face reminding me of a puppy who needs a pat on the head after a job well done.

I give him a nod. "Terrific. Thank you, Kyle."

"Anytime," he says. "Just doing my job."

He lingers for a moment and shuffles his feet. It looks like he wants to say something but then I see his eyes dart around the room, and he just gives me a small smile before walking out of the room. The moment the doors slide closed, I hear Fountains of Wayne's "Stacy's Mom" playing from Astra's phone. That sets Rick and Mo off and they howl with laughter. Astra, though, has her back to me and is pretending to be working but I know she's got that smug smirk plastered on her face.

"Funny. You are hilarious. Had that all cued up and ready to go. Awesome," I say.

She finally turns and flashes me a grin, satisfied with her own cleverness as she cuts the music off. "What can I say, babe? You've got it going on."

I roll my eyes again and this time, give her the gesture with both hands which only makes Mo and Rick laugh even harder. I shake my head and walk over to the boxes and take the lid off the first one. Inside are files marked with dates. Some of them have multiple pages, some only a single sheet. I pull the first one and see it's a neatly typed letter inviting Mrs. Osweiler to drink a gallon of bleach then shoot herself in the face. The note, of course, is unsigned. Because nothing says courage like an anonymous threatening letter.

The laughter behind me ebbs as Astra and Mo join me at the

boxes. They each take the lid off one and start to sift through the contents.

"Some of her case files are in this box," Astra notes. "I think Mr. Osweiler put them in here by accident. There's no way an attorney would include them."

"What should we do with them?" Mo asks.

"Go through every page of them," I shrug. "Look for names. Leads. It's a gift that fell into our laps."

"Won't that taint any potential court case?" Astra asks.

I shrug. "Not if we don't mention where we got the names," I say. "It's not like we stole the files or forced him to break privilege. His mistake is our gain. I say we use it and let the attorneys hash it out after we nail whoever abducted Mrs. Osweiler. If he gave it freely to us, that's on him, not us."

"Works for me," Astra says.

"I've got a couple of thumb drives in this box," Mo calls out, holding up a plastic baggie.

"Those are probably the audio recordings of threatening messages people left her," I muse. "Mr. Osweiler said there were some."

"Looks like we've got a lot to go through," Astra notes.

I nod. "Well, let's get to it then."

"What are we looking for?" Mo asks.

"Anything that seems like it could be more than just some idiot's impotent rage," I tell her. "Something that seems like it could lead to something else. Something real."

Astra and Mo both nod as they grab a box and return to their workstations. I'm glad Scott sent it all along, but this is going to take us all day to get through and I can feel the pressure of the clock ticking. If she truly was abducted and didn't just run off with somebody, then the longer she's out there missing, the less likely it is things are going to work out the right way. The trouble is, we don't yet know which scenario is the most likely. Right now, we're just taking shots in the dark, hoping we hit something.

"Rick, can you get enough from that video to run it through facial rec?" I ask.

He grimaces. "To be honest, I don't think so," he replies slowly. "This isn't CSI. I can't zoom and enhance. But let me try something here. It'll take me a bit of time, but I might have a workaround."

I hold up a handful of the files from the box in front of me. "We're going to be here a while, so take the time you need."

"You got it," he says.

The room falls silent as we all tuck into our tasks. I honestly have no idea what I'm looking for as I pore through the files. I'm just hoping something pops—and pops soon. If we don't catch a break and refine our investigative path forward soon, there may be no happy ending to this story for anybody.

It's closing in on ten. We've been at this all day and haven't come across a single viable lead and I'm getting frustrated.

"Okay guys, let's call it a night," I sigh. "Go home. Get some sleep and we'll keep pounding away at this in the morning."

I'm hoping with a little time away and fresh eyes, we'll be able to find something that can help point us in the right direction. Or in any direction at this point. Astra, Mo, and Rick all pack up and head out as I walk into my office to grab my things. As I set my bag down on my desk though, my cellphone rings. I look down at the caller ID and see it's coming from a restricted number, which tells me it's most likely Kit on the other end of the line. Not wanting to miss her call, I connect it and press the phone to my ear.

"Wilder."

"Agent Wilder, this is Sandy Inman," she replies. "Of the Churchill."

A white-hot shot of adrenaline shoots through me when I hear her voice. I've been waiting for this call. Hoping for it. Other than threatening her with bad media exposure, I have no real leverage to get that list of names from her, and Inman is smart enough to know that. I'm just hoping that she's calling to give me good news.

"Yes, of course. I've been hoping you'd call," I say evenly.

"I'd like to talk to you, but can you meet me?" she asks. "I'd rather speak in person. Do you know the Triangle over on Colton?"

"I do," I reply.

"Good, can you meet me there in half an hour?"

"I'll be there."

I disconnect the call, feeling a surge of adrenaline. We may be getting a little help from an unexpected place after all.

CHAPTER TEN

The Green Triangle Tavern; Downtown Seattle

The Triangle, as it's called by most people, sits on a quiet side street, nestled in among some other shops that usually close well before things get rockin' in the evening around here. This section of the city is usually alive and vibrant with nightlife. There are probably a hundred different bars and restaurants that each cater to the different tastes of the thousands of people who flock here every night. They say if you can't find something that suits your taste down here, you're either not trying hard enough or you're way too picky.

It's the last place I would have expected Inman to want to meet. Personally, I think she seems a little too uptight for the lively, free-flowing vibe of the area. I would have thought she would have felt more comfortable in some stodgy, staid old lounge where people sit with their glasses of scotch and a cigar discussing stock prices and market fluctuations. But then, perhaps it was wrong of me to judge a book by its cover. I know that I'm not the same person outside the shop that I am inside it. We all have work faces and real-world faces we wear.

The Triangle's not too far from the office, so I make it about ten minutes early. I walk in and find a boot near the back of the place and take a seat to wait for her. Compared to some of the other bars in the area, the Triangle is pretty plain. There's no theme to it and there aren't a lot of bells and whistles to the place. It's longer than it is wide, reminding me of an old shotgun house. The walls are all aged and weathered red brick and the bar takes up the entire left side of the building. It's long and made of polished light-colored wood with brass fixtures.

Stools run the length of the bar, a row of tables lines the center of the building, and a row of booths run along the right-hand wall. Framed posters of old movies, concerts, and music festivals from over the years hang on the wall above the booths, and half a dozen TVs hang on the wall behind the bar, each of them tuned to a different game. An oldies station drifts from speakers mounted around the place, but it's not too obnoxious. The TVs are muted and the music isn't loud, making the Triangle a great place to come for a quiet drink and a conversation. Maybe that's why Inman picked it. That and it really is kind of out of the way and not a place you're likely going to be spotted by anybody who isn't following you to begin with.

A waitress approaches the table with a warm smile on her face. She's probably in her thirties, with dark hair tied back in a braid, olive-colored skin, and dark eyes. The black skirt she's wearing hangs to the middle of her thigh, and she's got a white button-down topped off with a black bow tie, and a short, dark apron around her waist.

"What can I get you?" she asks.

"I'd like a glass of scotch please," I tell her. "Top shelf, not what's in the well."

The waitress gives me a nod and I see Inman walking up behind her, so I gesture.

"And whatever she's having," I add.

"I'll take a Gibson, please," Inman says as she slides into the booth.

"Comin' right up."

Inman slips out of her jacket, letting it pool onto the bench behind her, then unwinds her scarf. It's a cool night but it's not that cold. All those layers seem a bit much. But maybe she's just a bit thin-blooded and I'm being judgmental again. I should be thankful that she's meeting with me when she didn't have to. Or at least, I'm hoping that I'm going to be grateful by the time this is all said and done.

Inman shifts in her seat and folds her hands on the table in front of her. But then she clears her throat and drops her hands into her lap. Her eyes dart around the bar and she can't quite seem to sit still. It's not hard to see that she's nervous and doesn't necessarily want to be here. I suppose I can't really blame her. But she finally lets out a breath and takes a beat before finally turning her eyes to me.

Before she can start speaking, though, the waitress arrives with our drinks. She sets them down in front of us and departs with a smile. I pick up my glass and take a sip as Inman downs half her drink in one swallow. The glass is trembling in her hand as she sets it down, then wipes her palms on her pants. She gnaws on her bottom lip and looks up at me.

"Thank you for meeting me," she starts.

"Thank you for calling," I reply. "To be honest, I didn't think you would."

"I wasn't sure I would either, until about two minutes before I called you."

I take another drink as I wait for her to continue. Inman is torn. That much is clear to see. Her loyalty to the hotel is admirable, but it's almost pathological. I don't understand it. I mean, it's a hotel guest registry. She's not guarding national secrets or the nuclear codes or anything like that. She looks up at me and a gentle smile crosses her lips. She seems to be intuiting my thoughts.

"About ten years ago, I met Mr. Philon—he's the owner of the Churchill," she says. "At the time, I was in pretty bad shape. I was strung out—I did a lot of coke and some other things back in the day. It was always available at shoots, and I just fell into that lifestyle."

"You were a model?" I ask, giving myself a high five for being right.

She nods. "For a little while, yeah. Modeling and a few bit roles in a couple of movies. Long enough to ruin my life," she mutters.

"An all too common story, unfortunately."

"Yeah. The lifestyle made me crash hard. I spun out and was in a really bad way," she says softly. "But Mr. Philon saw something in me that I didn't even see in myself. He pulled me out of the gutter, helped me get clean, and gave me a job. I've worked my way up to where I am now. But I wouldn't be here if he hadn't rolled the dice on me."

"So, that's why you're so loyal to him."

"Yes. That's why I'm so loyal to him. It's why I take my job so seriously and why I do the things I do to protect the hotel. And Mr. Philon," she explains. "I'm not naïve. I know the Churchill's reputation. I know the things that are said. But it's still my hotel. Everything that happens to it, I take personally. Anything that can hurt Mr. Philon, I take personally. And I will do whatever I can to protect him."

I sit back in my seat and take a sip of my drink, replaying her words in my head. Her issues with Mr. Philon and the Churchill are even deeper than I suspected. But I have to say, now that she's laid out her whole story, I understand why she's so loyal and why she this job so personally. I get it. And now I understand why she's so reluctant to help me. If getting her to help me weren't so critical, I'd feel bad for squeezing her as hard as I did.

"But I also don't want anything to happen to Mrs. Osweiler. I'm not as cold or heartless as I must have seemed in my office," she goes on. "The idea that she was taken from our property and could be in grave danger… it rattled me. I'm not a monster, Agent Wilder."

"I didn't think you were," I say.

A soft smile touched her lips. "Yeah, you did. But a woman in my position has to be tough. She has to cultivate a certain image," she says. "I think being a woman in your position, you'd understand that."

"I do," I nod. "More than you know."

"I also want you to know that I'm not doing this because of your threat to go to the media," she continues. "The backlash and negative press would be significant, but the Churchill would eventually recover from it."

"I have no doubt," I reply. "So, why are you doing this then?"

"Because it's the right thing to do."

She lets the statement hang in the air between us, giving me a chance to chew on it for a moment. Inman starts to gnaw on her lower lip again. Every moment of this is torturous for her and I can see the fear in her eyes. It's the fear of betraying Mr. Philon that was gripping her. I needed to make her feel okay about doing this.

"Ms. Inman—Sandy—you have my word that nobody outside of my team is going to see these names," I tell her. "We're strictly looking for Valerie Osweiler, no one else. I give you my word that we are not looking to cause problems for anybody. All we're going to do is cross-reference the names on that registry with names in Mrs. Osweiler's case files. I promise you it's a very narrow scope. I will not compromise the hotel—or you."

She frowns and looks down at her hands again. Inman takes a beat then digs in her bag and pulls out a small, silver thumb drive. She stares at it for a long moment, still trying to decide if she can go through with it or not. Inman drains the last of her Gibson and sets the empty glass down. She lets out a breath and sets the thumb drive down on the table and slides it across to me. When I reach for it though, she puts her hand down over it.

"You promise you'll protect the hotel?" she asks.

"And you," I tell her seriously. "I'll protect you both as much as I can."

She looks uncertain and skeptical of my answer, but she seems to accept it's the best she's going to get from me. Her drive to do the right thing by trying to help save a life overshadows her loyalty to the Churchill and she takes her hand off the drive. I pick it up and give her a solemn smile.

"Thank you, Sandy," I say. "I owe you."

"Just keep me and the Churchill out of it if you can and we'll call it square."

"I promise to do everything in my power to do that," I tell her.

She looks at me for a long moment then nods. "Good luck, Agent Wilder. I really do hope you find her alive and well."

I watch her walk out of the bar, leaving me alone with the adrenaline inside of me surging. I look at the thumb drive in my hand. There is going to be a lot of sorting and cross-referencing to do when I get this back to the office. It's going to make everything we did today look like a cakewalk. But this is the first tangible lead we've had since getting the case passed off to us. The name of Valerie's abductor is in the files on this drive, and somehow, we've to got to figure out which one it is.

That clock for Mrs. Osweiler is ticking and seems to be running faster.

CHAPTER ELEVEN

Criminal Data Analysis Unit; Seattle Field Office

"WELL, YOU'RE IN DIFFERENT CLOTHES, SO I ASSUME you went home at some point last night," Astra observes. "But what are you doing here so early?"

She's coming through the doors to find me already sitting at one of the workstations, clacking away at the keyboard. She thrusts a cup of coffee into my hands, and I take a sip, savoring the dark, rich brew as it slides down my throat. My eyes are grainy. I feel caught in the grip of exhaustion on one side and determination on the other, and they are playing one hell of a game of tug-of-war with me. I feel ready to drop but want to keep going. I've only barely scratched the surface of the data Inman gave me.

"Bless your soul for this," I tell her.

"When did you get in?"

"A little after three," I reply.

"Why in the world would you come in that early?"

"I couldn't sleep," I tell her. "Sandy Inman called last night and asked me to meet."

Astra's eyes widen. "Did she now?"

I nod and then fill her in on all the details of our meeting. Astra sits down at her workstation and takes it all in, looking as surprised as I was that Inman had called me in the first place. When I'm finished with the story, she sits back in her chair.

"That's quite the story," she says. "I feel bad about giving her such a hard time."

"Don't lie. You've got no feelings."

She gives me a lopsided grin. "Okay, that's true," she admits. "But good for her. It takes a lot of strength to pull yourself up out of the gutter like that."

"That's what I thought too," I reply. "Anyway, that's what I've been doing down here all night—sorting through the names in the register and trying to cross-reference them against Mrs. Osweiler's caseload."

"Any luck so far?"

I shake my head. "None. But I've been at it all morning and I'm barely through this list," I reply. "I'll never understand how techy people like Rick and even Mo can do things so fast."

"Don't beat yourself up too much about it. They don't nearly burn their houses down in a drunken stupor as well as you. We all have our own unique skill sets."

"Oh, that reminds me, your transfer went through to the mail room," I fire back even as the exhaustion in my voice betrays my tone. "I'm swapping you out for Kyle."

She guffaws and takes a drink of her coffee as the doors slide open. Rick and Mo come walking through laughing and talking with one another.

"You two are in early," Mo notes.

"Because we've been here getting things done while you two slept in," Astra says.

"Nice try. I saw you pull in," Rick responds with a laugh. "I saw Blake's car already here though, so I guess she's the one getting things done."

I give Astra a grin. "Busted."

"Whatever," she says with a laugh.

"So, what do you have?" Mo asks.

"We got the guest register from the Churchill," I say. "One hundred and thirty-seven names. I've been running backgrounds and cross-referencing them against Mrs. Osweiler's caseload since about four in the morning. I've made it through thirteen of them so far."

"Thirteen?" Rick asks. "That's it? What have you been doing with your time all night, playing solitaire?"

I shoot him a dirty glare. "I'm wearing my gun, Rick. Don't tempt me."

He grins. "There are witnesses."

"I didn't see anything," Astra says.

"I was out for coffee," Mo adds.

He looks at them, an expression of faux hurt on his face. "Ladies, you wound me so."

They set their things down at their workstations and take their seats, waiting for their marching orders.

"Mo, Astra, I'm sending you a copy of the list of registered guests. If we divide it up, we'll get through it faster," I say.

"You certainly couldn't get through it any slower," Rick quips.

I turn to him. "I've had like no sleep, I'm wired on coffee, and I've got a twitchy trigger finger this morning," I say. "Keep pushing me, Scanlon."

He chuckles. "Easy now. It's just jokes, boss."

"Not in the mood."

"I can tell," he replies. "My apologies."

"Where are you on the facial rec?" I ask.

"The footage was too grainy so unfortunately, nothing popped on facial rec," he tells me. "So, I tried something different."

"Different?"

"I wrote a program that would digitize the face, rendering it in 3D," he said. "It uses all the facial markers to build the model and accounts for variances in shape that the blurriness couldn't recreate. It's a lot like the sort of facial reconstruction software anthropologists use that allows them to render a face from a skull."

"Who knew? Boy's got skills," Mo cracks.

Rick grins. "More than you know."

"Okay, I'm officially grossed out now," Astra remarks.

He laughs. "Anyway, once I was able to render a few different models, I put those through facial rec. It's been running since I left last night," he goes on. "I set certain parameters in place and filtered it to guys with criminal records in the Seattle area. That will hopefully limit the number of hits we get. We can expand out from there if we don't get anything useful from the search."

"That's really great work, Rick. That's thinking outside the box," I say. "I'm impressed."

"Is it accurate?" Astra asks. "The last thing we need is to go kick in the wrong door."

"It's accurate-ish. It should be fairly close to the actual face from the footage," he replies. "There are certain variances that are broader than others, but once we have a comprehensive list of results, we should be able to narrow it down. I'm trying to limit it, but..."

He shrugs and spreads his hands out. I get it. There's only so much he can do. But what he's done could prove to be a big help. Yeah, we may have to track down a lot of guys who prove to be dead ends, but once we separate the wheat from the chaff, he may lead us straight to the guy. It really is terrific work. Rick turns to his computer and taps away at his keyboard. He mutters to himself as he works then turns back to us.

"We've got twenty-seven hits," he groans.

I sit back in my seat and blow out a long breath. This is going to take some time—time Mrs. Osweiler doesn't have. But there's nothing else we can do but keep working the leads we have, time-consuming though they may be. There has to be a way to narrow the list. I give it a moment then figure out a place for us to start.

"All right. Can you run those twenty-seven names against the guest registry?" I ask. "Let's see if he was a guest there."

"On it," Mo says. "Rick, send me those names."

"Comin' right up," he says.

Mo gets the list from Rick then bangs away at her keyboard as she runs the cross-reference. It takes a minute, but she frowns and shakes her head.

"Nothing," she sighs. "None of those twenty-seven were registered at the Churchill."

"We should have known it wouldn't be that easy," Astra says.

"Yeah, tell me about it," I mutter. "All right, I guess we have to do this the old-fashioned way. We're going to have to go knock on doors."

"That's fun."

I shrug. "It is what it is," I reply. "Any results on her socials?"

"Nothing," Rick answers. "Unless you consider a penchant for posting pictures of food and inspirational quotes unusual."

"Boring and trite but not unusual," Astra says.

"There's nothing I can find. No flirtations, no suggestive remarks. No nothing," he tells us. "As far as I can tell by what she's posted on her socials, she was a Girl Scout."

I frown and shake my head. "I don't buy it. You don't get to her position without having a few skeletons in your closet."

"That's pretty cynical," Mo raises an eyebrow.

"That's just reality. People in positions of power have typically buried some bodies along the way. It's science," Astra points out, making Mo laugh.

"If she does, she's smart enough to bury those bodies deep—and not put any trace of it on social media," Rick says.

"Okay well, divide the list up. Astra gets one half, I get the other and we'll pound the pavement," I say. "Rick, Mo, I want you two to go through the guest registry. I want you to run backgrounds on the names, then cross-reference those against Mrs. Osweiler's caseload.

You guys are obviously better at that stuff than I am. Just remember, we're on a clock here. Faster would be better."

"On it," Mo says.

"Lists have been divided and sent to your phones," Rick says. "Happy hunting."

I turn to Astra. "Stay in touch with me," I tell her. "And be careful. We don't know exactly what we're dealing with yet."

"You too. Watch your back," she replies.

CHAPTER TWELVE

El Rancho Mexican Cocina; Queen Anne District, Seattle

"I'M ZERO FOR NINE," I SIGH. "HOW ARE YOU DOING?"

"About the same. Everybody's got solid alibis," Astra replies.

"We're going to have to do our due diligence, but yeah, everyone I've talked to so far have alibis too," I say. "That and I'm not getting that ping off them that tells me they're lying."

"Petty criminals being honest. Who'd've thunk it? The world may actually be ending." she muses.

I switch the phone to my other ear and stare through the windshield at the restaurant across the street from me. Even though I've still got a few names on my list to go, I'm getting the sinking feeling we're going to have to expand the search—or consider other lines of investigation entirely. We're getting nowhere and the clock on Mrs. Osweiler is still running. Most abduction victims don't last very long and the fact that she's been missing for days now doesn't bode particularly well. But until we find a body, I'm determined to keep working this as if she's alive and waiting for us to come rescue her. I won't give up on finding her. I refuse.

"I'm at number ten," I tell her. "After this, I'm going to grab something to eat. I'm starving. Let's hook up and compare notes."

"That sounds good to me. Give me a call when you're done with your guy and we'll figure out where to meet," she replies.

"Will do. Talk to you in a bit," I say and disconnect the call.

I get out of the car and slip my phone into my coat pocket, then head for the restaurant, pushing the button on the fob to lock my car. It's a cool afternoon with a thick blanket of slate-gray clouds overhead. It doesn't feel like rain and there's nothing in the forecast that I saw, but then, who really knows with the weather? El Rancho is a hole in the wall that's been around for a generation. I've only been here a handful of times, but the food has always been top-notch.

Pulling the door open, I'm immediately overwhelmed by a wave of amazing smelling aromas of beans, rice, cilantro, and warm tortillas that make my stomach rumble with appreciation. If I weren't here to track down a suspect, I might not be able to wait for Astra to eat. But food is going to have to wait because a woman is missing and I'm here to do my job.

A young woman, no more than twenty or so, approaches me as I step through the door. She's a dainty little thing, no more than five-three, with large eyes the color of chocolate and thick dark hair that's tied back. Her skin is a golden caramel color and has that smoothness that seems to favor the young. She's dressed in green and white skirts and a white peasant blouse that has red, pink, and yellow flowers stitched into the fabric.

"Welcome to El Rancho," she smiles brightly. "Table for one?"

I flash my badge and the girl's smile immediately falters. Her large doe eyes grow even wider and she wrings her hands together in front of her.

"SSA Blake Wilder," I start. "I'm looking for Jake Milburn."

Though she still looks anxious, I see a slight ease in her

shoulders as she lets out a small breath of relief. I'm used to that sort of reaction when I show up and badge somebody. Even if they didn't do anything, they always seem to feel like they did.

"I—uhh—I can go get him for you—"

"No, that's all right. Just tell me where he is," I interrupt. "I'd rather go speak to him myself."

"Oh, okay. He's in the back," she says. "He works in the kitchen."

"Great. Thank you. And please, just stay up front if you would."

"All right," she says slowly, a note of worry in her voice.

I subtly reach my hand beneath my coat and unsnap my holster. Jake Milburn isn't the most hardcore criminal I've ever come face to face with, but he does have a couple of assault charges in his jacket. They were the result of a couple of bar fights, but they show he is capable of violence and I'm not one to take stupid chances. In my line of work, I've discovered that anybody can be capable of horrendous things—especially when they feel their back is against the wall and they have nothing to lose.

I push through the swinging door that leads me into the back of the house. It's hot, stuffy, and somehow manages to smell both horrid and amazing all at the same time. There are a couple of guys working the grill, poking at a sizzling portion of chicken and peppers that's already making my mouth water. Standing at the sink near the back is the man I'm looking for. He happens to look up as I step into the kitchen. A burst of fear crosses his eyes and I already know what's about to happen.

"Come on, Jake. Don't make me chase you," I say. "I'm really not in the mood."

But sure enough, as if my voice acted like a starter's pistol, he's off. He slams through the back door and sprints into the alley behind the restaurant.

"And he's running. Fantastic," I mutter to myself.

The other men working the grills in the kitchen are looking at me, curiosity painted on their faces. In the mood for it or not, I have to give chase, so I groan and take off after him. I push through the door and turn down the alley. Milburn has a good lead on me already, so I grit my teeth, put my head down, and run as fast as my legs will carry me.

Lucky thing for me that Milburn isn't the fleetest of foot and I'm quickly able to make up some ground. At the mouth of the alley, he takes a left, and then we're out among the foot traffic, dodging and weaving around the startled pedestrians.

"Milburn, stop!" I shout. "FBI! Stop!"

He looks over his shoulder at me and I'm close enough now to see his eyes widen when he realizes his lead is evaporating. He grabs hold of a young woman and throws her to the ground in front of me. She screams and hits the ground with a hard thud. I hurdle her without breaking stride and keep closing the gap between me and Milburn. I know I should stop to make sure the girl was all right, but her boyfriend is already at her side so I'm sure if she needs help, he'll get it.

Just ahead of me, Milburn cuts down an alley and seems to pick up a little bit of speed. I slip in a wet spot and nearly go down but manage to keep my feet—though just barely. That gives Milburn a precious second to open the gap between us that much more. Cursing under my breath, I grit my teeth and keep running. My lungs and legs are burning like they're on fire, but I push myself forward, driving myself harder. I'm not going to let him get away.

"Milburn, stop!" I scream. "FBI. Stop running!"

He doesn't, of course, and he reaches the mouth of the alley and cuts left, heading away from El Rancho. I cut the corner and dash after him. People on the sidewalk are jumping out of his way, startled by the man running headlong toward them. I'm gaining ground on him and when Milburn looks over his shoulder again, he cuts between a pair of parked cars, heading across the street and toward an underground parking garage. He's no doubt hoping to lose me in the darkness among the parked cars down below.

The squeal of tires shakes the air around us. It's quickly followed by the gasps and shrieks of the pedestrians on the street all around me. I hear a hard thud and then a sound like wet meat slapping concrete. I dart between the cars beside me to see Milburn lying motionless in the street. I gasp and my stomach clenches so tight, it's almost painful. As I run toward him, Milburn struggles but manages to get himself into a sitting position. At least he's alive.

The driver of the car is getting out, his face pale, his expression one of absolute horror. A crowd starts to form around us, so I flash everybody my badge.

"FBI," I announce. "It's all under control."

Milburn is looking up at me with a look of fear on his face. His pants are torn, and his knee scraped and bleeding. He's also got some abrasions on his face and he's holding his arm like it's bothering him. Even though I see no bones protruding through the skin and he doesn't look like he's going to die, I'll still need to call an ambulance and have him checked out. If he were bleeding internally or something and keeled over while I was interrogating him, I know it would be a very bad look, so I call it in and get an ambulance on the way.

"Don't kill me. Please don't kill me," he wails as tears stream down his cheeks. "Tell Amaras I'll get him his money. I swear it. Please don't kill me."

I cock my head and look at him. "Who in the hell is Amaras? And why do you think I'm here to kill you?"

Milburn looks at me in silence for a moment, looking as if he's trying to decide if I'm putting him on or not. I squat down beside him and look him in the eye.

"Y—you ain't here to kill me?" he asks.

"Why would I kill you?"

"Because I didn't pay Amaras what I owed him," he replies.

"Who is Amaras?" I ask again.

"You really don't know?"

"Would I be asking if I did?" I snap.

"He's a bookie. Works for the Armenians," he says.

I stare at him for a long moment, processing everything he said. And all I can do is shake my head. Of everything he said, I think the idea that I look like I could be mobbed up is the most offensive thing. I may not like that people can tell I'm a cop just by looking at me, but I definitely don't like people thinking I'm a gangster either. Especially as if I'd work for an organization as monstrous as the Armenian mob.

I've tangled with them before. Their leader, Stephen Petrosyan, once ordered the grisly murder and dismemberment of Ben Davis, a young man who'd been dating his daughter. Needless to say, he disapproved—and had the boy murdered and his remains cut apart, stuffed in a barrel, and drifted down the river. I got so close to nailing him for the crime, but he slipped right out from my fingers. One of his men took the fall, but I know to my bones that Petrosyan was the one responsible. I just can't prove it.

"Do I look like an Armenian tax collector?" I ask. "I mean, seriously?"

He shrugs. "I got no idea. You never know who they'll send after you," he says then pauses for a moment as if considering his next question. "So, if you ain't here to collect the money or kill me, who are you, and what the hell do you want?"

I hold my badge out for him. "FBI," I repeat for what feels like the tenth time. "I have some questions for you."

He mutters a string of curse words under his breath. "I think I'd have preferred the Armenians after all."

The sound of sirens reverberates through the air around us. The crowd has backed off like I asked them to, but they're still hovering, all of them jockeying for a position, hoping to see all the blood and gore. There is none, disappointing many of the rubberneckers. But then the EMT and fire crew roll onto the scene and as they rush toward us, I get to my feet.

"You're going to the hospital to get checked out. But when you get a clean bill of health, as I suspect you will, I'm going to drag you into my interrogation room so you and me can sit down and have ourselves a nice chat," I tell him.

"Awesome," he mutters. "Really lookin' forward to that."

CHAPTER THIRTEEN

Interrogation Suite Beta-3; Seattle Field Office

As I'd thought, Milburn was treated and released into my custody. He's got some bruises, cuts, and scrapes, but there's nothing broken and he's otherwise in one piece. Now he's sitting at the table in the interrogation suite waiting for us. Astra and I stand behind the two-way glass in the observation pod, watching him. Through the window to our right, I can see there's another interview in progress, but the other two suites are currently unoccupied. Must be a slow day in the world of crime, I guess.

The tech, a woman in her mid-thirties or so named Iris, is at her station in the pod. She's got a pair of noise-canceling headphones on as she works all the audio and visual equipment for all the interview suites, preserving the records in case they're needed for trial. I watch the different lights and digital equalizers going up and down in time with the voices in the other interview suite. Iris is making adjustments on the fly, ensuring nothing is garbled and everything comes out clean and crisp.

"So, tell me again how he came to be in front of a moving vehicle?" Astra asks, a note of amusement in her voice.

I look at her and grin. "He ran into traffic without looking both ways first," I shrug. "His mother obviously didn't teach him that important lesson when he was young."

"Obviously."

"Shall we?"

Astra nods. "Let's."

We walk out of the observation pod and into our interview room. I close the door behind us, then Astra and I take a seat across from Jake Milburn. I set my things down and look up. He's not a bad-looking guy. A little too rough around the edges for my taste, but I know some women like that bad-boy appeal. Milburn is about five-ten with sandy blonde hair and crystalline blue eyes. He's got that stylish five o'clock shadow guys seem to cultivate and is lean and trim. The tops of a couple of tattoos peek out from under his shirt collar and trail up the sides of his neck. He reminds me a lot of one of those guys they use in male cologne ads where they're trying to cater to that bad-boy style.

"Before we begin, I need you to acknowledge for the record that you have been read your Miranda warning, Mr. Milburn," I start.

"Whatever," he grumbles.

"Mr. Milburn—"

"Fine. Yeah. I been read my rights," he snaps.

"And you acknowledge that you have the right to have an attorney present for this interview," I press.

"I don't need no lawyer."

"But you have the right—"

"I don't need a lawyer because I didn't do nothin'!"

"Mr. Milburn, are you waiving your right to counsel at this time?" I grumble.

"Yeah. Fine. Whatever. I waive my freakin' right to counsel, all right? You happy now?"

Milburn shifts in his chair and is wringing his bound hands together, the expression on his face that of a sulking teenager. He's gnawing on his bottom lip and refusing to look at either one of us. I let him sit for a moment, allowing the tension in the room to grow. He finally can't take the silence anymore and raises his eyes.

"I don't feel so good," he mutters. "I think somethin's busted inside me. You have to take me back to the hospital or I might die."

Astra looks at me. "I'm not quite buying the performance. You?"

I shake my head. "It lacked conviction."

"Right. I wasn't emotionally invested."

"You two are lettin' me die here. My blood is gonna be on your hands," he spits.

I frown. "Still doesn't pack that emotional punch."

"Are you friggin' crazy? Are you deaf? I said I'm dyin' here," he shouts.

Astra chuckles. "The doctors gave you a clean bill of health," she says calmly. "Nice try though. The performance sucks, but I'll give you a solid B for effort."

He glowers at her. "Crazy bit—"

"So, Jake," I cut him off. "You say you ran from me because you thought I was one of Amaras Kazarian's tax collectors."

He turns that cold, hateful glare to me. "That's what I said, ain't it?" he growls. "For Christ's sake, I'm the one who got hit by a car and you're the one with memory problems."

"We're merely establishing the record here, Jake. No need to be hostile," I say.

"And let the record reflect that Amaras Kazarian is a known member of the Elezi crime family, headed by one Sarvan Petrosyan, also known as Stephen Petrosyan," Astra mentions. "Kazarian is known to be involved with bookmaking and prostitution."

Milburn claps his bound hands together as much as he's able to. "Very good. You know your stuff," he says. "And now you know why you need to uncuff me and let me out of here. If they get wind of you picking me up, they're going to think I'm cooperating, and then they're gonna kill me."

He's unfortunately not wrong. The Armenian mob does not play around—as I know all too well. If they so much as think you're a snitch, that's usually good enough for them and we end up pulling your body out of Puget Sound. If there's a body to be found at all. These guys don't take chances.

"This is what we call a teachable moment, Jake," Astra says. "This is exactly why it's so important that you don't run from law enforcement. Misunderstandings like this can be avoided if you would have just stayed put."

"How was I supposed to know she's a cop? She didn't say she's a cop," he argues.

"You hardly gave me a chance. You took one look at me and bolted," I say. "All I wanted was to ask you a few questions."

He shrugs. "No way I could've known."

"You could have if you hadn't run away the second you laid eyes on me," I reply. "But that's neither here nor there. You're here now so we need to ask you some questions."

"You're gonna get me killed, lady."

"Maybe you should think about the company you keep," Astra comments with a shrug. "And you wouldn't have worries like these."

He scowls at her but says nothing. I watch him closely as a theory starts to form in my mind. Mrs. Osweiler had won a couple of cases against Armenian mob-owned companies. I don't think it was anything earth-shattering, but they usually don't like losing at all, so no doubt they would have taken it personally. So, as my burgeoning theory goes, they get a guy like Milburn, up to his ears in debt to them, to take her out on their behalf.

My theory is definitely shaky and has got a lot of holes—holes that could totally destroy it unless I'm able to plug them. But it seems like a good place to start.

"We're looking into the disappearance of a woman, Jake. She's a prominent attorney here in Seattle and she's been missing for days now," I start.

"And what's that got to do with me?"

"Because you were outside the Churchill hotel the morning she went missing," Astra says. "The Churchill, by the way, is the last time she was seen."

He looks from Astra to me and shakes his head. "I—I don't got any idea what you're talkin' about," he stammers. "I didn't kidnap nobody."

I pull the still image from the traffic cam footage out of the file and set it down in front of him. Milburn looks at it for a moment then raises his gaze to me.

"That ain't me," he frowns.

"It's not?" I ask.

He shakes his head. "No, it ain't. Look, that guy has hair that's longer than mine."

"Nothing a pair of scissors couldn't account for," Astra counters.

"I'm tellin' you, I ain't never been to the Churchill," he growls. "Do I look like the kind of guy who can afford a room there? Do you really think I'm playin' sugar daddy to some chick barely out of high school?"

"No, we know you're not that wealthy. We think you went there on the Kazarian's orders—maybe even Petrosyan himself, for all we know—and abducted the woman we're talking about to help satisfy the debt you owe them," I say.

He shakes his head vigorously. "No. I didn't do that. I got no idea what you're talkin' about. I didn't kidnap no woman."

I take the DMV photo of Mrs. Osweiler we'd printed out and set it on top of the other picture in front of him then tap on it.

"Valerie Osweiler," I go on. "She's a labor attorney here in Seattle. She's won some cases against the guys you owe money to, which undoubtedly upset them."

"You see where this is going, Jake?" Astra presses. "They're upset about losing to her in court, and since you obviously suck at gambling, you owe them. Big time. Then one day, they lean on you to help them out with their little Valerie Osweiler problem."

"No. That ain't what happened."

"Then what did happen, Jake?" I ask. "Tell us what happened and maybe we can work with you. Get you into witness protection or something."

"Nothin' happened. I'm tellin' you, nothin' like that happened," he shrieks. "I don't know that woman. I ain't never seen her before in my life and I damn sure didn't kidnap her!"

"We have you outside the hotel—"

"That ain't me!" he roars and angrily stabs the picture with his finger. "And I'm tellin' you, I never laid eyes on this woman in my life."

"Jake, we don't have time for this. We need to know what you did with her, and we need to know now," I snap.

"I really don't know what to tell you, lady," he huffs. "This has nothin' to do with me."

Silence descends over the interview room, and I look down at my hands as my frustration builds. Milburn stares at the still image from the traffic cam footage. He starts tapping on it with his finger and looks up at us excitedly.

"I can prove this isn't me," he says.

"How?" I ask.

I see him stabbing his finger on the time and date stamp in the corner of the photo and groan as a bad feeling envelops me. Apparently one of those holes in my theory is about to become unpluggable.

"I was with my parole officer at the time this picture was taken," he explains. "You can call and check it with him. He'll tell you I was sittin' in his office right in front of him."

Astra and I exchange a look, both of us frowning. It looks like our once-promising lead has turned to dust right before our very eyes.

"We're going to check your alibi and if we find you're lying to us, you are not going to have a good time, Jake," I say. "You might wish you were back with Amaras after all."

"I'm telling the truth, I swear!" he exhales in frustration.

"Just sit tight," Astra tells him.

"Like I can do anything else," he mutters. "But can you hurry it up? I really have to pee."

Astra and I get up and head back into the observation pod. Astra makes the call and I can see by her face that Milburn's alibi is checking out, which makes my stomach churn. We've wasted all this time on Milburn and have absolutely nothing to show for it. She disconnects the call, an expression of deep disappointment on her face.

I sigh. "Cut him loose."

CHAPTER FOURTEEN

Guerrero's Taqueria; Beacon Hill District, Downtown Seattle

After coming up empty with Milburn, Astra and I moved on to one of the few remaining names on the list. And it just so happens that our latest person of interest works at this taqueria. Which works out well. I'm famished. I guess the universe decided to throw me a bone for a change, which is nice.

We sit at a table on the covered patio, munching away while keeping an eye on Alex Moore, who's working behind the counter. Moore has a rap sheet that includes several assaults, armed robbery, grand theft, and a sexual assault. He's been in and out of state-run facilities for nearly half of his thirty-three years on this planet.

"I have a very bad feeling about how this is all going to turn out," Astra says.

I wash my food down with a swallow of soda and nod. "Yeah. So do I. Mrs. Osweiler's been missing for days now. That doesn't bode particularly well."

"I'm just hoping she skipped town with a boyfriend."

"Yeah, I hope so too," I nod. "I'm sure it won't bring Mr.

Osweiler much comfort, but I think it'll be better for him than finding out she's been murdered."

"I think so too, but..."

Astra lets her words trail off, but she doesn't need to finish the sentence. The unspoken sentiment is more than clear. The likelihood that we're going to find her alive diminishes with every minute that passes. It's a grim thought, but it's a statistical fact. If I'm being honest with myself, it's likely she's already dead. But I'm not giving up hope. Not until I know for certain that she's gone.

"I thought we really had something with Milburn," Astra sighs. "Your theory fit perfectly. I really thought he was our guy."

"Like you always say, things are never that easy for us. That was the equivalent of having it all wrapped up with a big red bow."

"Tell me about it."

"It's why I'm not expecting much from this guy," I say. "I'm sure he'll have a solid alibi. But we have to do our due diligence. The one rock we don't turn over is the one the answer is going to be hiding beneath."

"Mo's right. You are pretty cynical."

I shrug. "I like to think I'm realistic."

She grins. "I like to think I'm wealthier than Elon Musk and Jeff Bezos combined. Doesn't make it true now, does it?"

I laugh. "Shut up."

The laughter fades and we finish our meals in silence. My mind is consumed with a thousand different thoughts about this case but can't settle on anything solid. None of our leads have panned out to this point, but I still somehow feel like we're close to breaking something open. Maybe even finding her. All we need is to get one lucky break. We just need one thing to go our way. If we get that, we might be able to crack this and hopefully get Mrs. Osweiler back home where she belongs.

"I can't recall a case in recent memory where we've been stumped this hard this long," Astra notes.

"That makes two of us. I mean, we've got absolutely nothing but wishes and hopes at this point," I reply. "We don't have one tangible thing to cling to. No leads, no nothing."

"Are we losing our touch?"

"Oh, don't you start being cynical too. That's my job," I say. "But I like to think this is more of this case being an absolute crapshow from the start. I mean, she'd already been missing for a couple of days before we ever got the folder. I don't have to tell you how critical those first days are."

She shakes her head. "Nope. You don't. They put us behind the eight ball from the jump. And it hasn't gotten easier since."

"We'll keep doing what we're doing and following every lead," I shrug. "And for my part, I'll keep hope alive that this could have a happy ending. But that voice in the back of my head is telling me I'm being naïve. I hate that voice."

"I hate that your voice is usually right."

I drain the last of my soda and look behind the counter. Moore is taking his apron off and speaking quietly to another man who's standing back there with him. I sit up.

"Looks like our guy is taking a break," I say.

"Let's go ruin it for him."

"Might be the highlight of my day."

We get up and throw our trash away then walk around to the rear of the building just in time to see Moore stepping out. He leans against the building as he lights a cigarette. Moore takes a deep drag on it then exhales a thick plume of smoke. He glances over at us, and a sour look crosses his face as Astra and I approach him.

Moore isn't a big guy. Five-nine at most, with shaggy brown locks and brown eyes. He's pretty average in appearance. The stubble on his face isn't like Jake Milburn's—it's not stylish, it's just slovenly. His clothes, like his hair, look like they haven't been washed in a while and he just has a disheveled look about him. If I squint, I can see that the shapes of his facial features look just like Milburn's—but his presence is just completely different. He's the sort of guy you'd forget five minutes after meeting him.

"Come on," he says after we introduce ourselves. "I'm clean. I'm keeping myself out of trouble. I haven't done anything wrong."

"Is that so?" I ask.

He takes another drag and angrily blows out the smoke. "Yeah, that's so."

"Then you shouldn't mind answering a few questions," Astra says.

He sighs. "Like I have any other choice?"

"No, you don't. Not unless you want us to violate you and revoke your parole for failing to cooperate with an investigation," I tell him.

"You wouldn't want to do the rest of the time on your sentence now, would you, Alex?" Astra asks. "I mean, what do you have left on that bid? Three years?"

"Three years and six months," I clarify. "And I'd hate to have to report back that you weren't cooperating in a high-profile case. I don't know how happy your PO would be to hear about that."

"Come on, why are you guys always bustin' my chops like this?" he whines. "I haven't done anything. I'm clean. I swear it. I've got a regular job, my own place. I'm even paying taxes. Why do you people have to keep coming around and giving me grief?"

"Maybe because you keep giving us reasons to give you grief," I say.

"I haven't done—"

"Anything, yeah you keep saying that," Astra cuts him off. "The trouble is, we don't believe you. In fact, we know different."

"I have no idea what you're talking about," he says.

I pull the photo out of the folder in my hand showing him—or who I hope is him—sitting in front of the Churchill and thrust it at him. Moore hangs the cigarette from the corner of his mouth and looks at the picture. I see the flash of concern cross his face. It's subtle and he covers it quickly, but it was there. That's how I know we've got him. He's the one in the photo. The realization sends a hot bolt of adrenaline shooting through me.

"That's you," I tell him.

"It's not," he replies weakly.

"Don't bother lying to us, Alex. We don't have time for it," I say. "Where is Valerie Osweiler? If we get her back unharmed, things might not go so bad for you."

"Who?" he asks.

"The woman you were clocking and then followed into the hotel," Astra says.

He shakes his head, an expression of genuine confusion on his face. "I have no idea what you're talking about."

"Alex, the woman you followed into the hotel is missing. She's been missing since the day this photo of you watching her was taken," I press. "We have you on video following her into the hotel."

"Do you really want to spend the rest of your life in prison?" Astra adds. "Talk to us and maybe we can get you out of prison while you're still upright."

Moore opens his mouth to reply but closes it again, letting his words die on his lips. Maybe the message that lying to us isn't going to work has finally made its way through that thick skull of his. He takes another drag of his cigarette and lets the smoke drift out of his half-open mouth. He seems to be thinking about the next words he's going to say, then nods to himself and raises his eyes to me. He licks his lips nervously and nods.

"All right, fine. I was there. And I saw your missing woman," he admits. "But I didn't have anything to do with her disappearance."

"Then why did you follow her into the hotel?" I ask. "Why were you watching her?"

He shuffles his feet and draws from his cigarette again. Moore looks down at the ground and seems to be thinking about what he's going to say. But he raises his head and meets my eyes again and sighs.

"So, all you're interested in is finding this woman, right? You swear? Nothin' else?" he asks.

I groan. Typical. "If it has nothing to do with our case, we probably don't have time to deal with it," I say.

"But you had best tell us the whole truth, Alex," Astra grumbles. "If we find out you lied to us, I swear to God, we will rain hell down on you."

"Fine, fine. I get it," he says. "I... sometimes I find people's wallets for them, if you know what I mean."

"Oh, so you're a pickpocket?"

He makes a motion for me to quiet down and cuts a look left and right to make sure no one is listening. "Not so loud," he protests. It's just to supplement my income. I zeroed in on your girl because she had a big, fat purse and didn't seem to be paying attention. She was distracted."

"So, you're telling us that you followed her into the hotel and lifted her wallet?"

"That was my plan. But a security guard was hovering, so I never got close to her," he admits, still sounding disappointed about it. "I swear to God, that's all I did. I was outside the hotel because it's filled with fat cats, and they usually carry a couple grand around in their wallets. There's no better fishing hole in the entire city."

As he speaks, I'm watching him closely. It's a really convenient excuse I could wave off like nothing. The problem I'm having, though, is that I believe him. As maddening as it is, I'm not picking up on any hint of deception from him—and I'm really looking closely for it. But his voice is steady and his eye contact is direct. I'd really like to say he's being deceitful but no matter how hard I look, it's just not there. I look over at Astra and her expression tells me she's thinking the same thing.

I take the photos back from Moore and stick them back into

my folder. It seems more than obvious to me that Moore is not our guy and nothing I can do is going to change that. I look at Astra and give her a nod. He shifts on his feet and takes one last drag from his cigarette before dropping it onto the ground with a dozen others and crushing it beneath his foot.

"So, we're cool, right? You're not going to violate me for what I told you, right?" he asks, a waver of nervousness in his voice.

"Not right now. But don't leave town," I tell him. "We'll likely have more questions for you."

He nods. "I won't. I'll be here. You know where to find me."

Astra and I turn and walk back to the car, feeling frustrated beyond belief. We get in and sit there in silence for a moment.

"Well, that was a bust," Astra groans. "We're coming up empty left and right."

"Every time we think we've got our guy, we get our legs cut out from under us."

"So, what now?"

I purse my lips and think for a moment. A thought occurred to me earlier, but I'd dismissed it. Now that we have no other viable leads though, it's probably time to revisit it. I start the car and pull out of the spot. As I turn onto the street, Astra turns to me.

"Got an idea?" she asks.

"Not saying it's a good one, but yeah. I've got an idea."

"Great. I'm glad you do because my head is completely empty," she says.

"And that's different than any other day how exactly?"

She laughs. "Screw you."

As we drive, that clock ticking in my head grows louder and I feel a tremendous weight pressing down on me. It's heavy and suffocating. We've been stymied at every turn and a cold sense of dread grips me even tighter. This isn't going to end well. I can feel it.

CHAPTER FIFTEEN

Hawkins, Lott, Berman, and Todd; Downtown Seattle

“And what is it we’re doing here?” Astra asks as we take the elevator up.

“Digging. Investigating,” I say. “You know, working the case like the trained investigators we are.”

She laughs. “We’re walking into one of the most prestigious law offices in Seattle, if not all of Washington itself. What do you imagine we’re going to learn here?”

“No sure yet. Something, I hope,” I reply.

“You know they’re going to have everything buttoned up and locked away. They aren’t going to tell us anything. That’s just what lawyers do,” she says. “It’s like they never learned that sharing is caring when they were children or something.”

“Well, it’s on us to turn over every rock whether there’s something underneath it or not anyway. That’s the job,” I point out.

She nods. “Fair enough.”

I know she’s right. When we start probing, the lawyers in the firm will likely circle the wagons and refuse to give us anything other than their thoughts and prayers we find Mrs. Osweiler. I know in most cases they're bound by law and can't violate any sort of attorney-client privilege. I get that. But at the same time, I'm hoping somebody will push those bonds just a bit to give us any information that could prove helpful.

We've gotten glimpses of the case files she had at home—which I'm sure the partners in the firm would be aghast to know. But we took a very targeted approach to what we looked at. We were looking for the names of disgruntled clients or people who would be angry that she'd beaten them in court. Of course, we're not going to tell the firm that we've snooped through the files we did. That would open up a Pandora's Box of trouble for us.

But earlier, when I got to thinking about the case files we'd seen, it made me wonder about other cases she might have been working. She may not have had all her case files at home. In fact, she probably didn't. Maybe some of them were too sensitive to leave the premises or there wasn't any work for her to do on them at home. But I'm willing to bet my salary that she's got more case files here. And while I know snooping through them is out, I'm hoping against hope the partners might be willing to divulge the names of the people they were suing.

The elevator doors slide open and we step into a lobby that's done in marble and dark woods, with everything polished to a near mirror shine. The walls in the lobby are lined with photos of the named partners, all posed with solemn expressions on their faces, as if that's supposed to impart confidence that they'll take your case seriously. The atmosphere is staid and hushed. I have to admit, the office carries a certain gravitas. Pictures aside, the feeling when you get off the elevator is one of power and success.

"May I help you?"

The receptionist sits behind a desk across from the elevator. She's a blonde with her hair up and a pair of glasses over her blue eyes. She's got gorgeously delicate features and makeup that looks like it was applied by an expert, highlighting all her best features.

She gives us a smile bright enough to light up the entire city. Putting her up front to greet people is a smart move. The woman takes the edge off an otherwise dour and stodgy atmosphere.

Astra and I badge her. "SSA Wilder and Special Agent Russo," I say. "We'd like to speak with the managing partner—Ms. Hawkins, I believe."

The woman eyes our credentials for a moment but unlike nearly every other person we badge, the receptionist doesn't bat an eye. She remains cool and collected as she returns her gaze to mine.

"And may I tell her what this is about?" she asks with a haughty tone in her voice.

"It's an investigative matter," I reply.

"Regarding?"

"Regarding matters I'm not at liberty to discuss with you," I respond. "Now, please tell Ms. Hawkins we're here or we'll go find her ourselves."

The receptionist's demeanor turns icy as she picks up the phone. She presses a couple of buttons then holds the receiver to her ear, her eyes never leaving mine.

"Ms. Hawkins," she says into the phone. "There are a couple of FBI agents out here who would like to speak with you."

She pauses for a moment as she listens to the response.

"No, they won't say what it's about. They'll only speak with you," she says and pauses again. "Right away."

She hangs up the phone then looks up at us. I'm half-convinced she's about to tell us to get stuffed and to leave. Ms. Hawkins would certainly be within her rights to send us packing without talking to us. It's not like we have a warrant. But I'm hoping she can guess why we're here and wants to help. The receptionist gets to her feet.

"If you'll follow me, please," she says curtly.

Astra and I follow her through a doorway then through a warren of corridors, passing an open bullpen filled with cubicles, likely for the paralegals, and a break room enclosed within glass walls. We take a right and find ourselves in a short corridor that ends in a doorway. The receptionist knocks, then opens the door and steps aside to let us enter. She closes the door behind us, and we find ourselves standing in the office of Bea Hawkins, managing partner of the firm.

I'd expected somebody older, to be honest. But I'd put Hawkins in her late thirties or maybe early forties. She's got a youthful appearance that makes it hard to tell for sure. Hawkins' thick auburn hair is tied back, and she's got a round face. Her eyes are large and dark—doe eyes that convey a sense of innocence. But one look into their depths shows a woman who's seen some things in her day.

She gets up and comes around her desk to greet us. She's wearing a smart, dark blue pantsuit with a cream-colored blouse that's all beautifully tailored and fits her like a glove. Like the office, Ms. Hawkins has a gravitas about her that can't be denied. She's a small woman, five-four or so at most, but she has a presence that makes her seem so much larger than she actually is.

"I'm Bea Hawkins," she greets us. "Please, let's have a seat."

We let her guide us to a sitting area. Sitting atop a large Persian rug on the right side of the room is a plush-looking sofa and a matching loveseat that are separated by an elegant glass coffee table. Astra and I sit down on the sofa and I look around. Hawkins' office is stately. Her large, ornately carved desk is on the other side of the room and the wall behind it is built-in shelving filled with books, journals, plaques, photos, and personal knickknacks. The walls are deep forest green and three archway windows throughout the room give her a commanding view of the city beyond the glass. It's gorgeous.

"I have a feeling I know why you're here," Hawkins starts. "And have you made any progress on Valerie's case?"

"Some, yes. But we also seem to be running into more dead ends than viable leads, to be honest," I admit.

Hawkins looks away and seems to be doing her best to control her emotions, but I can see her eyes shimmering as the tears well within them. She draws in a breath and it's shaky as she exhales but she manages to get a grip on herself. She turns and looks at us again.

"I apologize. This is very difficult. Valerie is a good friend and I'm worried about her," she says. "I know the longer she's missing, the chances of her being found alive are diminished, and I..."

She bites off her words and covers her face with one of her hands, unable to keep her emotions in check. I watch Hawkins closely and her outburst feels genuine. I don't pick up on anything false or performative as she quietly cries. She takes a minute to gather herself. She dabs at her eyes with a tissue she pulled out of the pocket of her blazer, then takes another breath and seems to count to five before looking up at us again.

"I'm sorry," she says.

"No need for you apologize. This has to be difficult for you," I say.

She nods. "Very," she says. "But what is it I can do for you, Agents?"

"First, I wanted to know if you knew of anybody specifically threatening Mrs. Osweiler," I start.

She gives me a wan smile. "If we weren't being threatened, that would mean we're not doing our jobs very well," she says. "Everybody who litigates for our firm gets threatening letters and phone calls. It's just standard operating procedure around here."

"Well, do you know if she was worried about any of the threats she received in particular?" Astra asks. "Did she mention anybody by name or seem unusually scared?"

Hawkins shakes her head. "No, not that I can think of. She never mentioned anybody or any particular threats to me," she says. "To be honest, we all usually just brush off the multitude of threats we receive. If we let them all get to us, we'd all be huddled in a corner, shaking like leaves and bawling our eyes out."

"All right, tell me this," I say. "Do you know if she was having an affair with anybody? Was there another man in her life, Ms. Hawkins?"

She puts her hand to her chest and stares at me like I've lost my mind. But Hawkins quickly regains her composure and shakes her head.

"No, she wasn't having any affairs," she says. "Not that I know of. And believe me, I know everything that happens around here. If Valerie was having an affair, I'd know."

"Are you certain of that?" Astra asks.

"One hundred percent. Valerie told me everything," she confirms.

I have to keep myself from rolling my eyes. If I had a dollar for everybody who claimed their friend, child, spouse, or whoever, told them everything—and then have it turn out that they didn't—I'd be filthy, stinking rich right now. But I'm not going to argue the point with her. She obviously believes she knows better and I'm not going to burst her bubble.

"Ms. Hawkins, it would help us a great deal to find Mrs. Osweiler if we knew what she was working on," Astra says, seeming to read my thoughts from where I was about to pivot. "If you could perhaps, give us a look at her current caseload and let us see who might have—"

"You know I can't give you access to our files," Hawkins interrupts. "I can't break attorney-client privilege."

"We understand that, Ms. Hawkins," I say. "And we're not asking for access to your complete files. All we want to know are some names of people she was litigating against. If we can find out who—"

"I'm sorry, Agent Wilder," she cuts me off. "As much as I want Valerie found, I cannot jeopardize the integrity of our office."

"But we may not be able to find her if you can't provide us with some names or some information about what she was working on," Astra presses.

"I would do anything to help find Valerie—"

"Except actually providing information that could help us do that," Astra growls.

Hawkins swallows down a response that would no doubt be biting. Instead, she closes her eyes and takes a moment to compose herself before addressing us again. When she opens her eyes again, she looks at me, apparently not wanting to deal with Astra again.

"I might be able to have a special master appointed who can review the files and then provide you with information that will not compromise our cases," she says.

"A special master might take weeks," I say. "We don't have weeks. More importantly, Valerie doesn't have weeks."

"That's unfortunately the best I can do," she responds.

"No, that's the best you're willing to do," Astra snipes.

Hawkins finally turns to Astra, her eyes narrowed, her jaw clenched, and her demeanor colder than an Arctic wind.

"Agent Russo, I am bound by law and by ethics. If I were to turn over my files to you, I would be subject to a disciplinary hearing and even disbarment. As much as I love Valerie and want her brought home safely, I cannot violate the oath I took as an attorney. Nor am I willing to throw away my career like that," she says curtly. "I love being a lawyer and I love the good we do in this office. We help more people than I can count, and I can't jeopardize our reputation, nor my own license, on a fishing expedition. I won't. So yes, I suppose you're right. That's the best I'm willing to do. It is unfortunately a matter of the greater good. If I'm disbarred, how many people that I could have helped would end up suffering?"

Astra looks away, an abashed expression on her face. As much as I want to argue with Hawkins and tell her to stuff her greater good morality straight up her backside, I don't. And I don't because I know she's right. We're putting her in an impossible situation. We're asking her to betray every oath she's taken and every value she holds dear because we're having trouble building a case—and for the high possibility that we'd still have nothing to show for it afterward. I hate to say it but, in her place, I'd probably tell us to take a walk too.

"All right, Ms. Hawkins. I understand," I tell her. "And we're sorry for imposing on you this way."

She shakes her head and gives Astra an apologetic look. "It's all right. I know we're all probably wound tight right now. And I'm sorry for jumping down your throat, Agent Russo. If I could legally and ethically give you what you wanted, I would turn it over faster than a heartbeat. Please believe that."

Astra gives her a smile. "No need to apologize. I was out of line," she says. "And I do believe that."

With nothing more to say, we all get to our feet. There's a moment of awkward silence as we all stand there staring at one another.

"Well, I suppose we should go," I say. "Thank you for your time."

"I truly am sorry I can't be more help," she replies. "If it's not too much trouble, would you mind keeping me abreast of any developments?"

"I understand, Ms. Hawkins," I say with a nod. "And we will."

Astra and I take our leave and head out of the office. We pass the reception desk and see the blonde has been replaced by a brunette who gives us a friendly smile as we walk to the elevator. As we descend, the thought passes through my mind that I have no idea how to tell Rosie this case is going nowhere. We're stuck in the mud and can't get out. We don't fail often. Even when the odds seem overwhelmingly stacked against us, we usually get our guy.

But this one feels different, and the thought of failure is even more oppressive than normal. The mere thought of not finding Mrs. Osweiler leaves a bitter taste in my mouth.

CHAPTER SIXTEEN

Hawkins, Lott, Berman, and Todd; Downtown Seattle

WE GET OFF THE ELEVATOR ON THE GROUND FLOOR AND head across the lobby. Just up ahead standing off to the side of the coffee cart, I see the blonde receptionist from upstairs. She's got a cup of coffee cupped in her hands, but our eyes meet, and I can tell she's been waiting for us. She gives me a small nod that confirms my thought, then turns and heads out of the building, obviously wanting us to follow. I glance at Astra, who shrugs.

"Let's follow the white rabbit," she whispers to me.

"And down the hole we go."

We exit and follow her at a distance through a courtyard nestled between three tall office buildings. The way she gave me a subtle nod inside tells me she's a little worried and needs some discretion, so I'm content to let her lead the way. She'll let us know when and where she feels comfortable stopping.

The receptionist crosses the crowded courtyard and enters one of the other buildings. Astra and I follow and see her sitting at a table near a coffee cart on the far side of the lobby. The design of this building is identical to the one that houses her law firm, right down to the planters full of plants in full bloom and the vendor carts. We sit down at her table, which is partially tucked behind one of those planters. Anybody walking by would get a good view of me and Astra, but she is carefully screened by the broad leaves of the bush in the planter.

We sit in silence for a moment as the woman shifts in her seat. She clutches her cup of coffee in both hands and stares down at it intently. She's obviously wrestling with something heavy. Gone, though, is the icy demeanor and haughty attitude she'd thrown at us in her office, and in its place is one of uncertainty. Perhaps even fear. She gathers her nerve as best she can and looks up at us.

"My name is Casey," she introduces herself.

"I'm Blake and this is Astra," I say.

I'm hoping that using our names rather than ranks will make her a bit more comfortable. She gives me a small smile but honestly doesn't look anymore at ease than she did when we sat down at her table. Astra and I share a glance as Casey continues to fidget with her cup.

"So, we got the impression you wanted us to follow you somewhere more private," I say. "Did you have something to tell us?"

Casey looks up at me but flinches and looks back down at her cup. This radical shift in her personality is strange. Upstairs she was confident and cold. Or at least she did a good job of fronting that way. Down here though, outside of that ivory tower, she's an entirely different person. She seems like a scared little girl more than anything.

"I—I really shouldn't say anything. If they knew I was talking to you, I'd lose my job," she says. "They never want us talking to anybody, regardless of how trivial or irrelevant something might be. They fear anybody saying anything that can cast the firm in a bad light."

"So why are you risking it?" Astra asks.

Casey raises her head and looks at Astra, an expression of indignation on her face. It's the first trace of the woman we met upstairs I've seen since we spotted her at the coffee cart waiting for us. Casey sits up a little straighter and squares her shoulders.

"Because Valerie is my friend. She's the kindest person I've ever met. She's been helping me get ready to take the bar," Casey says with conviction in her voice. "I want you guys to find her safe. I fear the worst already, but I'm hoping for a miracle. And if you guys have more facts to work with, you might be able to pull one-off."

"All right," I nod. "So, we're here. Talk to us. What is it you know?"

Casey seems to deflate and slumps a bit in her seat. That brief gust of bravado seems to have blown out again, leaving her flatter than before. She runs the tip of her finger around the lid of her coffee cup, her lips pursed, still seeming to be struggling with whether to tell us what she knows.

"Do you know if she was being threatened?" I ask. "Was it by somebody whose case she was working on? Somebody she was suing maybe?"

"I don't have access to any of the attorneys' case files," she replies. "They keep those cards very close to the vest. Only they and their paralegal know what's going on with any case. I'm just a receptionist so I'm not in the loop."

"All right, so was she having problems with somebody in the office?" Astra asks. "Was she threatening to blow the whistle on somebody for sexual harassment or anything like that?"

"No, nothing like that either," she says. "Not that I know of, anyway."

This game of twenty questions is really starting to irritate me. I understand her reticence. Especially if talking to us can cost Casey her job. But she's here. She led us here, obviously wanting to unburden herself, and now that we're here, she's playing hard to get. Knowing it's not easy for her though, I'm doing my best to cut her a little slack, but I need to subtly dial up the pressure.

"What is it you know, Casey?" I ask as gently as I can. "If it can help us find Mrs. Osweiler, please tell us."

"You want us to find her, don't you?" Astra adds.

Casey nods. "I do."

"Well, we can't do that without you. We need your help," I say. "Valerie needs your help."

Casey sniffs and wipes away a couple of tears that rolled down her smooth cheeks, the warring emotions etched upon her face. But then she nods to herself as if coming to a decision. She raises her gaze to us again, a glint of determination in her eyes.

"Valerie—I'm sure she was having an affair," she says.

Astra and I exchange a glance, then turn back to her again. "Are you sure about that?" I ask.

"Not one hundred percent. More like ninety-nine point nine. I overheard her on the phone a couple of times and the conversation didn't sound work-related, if you know what I mean," she replies. "She was usually careful about taking personal calls behind closed doors, but there were a few times I saw her talking to somebody on a cellphone—one that wasn't her regular phone. And the snippets of conversations I heard were... they were... well, they sounded romantic."

"Are you sure she wasn't speaking to her husband?" I ask.

Casey gnaws on her bottom lip, that look of uncertainty crossing her face again. She looks down at her coffee cup, frowning, seeming to draw into herself again. I can't afford to have her shut down on me again but I'm not sure how to keep her talking.

Ever the emotional one, Astra reaches across the table. Casey flinches when Astra takes her hand and gives it a squeeze. But she looks up at her and I see some of that uncertainty on her face melt away. Not a lot, but some of it. That's a start. That's something we can work with to get her to open up.

"It's all right, Casey," Astra soothes her. "You can talk to us. We're here to help. We want to find Valerie. That's all we want right now, but we need to know what you've seen and heard."

"What if I'm wrong, though?" Casey asks, her voice trembling. "What if what I thought I heard or saw wasn't what really happened? I mean, I could have taken everything out of context. Or maybe I misheard something. Or maybe..."

Her voice trails off and she sniffs loudly again. Casey seems to be trying to talk herself out of whatever it was she'd overheard. I just need her to keep talking.

"It's possible. But we need to investigate every possible lead. Even if it turns out to be nothing," I tell her. "And you never know. It could turn out to be everything. You never know, Casey. The smallest detail could turn out to have the biggest impact."

She nods and takes a deep breath as if to try to hype herself up. "You're right. Okay."

I nod encouragingly. "So, how do you know she wasn't speaking to her husband?"

Casey looks at me, a new light of determination in her eyes. "Well, there was the different phone for one thing," she says. "I mean, if it's her husband, why was she using a burner? It was one of those cheap, pay-as-you-go things."

"All right, that's getting us somewhere, Casey. Really intuitive," Astra nods. "What else told you it wasn't her husband?"

"Because when she talked to her husband, she had a different tone. A different way of speaking," she explains. "It was almost cold and businesslike. I rarely ever heard the sort of warmth in her voice when she spoke to her husband that I heard when she was speaking with this other guy."

"Do you know who the guy she was speaking to on the burner was?" Astra asks.

She shakes her head. "I don't know. I'm sorry, I never spoke with her about it," she says quietly. "It didn't seem like my place to ask."

"No, of course not. I get that," I say. "But do you think it was somebody at the firm?"

Casey shrugs. "I don't know. It wouldn't surprise me. I mean, they spend so many hours there, it's not like she's out hitting the clubs, trolling for dates or anything like that."

"If you had to guess, who might she be involved with at the firm?" Astra asks.

"I don't know. I don't know that I could even speculate," she replies.

"Well, was there somebody in particular she was close to?" I ask. "Was there somebody she worked with more than others or..."

"I guess if I had to say, she spent most of her time with Mr. Foles," she tells us. "He kind of mentored her and I know they're close."

"Have you ever seen them together? Do they ever act inappropriately with each other, even subtly?" Astra asks. "Have you ever seen any indication they might be having an affair?"

She shakes her head. "No, nothing like that. They were nothing but professional at the office."

"So, what makes you think they were having—"

"I don't know that. You asked me to guess, and I said she was close with Mr. Foles," she points out defensively.

"All right, that's fair. I hear you," I say. "Who is Mr. Foles?"

"Patrick Foles. He's one of the partners."

"Not a senior partner?" I ask.

She shakes her head. "No, but I don't think he cared about that. He liked being in the courtroom. He said there was no bigger rush for him," she says. "I mean, he's a good guy. Always has a kind word for everybody."

"We'll look into him," I say. "But you have no idea who else it could have been?"

She shakes her head. "No. No idea. I'm sorry."

"Do you know if her husband knew she was having an affair, Casey?"

"I don't know. I overheard a couple of tense conversations with him, but I couldn't tell you what they were about," she tells us. "I just know there wasn't a lot of warmth between them."

I nod. It's not much, but it does give us an avenue to look at. But we need some more information first, rather than go running off half-cocked.

"I need to get back to the office," Casey says.

I give her a gentle smile. "All right. Thank you for your help, Casey."

She shrugs. "I don't feel like I helped all that much."

"Like I said, the smallest detail can have the biggest impact. You just never know," I say. "You've given us some things to look at and we appreciate that. I know it wasn't comfortable for you."

Casey nods. "I hope it helps. I hope you can find Valerie and bring her home."

"So do we."

Casey stands and walks away, leaving Astra and me there to mull things over. A burner phone and whispered conversations would definitely seem to indicate an affair. Astra looks at me with a wicked grin on her face, obviously having come to the same conclusion herself.

"Scott Osweiler's back in play as a suspect," she says.

"Maybe."

"Come on. Secret phone and even more secret conversations? Has to be an affair."

"Could be a hundred other things too."

"That fifty bucks is already burning a hole in my pocket," she says.

I laugh softly. "Dream on," I say. "Come on, we need to get back to the shop and get all up in Foles' life as fast as we can."

We get up and head for the doors. As we head for the parking lot, I call Rick and tell him to start digging into Patrick Foles. If there's something to be found, Rick will find it. But with the way everything has been breaking for us in this case, I'm not expecting much.

And all the while, the window on Valerie's survival closes that much more.

CHAPTER SEVENTEEN

Criminal Data Analysis Unit; Seattle Field Office

"OKAY, TELL ME WHAT YOU GOT," I CALL OUT BEFORE the doors have even finished opening.

"Just about nothing," Rick calls back.

Astra takes her seat at her workstation and I take up my usual position at the front of the room and start pacing. That wasn't the news I wanted to hear, though I was expecting it. Nothing about this case is going our way and everything is a problem. The news that she has a boyfriend, though, has rekindled my hope that she's alive. I know it's a slimmer chance than winning the lottery, getting struck by lightning, and finding a flying pig all on the same day, but part of me still hopes she just decided to skip town with him.

"So, I did as deep a dive on Patrick Foles as I could in the time I had," Rick starts. "But this guy reads like a Boy Scout."

"How so?" I ask.

Rick taps at his keyboard and the screens behind me come alive with his photograph from the firm. He's a very handsome man with flecks of gray peppering his dark hair. His neatly trimmed beard and mustache hold the same salt and pepper, his piercing green eyes convey strength and wisdom, and on top of it all he's got a strong jawline, and a patrician nose. He looks like he's straight out of central casting for a handsome older gentleman of noble lineage. If you were looking for somebody to play, say, a king or the President of the United States, Patrick Foles would be your guy.

"I think I feel my daddy issues coming back," Astra comments with a laugh.

"Figured you might," I reply. "Good thing you have Benjamin waiting for you at home."

"For now," she tips me a wink.

"Ladies, if you're done being degenerates and objectifying Mr. Foles?" Rick asks.

"Please, go on," I reply with a laugh.

"All right, well, Foles is fifty-four. Been married for twenty-seven years to his wife Beth. They have one child—sixteen-year-old Amelia. She attends a boarding school in France," he says. "Has a light social media presence, but what there is shows a man very much in love with his wife. Seems to be the picture of a family man."

"Lots of guys come across being very much in love with their wives," Astra points out. "Those same guys usually end up taking their eighteen-year-old mistresses to the Churchill."

"That's true in many cases," Rick acknowledges. "But I don't get that vibe from Foles."

"No?" I ask. "Convince me. Build your case."

"All right, well, the Foles are heavily involved with their church. Patrick is a deacon," he starts.

"Dennis Rader, also known as the BTK killer, was his church council president," Astra counters.

"Okay, well, the Foles also sit on the board of several charitable foundations," Rick continues undaunted.

I laugh softly. "John Wayne Gacy did a lot of charity work."

Astra laughs and gives me a high five. "She's got a point, Rick."

"Well, here's something you can't refute," he says.

A picture of Patrick and Beth Foles pops up on the screens behind me. It's a candid shot of the couple in Hawaii, and the moment I see it, I realize Rick is right. It can't be refuted. The picture is of them at sunset at what looks like a luau. They're sitting side by side, their faces turned to one another. Beth is caught with a wide smile on her lips and Patrick is looking at her with an unabashed look of the purest love on his face I've ever seen.

"Blake, we need to get you a man who looks at you like that," Astra says.

"I was just thinking that," I reply.

"I bet your neighbor the cop would look at you that way if you let him," Mo pipes up.

I turn and look at her completely aghast. "I guess you've been talking to Astra."

Mo laughs and gives me a shrug. "Maybe."

"So, I take all that to mean you agree with me? I mean, that is not the face of a man who is cheating on his wife, am I right?" Rick crows.

My gut tells me he's right. The look on Foles' face is one of pure devotion. The way he looks at his wife makes it seem more than clear he is a man wholly and completely in love. That opinion seems to be supported by a brief perusal of his social media page, where he does nothing but post their adventures together: mountain climbing in the Andes, visiting the Grand Canyon, smiling cheerfully on a gondola ride in Venice, sitting back to relax on beach resorts in tropical towns I can't even pronounce the names of. And the photos that are not of their vacation getaways are just as romantic. Rick keeps scrolling at pictures of the couple attending the opera, beaming proudly at their daughter's cello recital, and enjoying candlelit dinners at the finest restaurants Seattle has to offer. It's like they've been living one long honeymoon.

Of course, it may all be theater. All of the over-the-top declarations of love and devotion could be to create the image of a man in love. But that's not the read I get on it. I actually think it's genuine. It's the photo of him looking into his wife's eyes that sold it for me.

"Right?" Rick presses.

"Yeah, yeah," I admit. "I think you're right."

"Thank you," he says and stands, taking a quick bow before sitting back down.

"Even a busted clock is right twice a day," Astra cracks.

Mo turns in her seat and looks at him. "I'd like to know when Rick here became the expert on all things romantic."

"Excellent question, Mo," Astra says.

"Ladies, beneath this rugged and manly exterior beats the heart of a true romantic," he says. "I'm a modern-day Casanova."

"I'm going to be sick," Astra groans.

"While I think it's unlikely that Foles is our mystery boyfriend, it's still possible this could all be an elaborate front. I don't think it's likely, but he could still be Mrs. Osweiler's lover," I say. "I'm comfortable putting him on the back burner for now, though. We'll circle back to him if we can't find another viable investigative path."

"What is this world coming to when we can't find a viable thread, but Rick here is making sound deductions and logical points?" Astra complains.

"I might have something," Mo says.

I turn to her. "Talk to me. What do you have?"

"Conor Boyle, age fifty-eight," Mo starts. "He's affiliated with the Irish mob."

"We still have Irish mob in Seattle?" Astra raises an eyebrow.

"Remnants," I tell her. "They're a dying breed here. Most have moved back to places that have been traditional Irish strongholds like New York and Chicago."

"But there are still a few hanging on like ticks here," Mo explains. "When I was with the SPD, we had run-ins with some of them. Nasty lot, those guys."

"So what's the deal with Boyle?" I ask.

"He had a room at the Churchill the day Mrs. Osweiler was grabbed," she tells me. "She'd previously brought a suit against his strip club—the Cherry Patch—and cost him a small fortune. He didn't take it well and he left her a couple of messages for her expressing his displeasure with her. He stopped just short of outright threatening her, but if you read between the lines, his meaning was more than clear."

"All right, but what would she be doing meeting him there if he'd dropped veiled threats after she took him to the cleaners?" Astra asks. "That doesn't make sense."

I'm already turning it over in my brain, trying to find a logical thread. It seems to be too big a coincidence to have a woman go missing from a place where a guy who'd threatened her was staying. I hate coincidences. I think about it for a moment and a theory crystalizes in my mind.

"All right, what about this... Valerie was there to meet her secret boyfriend. Boyle spots her and sees a chance to exact a little revenge," I postulate. "It was a crime of opportunity and convenience, not one he planned out. Taking her was just a spur of the moment thing."

Astra grimaces. "A lot of what-ifs and leaps of logic there."

"I have to agree, boss. That theory has enough holes to strain pasta through it," Rick adds.

"They're not wrong, but it's also worth investigating since, you know, it's really the only solid one we have at the moment," Mo points out.

"She's right," I nod. "You know what I always say. We have to turn over every rock."

"And look at all the slimy things squirming around underneath," Astra adds.

"Exactly. Like it or not, we're obligated to follow every lead."

"Sounds good to me," Astra offers. "I've never met an Irish mob guy before. This could be interesting. I've always been into the accent."

"Don't get yourself too lathered up," Mo tells her.

On the screens, a picture pops up showing a man with a bulbous nose that's spiderwebbed with red veins, beady brown eyes, and iron-gray hair. Boyle's got thin lips, sallow skin, and dark circles beneath his eyes. Mo said he's fifty-eight, but he looks ten years older than that. I guess a life filled with booze, pasta, and cigars was catching up with him. Astra frowns.

"This just got decidedly less interesting," she mutters.

"Do we have an address on Boyle?" I ask.

"Yeah, I'll send his home address as well as the address for the Cherry Patch to your phone," Mo replies. "Apparently Valerie wounded it but couldn't quite put the stake through its heart."

"Well, maybe we can finish the job," I muse. "How are you doing on the rest of the guest registry?"

"It's a process but we're getting there. I'm still cross-referencing names against open cases filed with the court and the names we pulled out of the threat letters and recordings," she says. "Just thought I'd bring that to your attention first."

"That's good work. Thanks, Mo," I say. "Keep at it."

"Will do."

"And Rick, keep digging. See if you can find anything that can lead us to this secret boyfriend," I tell him. "There has to be something out there. A single breadcrumb to follow. Something."

"I'm on it," he tells me.

"We heading over to go talk to Boyle?" Astra asks.

"We are. But we're making a stop first."

"Where?"

"We're going to ask our old friend Scott face to face whether he knew about his wife's infidelity or not," I reply. "If he's hiding something, we're going to flush it out of him this time."

"I'm game. Let's go."

I can feel the faint stirrings of momentum building inside of me as we head to the car. But it's tempered by the knowledge that we could still be too late to save Valerie.

CHAPTER EIGHTEEN

Osweiler Residence; Windermere District, Seattle

Scott Osweiler opens the door to us and his shoulders slump. He doesn't look well. Hos hair is standing up in a hundred different directions, his clothes are rumpled, and he hasn't shaved since we were last here. I'm not entirely sure he's bathed either. The circles under his eyes are darker and deeper. I wonder if he's even slept since we last saw him. Osweiler looks defeated. He looks like a man who's already expecting the worst.

"May we come in, Mr. Osweiler?" I ask gently.

He doesn't say a word but turns and walks away, leaving the door open behind him. Astra and I step across the threshold and follow him down to the living room at the back of the house. The well-kept air of the house has fallen away and now, after only a few days, it's in complete disrepair. There are beer cans, empty vodka bottles, and food containers strewn about the place, and the aroma of body odor, booze, and rot inside is pungent. At least he's eating, I guess.

Osweiler walks over and picks up a vodka bottle that's about a quarter full and takes a long swallow of it. He swishes it around like mouthwash, then swallows. He sits down on one of the barstools at the island in the kitchen and looks at us with fear in his eyes and agony etched upon his face. This is a man in a full spiral just waiting for life to dish out another blow. I can't help but feel a twinge of pity for the man. He just looks beaten.

But I remind myself that he may have something to do with his wife's disappearance and this spiral may have been brought on by guilt. I still don't think it likely that he's the culprit, but I also believe he knows more than he's told us. The fact that he's withholding and not being transparent has set the warning bells clanging in my head and I can't just ignore them.

"Well?" he asks, his voice gruff and hoarse.

I glance at Astra and clear my throat before I speak. "We have not been able to find your wife yet, Mr. Osweiler—"

"Then why are you here?" he roars. "Why are you talking to me when you should be out there looking for her? You're not going to find her here!"

Osweiler covers his face with his hands and sobs quietly for a moment. His entire body shakes, and I can smell the fear and misery wafting off him. That odor is a very close second to the combined miasma of body odor and vodka that shrouds him. He finally looks up at us, his face a mask of the most exquisite agony.

"I'm sorry," he says softly. "That was out of line. I apologize."

"It's fine, Mr. Osweiler," I reply. "And please believe that we're doing everything we can to get your wife back to you."

He nods and drains the last of the bottle in his hand, then sets it aside. Astra and I exchange glances and I know if we're going to get anything useful out of him, we need to move quickly before he's pickled himself completely.

"Mr. Osweiler, I'm afraid we need to ask you some rather delicate questions. And I apologize in advance if we sound insensitive," Astra begins. "But we've developed evidence that your wife was having an affair."

I watch his face closely and though I still see grief and the fear of what we'll reveal next, what I don't see in his eyes is surprise.

"But you knew that, didn't you, Mr. Osweiler?" I ask.

He frowns and looks around the counter, scrounging for another bottle. Thankfully, he doesn't find anything and turns back to us, his frown deepening.

"Mr. Osweiler, I know this must be difficult for you, but by withholding that information, it cost us time—time we could have spent looking for your wife," I say.

"What do you want me to say?" he spits. "That we were having problems? That we were seeing a counselor for them?"

"Yes. That would have been helpful," Astra says. "Did you know she was having an affair with somebody?"

His face goes red, and he seems to be on the verge of another eruption, but the color in his face gradually ebbs and he deflates. Osweiler looks down and takes a beat to gather himself. When he's ready, he looks up.

"I didn't know that she was having an affair. I suspected it, but I didn't know. Not for sure," he admits softly. "I have no proof and there didn't seem to be any point in telling you about it because I would have sounded like a paranoid control freak."

"But by not telling us, you not only made yourself look like a suspect. You withheld what might be crucial facts from us, which have hampered our efforts, Mr. Osweiler," I say. "And you of all people should know better than that. Which only makes things more suspect."

His eyes narrow and his jaw flexes as he grits his teeth. "Are you seriously calling me a suspect? Do you really think I did something to my own wife?"

Astra shrugs. "Did you, Mr. Osweiler?"

He gets to his feet so quickly he knocks his barstool over behind him. He's wearing a look of unadulterated rage on his face, and he clenches his hands into fists. The man glares at Astra, trembling with fury. He somehow manages to keep from launching himself at her though, and I have to admire his restraint.

"You need to leave," he hisses. "Get out of my house and go find my wife."

"We're doing our best, Mr. Osweiler. But we just need to get a clear picture of things," I tell him. "Now, let's all calm down."

He cuts his eyes from Astra to me, and I see his anger beginning to slowly recede. He turns away and picks up the barstool, then takes a seat. As he does that, I go to his refrigerator and pull the door open, not finding a whole lot inside. There is a bottle of beer though, so I grab that, twist off the cap, and set it down in front of him. Osweiler downs half of it in one swallow. It takes a couple of moments, but he seems to calm down enough to speak to us.

"We can confirm that she didn't go to the airport the morning she went missing. She paid a driver off book to take her to the Churchill Hotel," I tell him.

He pales as he listens to my words and lowers his eyes, unable to meet my gaze. He looks like a man who hasn't just been beaten but entirely broken as well. The confirmation that his wife was cheating on him was the final straw. I hate to press him, but I have no choice.

"Now, you said you had suspicions that she was having an affair," I say. "Mr. Osweiler, do you have any idea who your wife might have been seeing?"

He shakes his head. "Not a clue. I confronted her about it once, but she denied it," he says quietly. "She wouldn't even admit to it in couples counseling. What a waste of time and money that was, apparently."

"What made you believe she was having an affair, Mr. Osweiler?" Astra asks in a gentler tone of voice than before.

He sighs. "I heard her in her office having whispered phone conversations. Whenever I asked, she just said it was some work thing," he replies. "I found a second cell phone. A cheap, prepaid deal. When I confronted her, she said it was for work. And when I pressed, Valerie flew into a rage and refused to talk about it."

"Why didn't you tell us all of this from the start?" I ask.

His eyes are red, and tears spill down his cheeks as he looks at me. "Because I'm ashamed. I'm embarrassed that my marriage is failing and there's nothing I can do about it," he says, his voice quavering. "I'm humiliated that she found somebody else she wants to be with and instead of being honest about it, she's running around behind my back like everything's normal. Because I'm devastated that she hasn't touched me in more than a year but is apparently screwing somebody else on the side. That's why, Agent Wilder."

Maybe I'm naïve or overly sympathetic, but his words strike me as authentic and coming straight from his heart. His pain feels legitimate, and it convinces me that Mr. Osweiler didn't have anything to do with his wife's disappearance.

In the moment of awkward silence that follows his confession, the doorbell rings, its chime shattering the quiet of the house. We all turn as we hear the door open and then the sound of a woman's voice.

"Scott? Are you home?" she calls.

Astra and I both turn to Mr. Osweiler. "That is Valerie's best friend, Wren."

A moment later, a leggy blonde with sparkling green eyes steps into the room. She's about five-six, fit and toned, with smooth skin the color of porcelain. She's wearing black skintight leggings and a snug long-sleeved t-shirt that shows off her physique. A sweatshirt is tied around her waist and she's got a ballcap on with her hair in a braid that falls to the middle of her back. Faint lines at the corners of her eyes and mouth tell me she's probably in her early forties but she could easily pass for somebody a decade younger. When she sees Astra and me standing in the room, she draws up short, looking from us to Scott uncertainly.

"Wren, this is Agent Wilder and Agent Russo from the FBI," he gestures to us. "They're working on Valerie's case."

A host of emotions scroll across her face as she looks at both of us again. Wren is carrying a covered dish, which she seems to remember belatedly. She walks over and sets it down on the counter and turns to us.

"Have you found her? Do you know where she is? Do you have any leads? Are you following up on those leads?" Wren peppers us with a host of questions.

I hold my hand up to stop her. "We're doing everything we can to find her, Ms. . . ."

"Keaton. I'm Wren Keaton," she says. "Valerie and I have been best friends since college. What are you doing here? Why aren't you out looking for her?"

"Wren," Scott says. "Relax. They're doing their job."

She wipes the tears away from her cheeks and shakes her head. "I'm sorry. I'm just… I'm worried out of my head. I'm sorry."

"Of course. I understand," I say. "We're just trying to get some follow-up information from Mr. Osweiler."

Keaton is jittery and rattled. She turns to the dish she'd brought in and taps the top of the glass lid.

"You weren't returning my calls or texts. I can't imagine how difficult this has been on you and I figured you weren't eating well… or bathing," she says to Osweiler. "You really need to take care of yourself, Scott. You need to stay strong. They're going to find her."

Osweiler shakes his head. "I appreciate the casserole, Wren. I'm doing all right."

"You don't look like it," she says. "And when Valerie comes home, she'd be furious if she found out I didn't try to take care of you. Now, you need to eat something."

"I'll eat later," he grumbles. "Thank you."

"Scott, I—"

"I said I'll eat later," he snaps, his tone firm and cold.

Keaton flinches at his words and looks away, a frown on her face. I glance at Astra and give her a small nod. One of the things I appreciate most about our friendship is that we can communicate without words. She and I are practically sharing a brain.

Astra turns to Mr. Osweiler. "You mentioned that your wife had a home office?" she asks. "Would you mind showing me?"

"For what?" he asks.

"I just want to take a peek and see if there's anything that can help point us in the right direction, Mr. Osweiler."

He nods weakly. "Yeah. Sure," he says. "Follow me."

He shuffles out of the main room and down a hallway with Astra right behind him. Keaton watches them go with concern etched into her features. She sniffs loudly and takes a couple of beats to compose herself. She finally turns to me.

"I'm worried about him," she says. "He doesn't look like he's doing very well. He's certainly not taking care of himself."

"He has a lot on his plate right now," I reply. "So, Ms. Keaton, you said you and Mrs. Osweiler were best friends?"

"That's right. We've been best friends since college. I actually introduced her to Scott," she nods. "They helped me get my business off the ground. They're great people and I just can't believe this is happening. Things like this shouldn't happen to good people."

Bad things happen to good people and bad people alike. Bad things don't discriminate. But that's not going to help the situation and I'm sure Keaton doesn't want to hear that sort of philosophical navel-gazing right now. Besides, it would be pretty insensitive of me to say that. So instead, I try to keep things focused on the investigation.

"Ms. Keaton, we've developed some evidence that Mrs. Osweiler was having an affair and I just need—"

"What? No. Uh-uh," she interrupts. "There is no way Val was cheating on Scott. That's just not possible."

"I'm sorry to say it's not only possible, but it's pretty much a confirmed fact at this point," I tell her. "She was at the Churchill Hotel the day she went missing."

Keaton shakes her head. "No way."

"Listen, I just need to know if you knew about her boyfriend," I asked. "I'm not trying to snoop and I'm certainly not judging, Ms. Keaton. I just need to know if you knew who she was seeing."

She shakes her head emphatically. "No, I told you. I didn't know she was even seeing somebody on the side," she argues. "I still don't believe it."

I study her closely and can see she's not being entirely truthful with me. She's holding something back. I don't know what it is though.

"Ms. Keaton, if you know something, now's the time," I tell her. "Anything you know might be able to help us find her."

"I swear I don't know anything. I didn't know she was seeing somebody, Agent Wilder," she tells me. "Like I told you, I don't even believe she was cheating on him."

I'm getting nowhere with her. She either really doesn't know anything or she's really determined to keep her best friend's secret. Loyalty is one thing. I appreciate loyal friends. But this is something else entirely. By keeping her best friend's confidence, she could be dooming her.

Shaking my head, I pull out a card and hand it to her. "Ms. Keaton, we're going to do our best to find your best friend. But having one hand tied behind our back because we don't have all the information isn't making it easier," I tell her. "So, if you can think of anything or when you're ready to talk, give me a call. And remember, the sooner you realize your actions are hurting your best friend, the better."

Ms. Keaton looks down at the card and frowns. But she doesn't budge an inch. We're not going to get anything useful out of her because she's choosing to take her best friend's secret to the grave. Or at least, to Mrs. Osweiler's grave.

CHAPTER NINETEEN

East Hill Anglers Club; East Hill, WA

EAST HILL USED TO BE A NICE, QUIET, SUBURBAN NEIGHBORhood about fifteen minutes outside of Seattle. It was the kind of place you could feel safe raising a family. Sadly, the area declined as drugs took hold over the years. Meth ran rampant and as the dealers and addicts moved in, the families moved out. Now, East Hill is a run-down shell of what it once was. It's a shame.

There have been a few efforts to gentrify the district over the years, but nothing has ever stuck. Not much money to be had here when investors would rather attract high-dollar clients in Capitol Hill or Belltown. It's like this place has just been left out to rot.

I pull into the lot of an old anglers club that's been shut down for years and park the car. I got a call early this morning to roll out to this location and I'd called Astra right after. There are half a dozen emergency vehicles already in place, the red and blue strobe lights shining like grim fireworks against the gloom of the day. The sky is cluttered with dark clouds and a heavy drizzle falls on the world. As I get out of the car, I find Astra already there waiting for me. The atmosphere is heavy and somber. Seems fitting for the morning's work.

Pulling my coat around me tighter, we head for the tape line without a word to each other. The club, designed to look like an old, rustic wooden cabin, has been abandoned for years. Split and splintered wooden boards cover the doors and windows that have long since been broken out and graffiti is scrawled over just about every conceivable surface. The asphalt in the parking lot is cracked and pitted. Tall weeds sprout from holes in the surface as nature reclaims the land.

There's already a crowd of onlookers pressing at the line to get a look at the body. Nothing brings a community together quite like the scent of blood in the air. We badge the cop standing at the tape line and he gives us a nod as he holds it up for us.

"All the action's around back," he tells us.

"Thank you," I reply.

We follow the stream of bodies coming and going from behind the clubhouse. As we come around the building, we see a small cluster of people standing beneath a gnarled, ancient oak tree that cants preciously over an old casting pond. The shell of an old boat floats half-submerged in the middle of the pond like an eerie buoy. The field behind the club is choked with tall, dry grass, tires, and a wide assortment of garbage. There is everything from the usual bottles, cans, and fast-food bags and wrappers, but there are also quite a few rusted hunks of scrap metal protruding from the weeds.

"Watch your step," I tell Astra.

She nods. "If I'd known we were coming to junkie heaven, I would have worn my steel-soled boots today."

I step lightly, taking care to avoid stepping on a hidden needle or something equally dangerous. Judging by the number of scorched tinfoil squares and empty plastic baggies, there are obviously a lot of junkies who do their thing out here. We make our way to where everybody is standing and when we see the body, my heart sinks into the pit of my stomach instantly. I share a look with Astra, her face as dark with emotion as the sky overhead is with clouds.

"Who found her?" I ask the nearest officer on the scene.

"Transient," he replies and motions to a man standing off to the side with another officer. "Out here picking up cans and he ran across the body."

"All right. If you could hold him there, I'll have some questions for him," I say.

"Yes, ma'am," he replies.

Astra joins me next to the body and we both squat down and look her over. There's a crime scene tech in a dark blue coverall kneeling by Mrs. Osweiler's head, jotting some notes down on his clipboard.

"How long has she been dead?" I ask.

He shakes his head. "Hard to say for sure, but judging by the amount of decomp, I'd have to say it's been a few days. At least," he says. "You can see her already beginning to bloat. The bloody foam at leaking from her mouth is another telltale sign."

I nod. That means it's more than likely she was killed the day she was taken. The day she was at the Churchill. Although that means we're off the hook as far as not finding her in time—she was dead by the time we got the case—it's a hollow sense of relief. And any sense of relief I feel is quickly washed away by a fit of dark anger that rises within me like a malevolent tide. Our case is far from over. It's just shifted tracks. It's gone from a missing person's case to a murder investigation.

Unfortunately for us, we still don't have much to work with. That bit hasn't changed, which sucks for us. But we can hopefully pull some evidence off her body that will give us a direction to run in. Given how screwy everything with this case has been to this point though, I'm not expecting a lot of help. Still, a girl can hope. I feel like I've been holding onto that a lot lately.

I let out a deep breath as I push all my emotions down and lock them away. I can't let them cloud my mind or my judgment.

"I'm assuming the gunshots killed her," I say.

"I won't have a final determination until I do the autopsy," the tech says. "But yeah, I'd say it's probably a pretty good guess."

The tech stands and I thank him as he walks off to speak with other members of his team who are poking around the makeshift junkyard the field has become over the years. It's hard to tell anything important from the junk. Finding evidence in this mess is going to be next to impossible. I don't envy them their job.

"There are two gunshot wounds in the center of her chest and another in the side of her head," I note. "I don't see a lot of blood here though. I'm thinking this is a dump site."

Astra nods. "Looks that way to me," she says. "This reads like a mob hit to me."

I purse my lips as I stare at Mrs. Osweiler's body. I can't see anything that refutes her point. Not at the moment, anyway.

"Yeah, it seems like that might become the primary track of investigation," I say. "Which means I guess we're going to have to go drag Conor Boyle in to answer some questions."

"Great. I'll bring the rubber hoses," Astra quips.

"SSA Wilder."

I turn at the sound of the stern voice to find Interim Deputy Chief TJ Lee standing there staring down at us. Astra and I exchange a quick glance then get to our feet.

"Detective Lee," I greet him.

"Interim Deputy Chief," he clarifies.

"Oh, that's right. You took over for Torres. I apologize," I reply. "It's nice to see you. How are you this morning?"

"What are you doing on my crime scene?" he asks, his voice cold and stiff.

I look at Astra and she shrugs. While Lee and I have never been best friends—he holds my close relationship with Paxton Arrington against me—we were always cordial with one another. We've helped each other on different cases at various times. There has always been a sense of respect between us—a sense of respect that's missing entirely right now. He's looking at me like he stepped in something that's now stuck to the bottom of his shoe.

"I'm sorry, Lee," I say. "But this is our crime scene."

Lee sniffs. "It's not a federal case. Seattle PD caught the case, and this is still our jurisdiction. Ergo, it's my crime scene."

His attitude is really irritating me. Mostly because I have no idea where it's coming from. He's just coming off unreasonably snotty. Even for him. I mean, he's always been a bit stuck up, but it seems like he's dialed that up to eleven. I stiffen my spine. Although I would prefer to work with local law enforcement when I can, if they're not willing to work with me, they can get stuffed for all I care.

Deputy Chief Torres learned that the hard way. I took sheer, absolute pleasure in locking him up for his crimes and making him look like a fool for the world to see. But honestly, I thought Lee would be grateful for it. He and I may not see eye to eye, but he's a good cop and takes the job seriously. I know he's under a lot of stress trying to steer the SPD back to the good graces of the public, but that's no excuse to take it out on me.

"Deputy Chief, this woman was being vetted for a spot in the DOJ," I inform him. "That makes it a federal case. But if you want more justification for our involvement with this case, we were ordered by the Director of the FBI himself asked my team to look into this."

Lee clenches his jaw as he stares at me and his cheeks flush scarlet. He gets that nearly apoplectic expression I've seen on Torres' face countless times over the years.

"I'm not going to let you strongarm me off my crime scene—"

"Forgive me, Deputy Chief, but as I said, this isn't your crime scene," I say. "The FBI is asserting jurisdiction over Valerie Osweiler's murder. You're welcome to assist, of course, but this is our case."

His face flushes an even deeper shade of red and he clenches his jaw so tight, he could probably shatter stone.

"Look. I'm not to type to bigfoot onto a case. Never have been.

You know that," I say. "But this has been our case from the jump and we're not going to turn it over. I'm sorry that obviously upsets you, but—"

"But that's not going to stop you from doing what you're doing," he sneers.

"What has you so upset about this?" I ask. "After all we've worked together in the past? What, are you mad that you won't be getting front-page coverage for this one?"

"How dare you," he growls. "This isn't the last you've heard from me about this."

Before I can respond, Lee turns and huffs away. I look at Astra and shrug.

"What in the hell was that all about?" Astra asks.

I shrug. "Beats me. But he's all worked into a lather about something though."

"He's never been such a jerk before."

"Right?" I say. "I have no idea what that was all about."

"Anyway, what's our next step?"

"We proceed as we would with any other murder investigation," I tell her.

I turn and walk over to the transient man who's standing off to the side. He looks to be in his late fifties, with long, greasy gray hair. His scraggly beard is the same color as the hair on his head and hangs nearly to his chest. He's wearing so many layers of shirts, sweaters, and jackets, he looks like he weighs fifty pounds more than he probably does if I judge by his sunken cheeks and nearly skeletal hands. His eyes are dark and rheumy, and he's got a slight tremble running through his body.

"Good morning, I'm Blake Wilder. I'm with the FBI," I introduce myself. "And what is your name, sir?"

"Lou," he replies, his voice surprisingly deep and gravelly. "Lou Glass."

"Okay great. Can you tell me what you saw, Mr. Glass?"

"Like I told these guys, I didn't see much. I was just makin' my usual rounds, lookin' for cans or anything else I could recycle and when I came back here, I found her," he tells me. "She was kinda covered up with a sheet—her head and chest anyway—so, at first I thought it was a mannequin or somethin'. But when I got close to her... well... I knew it weren't no mannequin. So I called the cops."

I nod. "That's good, Lou," I say. "So, you didn't see anybody out here? Nobody hanging around or anything like that?"

He shook his head. "No, I didn't see nobody."

"Okay, great. Now, you said you were making your usual rounds," I say. "When was the last time you were here?"

"I dunno. About four days ago, I guess. Maybe five," he tells me. "You gotta give it a little time between collections, you see. People always comin' back here to drink and get high or to... you know, have some place that's kinda private if they can't get no hotel room to do their thing."

"Yeah, it's classy," I say. "A real nice spot for romance."

He laughs. "Yeah, some people like to do it under the stars, I guess."

I smile. "Yeah, I guess. Is there anything else you can tell me?"

He shakes his head. "Nah. I didn't see nothin'. I just found her like you see her layin' there right now. That's all."

"Thank you, Mr. Glass," I say, then fish a fifty-dollar bill and my card out of my pocket and hand it to him. "You get something to eat with that. You need a hot meal. And if you think of anything else, my number is on that card."

He laughs. "I need about a thousand hot meals," he says. "But I'll start with this. I appreciate it, Agent Wilder."

I walk away and find the crime scene tech again. He's talking to one of his techs off to the side. They're laughing about something together.

"Excuse me," I tell him. "I know you're taking the body to King County, so I need to ensure Rebekah Shafter is assigned to the autopsy."

He looks at me, seemingly put off by me giving him orders. "Yeah, that's not really how it works—"

"That's the way it needs to work in this case," I cut him off. "Or you can explain why you're refusing to do as I ask to the Director of the FBI."

A sour look crosses his face, but he finally nods. "Fine," he relents. "Whatever. Rebekah Shafer, I got it."

"Good. Thank you," I say.

Astra and I walk away from the crime scene, and I feel my stomach churning. We were too late to save Mrs. Osweiler and her killer has almost a week's head start on us. All I can do is hope we can work the case and make up ground.

CHAPTER TWENTY

Criminal Data Analysis Unit; Seattle Field Office

"All right, we're pivoting now, people," I announce. "We're working a murder, not an abduction anymore."

Rick and Mo both fall silent and a solemn air hangs over the entire room. After leaving the crime scene, I drove to the field office and briefed Rosie on everything we discovered. She, of course, was upset that Mrs. Osweiler turned up dead. Like us, she'd sort of been expecting it but had been holding onto the hope it would turn out for the best. And also like us, those hopes had been shattered this morning. But she gave me the green light to hit the murder investigation and hit it hard. She may have suggested putting a bullet in the killer when we find him and I'm only half-sure she was joking.

"What do we know?" Mo asks.

"Not much more than we did yesterday. But we can start trying to build a profile that might help lead us to the killer," I say.

"We met Mrs. Osweiler's best friend yesterday," Astra adds. "She says she didn't know a thing about Mrs. Osweiler's affair. We're relatively certain she knows something but won't give it up. She's protecting her friend's reputation, apparently."

"Freaking girl code," Rick mutters.

Astra turns in her seat. "Oh, please. Like you boys don't have the bro code," she says. "You wouldn't drop the dime on one of your buddies who had some side action."

"I sure would."

"Then you'd be just about the only man on the planet who would," Astra says.

"What do I keep telling you, Astra?" Rick says. "I'm a different kind of man."

"He says that now," Mo says. "But when the chips are down, I bet he'd be like every other dude around and go to the grave with his friend's secret."

"What about you, Little Miss High and Mighty?" Rick says.

"Oh, you better believe I'll take my best friend's secret with me," Mo says. "At least I'm up front enough about it to admit it."

"This is all very enlightening," I say. "And it's probably a good thing that I'm learning that none of you have a shred of character or integrity."

They all laugh, which makes me smile, but I don't join in. I pace the room, waiting for it to die down so we can get to work. I'm feeling unusually anxious about this case for some reason. I feel a personal stake in it that I normally don't. I don't know why, and I can't even hazard a guess. But for whatever reason, finding Mrs. Osweiler's killer is important to me.

"Mo, did you do a workup on Wren Keaton?" I ask.

She nods. "Yeah, nothing remarkable about her. She's a personal trainer who owns her own gym and yoga studio," she shrugs. "I did find out that the Osweilers gave her the seed money to open it."

"Oh?" I ask.

"Don't get too excited. From what I've been able to find, she's already paid the money back," she adds. "So, there's no financial motive for Keaton to kill Mrs. Osweiler."

"Anything on her socials that hint at somebody her best friend was doing on the side?" Astra asks.

"Negative," she says. "Lots of fun candid photos of the two of them together. They were obviously super close, but if Keaton knows who Mrs. Osweiler's side piece is, she's smart enough to not put it on social media."

"All right, let's start with the basics. What kind of killer are we looking for?" I ask as I move to the whiteboard in the corner and pick up a blue dry erase pen. "He's organized. Mrs. Osweiler's body was found in a field which was not the kill site. It was a secondary dump location."

"It was obviously somebody who knows the area. A local, I'd say," Astra offers. "Somebody who knows you can dump a body in East Hill pretty anonymously."

"And even if somebody there sees you, they're not likely going to rat you out anyway," Rick chimes in.

"Also, somebody who's smart enough to abduct Mrs. Osweiler without leaving a trace or raising a single alarm," Mo adds.

"All good points," I nod, taking those down on the board. "And I'm thinking it's somebody she knows. Or is at least acquainted with. I'd say it's somebody she's at least somewhat comfortable with."

"Why would you say that?" Astra asks.

"Because if we're operating on the assumption that she was taken from the Churchill—and that's really the only assumption we have to work with at this point—they got her out of there without raising any alarms and without anybody even noticing," I explain. "Given how jealously Sandy Inman protects the Churchill's reputation, she would have noticed somebody slinging a woman over their shoulder and dragging them out."

"Good point," Astra acknowledges. "You profiler types are smart."

I flash her a grin. "Yes. Yes, we are," I say. "Mo, is there any overlap between Mrs. Osweiler and our favorite Irish mobster? Were you able to find any sort of link between her and Conor Boyle?"

She shakes her head. "Not yet. If there's a connection, it's buried really deep. But I'm still digging," she says. "If there's anything to be found I'm going to find it."

"What do we know about Boyle?" I ask.

"He's lived in Seattle for most of his life. His family emigrated here from Ireland when he was a child," Mo reports. "Took his first pinch for assaulting another kid when he was thirteen. His record isn't as long as you might think it would be."

"He's smart enough to avoid taking unnecessary collars," Astra says. "Probably has other people do his dirty work for him."

"Bingo," Mo nods. "He started running his own crew when he was sixteen. They stole cars and knocked off liquor stores. His entire crew got pinched trying to take out an armored car when he was nineteen, but they could never tie Boyle to it. They knew he was the mastermind but they couldn't prove it and so he never faced the consequences."

"I'd say that indicates an organized personality," Astra notes.

"I'd say that indicates a very organized personality. An obsessively organized personality perhaps," I say. "You'd have to be to run a crew with an invisible hand like he did for that many years."

"And we know, of course, there's a nexus between Boyle and Mrs. Osweiler," Astra says.

"Right. Mo?" I prompt.

"She sued him on behalf of his employees at the Cherry Patch—he was forcing them to work overtime without paying for it. Also never gave them breaks or lunch periods. All big, fat no-no's and he'd been doing it for years and years," she reports. "Mrs. Osweiler somehow got one of the girls to turn informant and once she did, the floodgates opened, and they filed a class-action suit against Boyle. Judgment went against him, and he was ordered to pay not just their legal fees but a pile of money in back wages and punitive damages. He almost went broke and lost everything, according to his financial records.

"That sounds like ample reason to murder somebody," Astra notes.

"I've heard of people being murdered for a lot less," Rick chimes in.

"Rick, any luck finding this secret cellphone Mrs. Osweiler apparently possessed?" I ask.

"No. Nothing just yet," he replies. "I'm not finding any phones registered in her name nor any charges on any of her credit cards to pay for it. But that's the name of the game with this kind of thing. She was probably paying cash for it, which makes it impossible to track."

"We have to hope it was with her belongings when she was killed," I say. "Rebekah will give us a shout when she's done with the autopsy and walk us through the results. When we're there, we'll get ahold of her things and see if the phone's there."

"How long is it going to take to get the autopsy results?" Astra asks.

"I called Rebekah earlier and asked her to put a rush on it," I tell her.

"And? What did she say?"

"Well, after she stopped laughing, she said she'd get to our body as soon as she could," I tell her. "But she's pretty backed up."

"All right, what are we going to do in the meantime?" Astra asks.

I flash her a mischievous smirk. "Let's go pay a visit to the Cherry Patch and rattle Boyle's cage."

"Excellent," she grins. "I haven't been to a strip club in a while."

"Hey, if you need volunteers, I'm right here," Rick calls.

"Yeah, pass," Astra says. "We're trying to solve a case, not catch a charge, degenerate."

"Funny. The woman practically sprinting out the door to go to a strip club is calling me a degenerate," Rick notes.

"Well, she's not entirely wrong about that," Mo adds.

"Hey!"

"Don't worry, Rick," Astra says. "I'll get a lap dance for you."

"Gee, thanks."

The three of them laugh together but my mood has slowly shifted, becoming as dark and gloomy as the sky outside. As we head out, my mind is consumed by the image of Valerie Osweiler's face. All I can see are her eyes, wide open and sightless, staring off into nothing. Even though I know there's nothing we could have done to save her, that she was gone even before we caught the case, I can't help but feel like we let her down. Like I failed her.

That feeling envelops me, squeezing the air from my lungs. But it infuses me with a sense of determination as well. We may have failed to save her in life, but we will not fail her in death. We're going to catch the person responsible. If nothing else, perhaps it will bring her husband some small sense of comfort and allow her soul to rest.

CHAPTER TWENTY-ONE

The Cherry Patch; Capitol Hill District, Seattle

"YOU ALL RIGHT?" ASTRA ASKS AS I PARK THE CAR. "You've been quiet since we left."

"Yeah, I'm fine."

I reach for the door handle, but Astra puts her hand on my arm to stop me. I turn to her with a frown to find her staring at me closely as if trying to read my mind. Heavy raindrops thrum against the roof, and the sky is so choked with storm clouds, they snuff out the light. It might as well be dark outside and not the middle of the day.

The gaudy pink and red neon from the giant sign that reads "The Cherry Patch," complete with a blinking pair of cherries, makes the raindrops on the windshield sparkle especially brightly in the gloom outside.

"What is it?" she asks.

I let out a long breath and slump back in my seat. "I just can't stop feeling like we failed her, Astra. That we weren't fast enough."

"You know that's crap," she says. "She was already gone when Rosie walked her file in to us."

"I know, I know," I admit. "It's not rational but I can't help how I feel."

"I get that. But you can't carry that burden around with you. You didn't put her there," Astra tells me.

"I know, I just—"

"Blake, come on. How long have we been in this together? You're doing that thing again where you take personal responsibility for the case. Like if you don't give it every iota of your energy, it won't get solved."

"Someone has to."

"And we will. We'll get to the bottom of this thing. We always do. But I can't have my bestie falling apart on me now. Not after all we've been through."

"You're right," I admit with an emotional sigh. "I'm just feeling rattled by this whole thing. Forgive me if..." I don't want to say that I might be a bit touchy about the subject of a romantic partner who turned out to have a secret life and later ending up murdered. But I don't need to.

"I get it. I'm sorry," she tells me, sympathy in her eyes. She squeezes my hand and we sit there for a moment in silence. "In the meantime, let's try to focus on our actual leads. I'm becoming convinced her side piece is who we need to be chasing."

"I thought you said it looked like a mob hit," I counter.

She nods. "But then I got to thinking that maybe, that's just how it was supposed to look. What we're supposed to think."

"Ahh. So, we're going to chase conspiracy theories now?"

She shrugs. "It's only crazy if I'm wrong."

That finally cracks through my gloom and I smile. "You know, it's also entirely possible the fact that she was trying to do some good in this world and for people like the women who work here that put her in the ground," I say, gesturing to the club in front of us. "I'm convinced it was somebody she'd crossed paths with in the courtroom who killed her."

"Maybe," she replies. "Either way, I smell another bet coming."

A rueful laugh passes my lips. "Since we've both moved off Scott Osweiler being a suspect, I'd say you already owe me fifty bucks."

She frowns and looks off for a moment. The look on her face tells me she realized she just walked into that one and that she doesn't actually seem to think Mr. Osweiler is a viable suspect anymore. Astra finally turns back to me with a wicked grin on her lips.

"Fine. Double or nothing then," she says.

"Deal."

"Great. Now, let's stop moping and go to the strip club," she winks.

"You are really inspirational," I say. "If this whole FBI thing doesn't work out, I think you've got a real future in motivational speaking."

"Yeah, I'm considering making a switch and becoming a life coach."

"Yeah, that should go well."

My spirits somewhat lifted, if only a little, we get out of the car and dash through the falling rain to the portico that extends from the doorway. Under the awning, we give ourselves a shake, knocking the raindrops off us, then walk down the faded, frayed, and stained red carpet that extends from the curb to the front door. A large man, six-three at least and built like a linebacker, with deep ebony skin and a pate that's shaved clean is sitting on a barstool just outside the door. He gives us a smile bright enough to chase away the clouds overhead.

"Afternoon, ladies," he says, his voice higher-pitched than I expected for a man his size. "If you're looking for a job, you want to see Ms. Mona. She handles all the talent."

I stare at him with my mouth hanging open for a moment. "Do we look like we're looking for jobs?"

He shrugs his massive shoulders. "We don't usually get a lot of good-lookin' women around here, so I just assumed," he says. "Apologies. No offense meant."

I flash him my badge and he immediately starts to laugh. "No, I guess you aren't lookin' for work. My bad."

"We're actually only here because we hear your lunch buffet is to die for," Astra says.

The man laughs. "It ain't half bad actually," he says. "Make sure you try the Irish taco bites. They're amazing."

"I'll do that," she says, then cuts a look back at me as if to say, *"Irish taco bites?"*

"Cover charge is ten bucks," he says.

I look at him. "Are you serious? We're feds," I sputter. "We're not here to watch women shaking their—we're here on official business."

He shrugs again. "Sorry. Nobody goes through the doors without payin' the cover—feds or not. I don't make the rules."

Astra laughs and pulls a twenty out of her pocket and hands it over. He takes it from her and tucks it into the fanny pack buckled around his waist. I guess they don't need to worry about somebody trying to snatch the day's receipts from Man Mountain here. More than likely if they tried to grab his fanny pack, he'd rip off their arm and beat them with it.

"Thank you very much," he says with that electric smile and gives Astra a wink. "And don't forget those Irish tacos."

"Looking forward to it," she replies.

He pulls the door open for us and we step inside. My ears are immediately battered by the bass that's thumping so hard, I'm half-afraid it's going to knock my fillings loose, and a voice so auto-tuned, it's almost unrecognizable as being human. We walk down a short hallway, push through a pair of black, beaded curtains, and step into the club proper, which is an immediate assault on the senses.

The entire room is cast in a red neon glow and on the main stage, a voluptuous woman in nothing but panties, heels, and tassels covering her nipples grinds and writhes around the brass pole on the stage. There are about a dozen men scattered around the club. Six or seven of them are sitting at the seats that sit along the stage and the rest are sitting at tables, enjoying that world-famous Cherry Patch lunch buffet.

"How in the world can anybody eat in this place?" I call over the music. "I can count a dozen different health code violations from here."

"Spoiler alert, men don't actually come here for the food."

"I certainly hope not," I reply.

A waitress in a short black skirt and black bikini top carrying an empty tray gives us a strange look as she walks by us. She's a pretty girl. Young, no more than twenty, I'd say. She has long brown hair, brown eyes, warm, tawny skin, and the kind of body men would kill for. I'm surprised she's serving drinks and not up on stage right now.

"Excuse me," I flag her down.

"What can I do for you?"

"We're looking for Conor Boyle," I say and show her my badge.

She grins and points to a door on the far side of the club I didn't notice before. "Conor in trouble again?"

"No, we just have some questions for him," I say.

"Bummer. The club always runs smoother when he's not here," she replies.

We laugh and thank her for the information. She bustles away, heading back toward the bar and Astra turns back to me with a wry expression on her face.

"And you know she doesn't have to work her ass off for a body like that," she grouses. "She just rolls out of bed all perfect and perky."

"You're one to talk, Miss August," I needle her.

She gasps. "Don't you dare!"

Back in another life, Astra had aspirations of breaking into modeling, even while we were at the Academy together. I remember her telling me, wide-eyed, that she'd booked a shoot with a high-end glamour photographer—and the look of embarrassment on her face when it turned out to be a guy printing homemade calendars in his basement.

"I think I still have a copy at home somewhere."

"Remind me to head over and burn the rest of your place down."

I throw my head back and laugh. "Come on, let's get this over with."

We walk toward the door the girl had pointed out to us. On our way toward it, we pass an alcove in the wall that's filled with a large buffet table loaded with heating trays.

"Oh, look at this," Astra says.

She grabs a plate and heads for the tray marked "Irish tacos," and uses the tongs to pull half a dozen of the finger foods out of the tray and set them on her plate.

"You're not serious," I scowl.

"What? I'm hungry," she shrugs. "And these come highly recommended."

"Fine, but when you come down with Hep C, don't come crying to me. And I'm not sure that's covered under your insurance."

"Hey, we're here to talk to a person of interest in an ongoing investigation," she shoots back. "I'm pretty sure it would be considered an injury sustained in the line of duty."

"Good luck with that."

We push through the door and find ourselves in a hallway that's painted red and has the silhouettes of naked women painted in black lining the walls. Black and white photos of half-naked women hang in frames on the walls.

"Classy," Astra mutters, then takes a bit of her Irish taco.

"You feeling faint yet?"

"Not yet," she replies. "I'll keep you in the loop."

We continue down the hall toward a door that's helpfully marked with Boyle's name. On our way, we pass an office on our left marked, "Manager," and a hallway on our right that, judging by the sound of women laughing and talking over one another, leads to the dressing rooms behind the stage.

We reach Boyle's door and I open it to find him sitting at his desk. He's got his feet propped up with a plate of his buffet food in his lap. On the wall in front of him are a pair of flatscreens mounted side by side. One is showing the woman dancing on stage, the other showing a porno flick. This guy is a piece of work.

His office is a tribute to smut. The pair of bookshelves against the wall behind his desk are literally filled with adult movies. The walls are painted a neutral tone that's actually kind of nice but are covered in pictures similar to the ones that line the hallway outside. The one thing that stands out to me, though, is just how clean it is. Even his desk is organized and tidy. Boyle is obviously a man who needs control and order. A man who is almost obsessively efficient. Like our killer.

"Who the hell are you then?" he asks, his voice colored with a faint Irish brogue.

We badge him. "I'm Agent Russo, this is SSA Wilder," Astra says. "And these Irish tacos are amazing."

He smirks as I close the door behind us. We take the seats in front of his desk, though to be honest, I'm not super thrilled about sitting in the chair without disinfecting it first. The words 'hepatitis' and 'MRSA' immediately come to mind. Boyle sets his plate down on the desk and sits up. Boyle is a wholly unattractive man. He's every bit as rough and slimy looking as the photos Rick had pulled up for us back at the shop. If anything, those photos were more flattering.

He gives us both the elevator eyes and it leaves me feeling greasy. If he's intimidated by our badges, he isn't showing it. He's clearly not impressed or afraid of people flashing badges anymore—I guess he's apparently used to dealing with law enforcement. I try to shut out the sound of the adult movie playing in the background, doing my best to ignore it and focus on Boyle who's looking at us with a smarmy smile on his face.

"So, what can I do for you ladies? You lookin' to make a career move?" he asks.

The grunting and groaning seems to be growing louder and more persistent. My face flushes with warmth because it's all I can seem to focus on.

"Hardly," I say and wave vaguely to the televisions on the wall behind us. "Can you please turn that off?"

He laughs. "I'm sorry, is that distractin' you?"

"Just turn it off."

"Come on, sweetheart," he smirks. "I can tell you got a wild side inside you somewhere. I got a magic eye for it, and I see it in you. You oughta let it loose sometime. You might not walk around lookin' like you're constipated all the time."

"You should probably keep your thoughts and your magic eye to yourself," I snap. "And turn that off. Now."

He chuckles and picks up his remote, muting the volume rather than turning it off. He apparently needs to prove he doesn't bend or bow to law enforcement.

"Trust me," Astra says with a grin. "What this one considers wild is rearranging her sock and panty drawer."

"Oh, there's more in there than that. I can see it," he says, his eyes locked onto mine. "You two should really consider comin' down for open pole night."

"Open pole night?" I raise an eyebrow.

"Like open mic night. Anybody can dance," he says. "It's a great time for all."

"Pass. We need to ask you some questions, Mr. Boyle," I say curtly.

"Come on. You're both gorgeous," he presses. "Do you know how much money a pair of lookers like you could make up on that stage? I bet more than you make workin' in that government job you two are workin'. And talkin' to some of my girls here, they say it makes 'em feel strong and powerful."

"You know what makes me feel strong and powerful?" I ask.

"Tell me," he says.

"Arresting scumbags like you."

He chuckles. "Sticks and stones, Agent Wilder."

I stare at him, undaunted. "You had a room at the Churchill last Thursday."

"Yep, I sure did."

"And what were you doing there?" Astra asks.

"Last Thursday, I was hostin' auditions. See, in addition to my club, I also run a small, independent film studio," he says and points to the screen showing the porn. "That's our work right there. Won a couple of AVN awards for that'un."

The pride in his voice makes my skin crawl. I look over at Astra and she looks back at me with an amused smile on her face. She's enjoying this all a little too much.

"So, you were meeting with actresses?" I ask.

"Yeah, you could say that," he replies.

"When you say meeting, you actually mean you were taking talent for a test drive," Astra says. "Casting couch stuff?"

He shrugs. "You don't buy a car without knowin' if it runs, am I right?"

"I wasn't sure I could be any more creeped out, but you two have proven me wrong," I mutter. "Congratulations."

"You're too uptight, babe," he says. "You just need a good f—"

"If you finish that sentence, I will shoot you," I say. "And the next time you call me babe or sweetheart, I'm going beat you senseless. Got it?"

He laughs and holds his hands up in mock surrender. "Fine, fine. But you're only provin' me point here."

"When you were at the Churchill, did you happen to see Valerie Osweiler?" I ask.

His face immediately grows hard and his cheeks flush with color. "I didn't. But I tell you, if I had, I'd be sittin' in a cell right now. I hate that woman. She cost me a bloody fortune."

"So, you didn't see or talk to her last Thursday?" Astra asks.

"I saw none but the talent I was auditionin'," he snaps. "Got video of every single audition if you'd like to see."

"Pass," I say.

"What's this about?" he asks.

"Mrs. Osweiler was murdered, Mr. Boyle," I tell him.

He stares at me for a moment, seeming to be processing what I said. Then he erupts in laughter. Tears of mirth spill from his eyes and he claps, his booming laugh filling the room around us. It takes him a full minute to calm down. Boyle wipes the tears from his eyes and takes a moment to catch his breath.

"A woman was murdered, we're here questioning you about it, and you laugh about it?" I ask. "Really?"

He shrugs. "Am I sorry she's dead? Nope. Not a bit, love," he says. "But I had nothin' to do with it. And I got the video footage provin' it."

"That doesn't necessarily prove it," Astra counters. "We don't know the exact time she was taken, so you could still be involved."

"Well, I'm tellin' you. I was busy all day Thursday. I can show you proof of my movements from six in the mornin' to two that night," he shrugs. "So, I don't know what to tell you ladies. You're welcome to come at me but that's an uphill climb."

"But you're not hiding the fact that you wanted her dead," I say.

He holds his finger up. "I didn't say that. I sure ain't sorry she's dead," he clarifies. "That ain't the same as sayin' I wanted it. There's a difference."

"That might be a distinction without a difference," I snap.

"If you say so."

"We're going to need proof of your movements that day, Mr. Boyle," Astra tells him.

"Give me an address and I'll have it sent along," he says.

I get to my feet, wanting nothing more than to get out of there. Astra stands and looks at him with a small smile on her lips.

"Every Thursday, huh?"

"Aye. Every Thursday," he says, leering at her as if he's already picturing her naked.

I stare at her, and she laughs. "What?" she raises an eyebrow. "I think Benjamin might like to see me put on a show."

"Good God. Let's go," I groan and set one of my cards down on his desk. "Email me the proof of your alibi to that address ASAP, please."

As we walk out of Boyle's office, he calls after me. "You should really take a lesson from your partner, Agent Wilder," he says with a laugh. "She could teach you a few things about loosening up!"

"I really could," she adds.

"Shut up," I groan with a shake of my head.

CHAPTER TWENTY-TWO

King County Medical Examiner's Office; Downtown Seattle

After leaving Boyle's club, we get a call from Rebekah Shafer over at the ME's office. She's finished her autopsy and wants us to come by to talk. As we drive over, my phone pings with an email from Boyle. Just as he promised, he sent me all the files—but the absolute last thing I ever want to do is open that file =, so I immediately forward it to Rick. Once I do that, I give him a call and put him on speaker phone.

"Uh, boss, did you get hacked? Why am I looking at all this porn?" he asks when he answers my call.

"Better question," Astra replies. "When did you object to looking at porn?"

"Because Conor Boyle is not a pleasant man to watch in action," he replies.

She shrugs. "That's a good point."

"It's Boyle's alibi. I need you to verify the time stamps," I say. "He said he was busy until two that morning and I just need to know if that's true."

"Good God, I'm not sure I make enough money for this. Do I at least get hazard pay?"

"Thank you, Rick," I say and disconnect the call.

Astra looks over at me and grins. "That was cruel."

I shrug. "We need to establish Boyle's timeline. I'm certainly not going to watch those."

"That makes me almost feel sorry for him," she says.

"You should be grateful I didn't assign that task to you."

"You're right. Rick's going to do a fantastic job."

I laugh. "It's good to be in charge sometimes."

We pull to the gate at the ME's office and flash the guard in the booth our badges. He looks at them closely, then nods and pushes the button to raise the gate. We drive in and find a spot to park then get out and walk back to the building. The doors open with a pneumatic hiss, and we step into the cool, air conditioning of the lobby. Why they're running the AC when it's cold, dark, and drizzling outside is beyond me.

We step to the reception window. "We're here to see Dr. Shafer."

The woman behind the glass nods and picks up her phone. She murmurs a few quiet words before hanging up and turning back to us.

"She'll be with you shortly," she says.

I give her a nod then Astra and I step back to the small waiting area. The air in the lobby is somber, as it always is. There's only one reason people come to the ME's office and it's never a happy occasion. As if proving my point, there's a thirty-something couple sitting down, huddled close together. They're clinging to one another and sobbing quietly. I can only imagine they're here to identify a body, perhaps a child, and I feel a stab of sympathy for them. No parents, if that's what they're there for, should ever have to bury their child.

A couple of minutes later, the doors to the back swing open and Rebekah steps through. She sees us standing there and offers a tight smile. Rebekah is an old friend from college. She's tiny, no more than five-three, with brown eyes and cool, fair skin. The bright pink that she'd had her pixie cut dyed last time I was here has faded a bit to a dusty bleached look. But the light in her eyes has not dulled one bit. She's always chipper and upbeat. Rebekah is one of those people who seems to genuinely enjoy every minute of life. I envy her that.

Astra and I head over to her and she greets us quietly. We follow her through the warren of corridors that lead us into the bowels of the ME's office. We turn a corner and walk down a short hallway that ends in an automatic door. It quietly slides aside, and we step in. Valerie Osweiler is laying on the stainless steel table in the center of the room, covered by a sheet. I can see the tops of the Y-incisions on her upper chest peeking out from underneath the sheet. Rebekah stands on one side of the table and we stand on the other, with Mrs. Osweiler's body between us.

"It's good to see you, Beks," I say with a smile.

"We really ought to hang out in places that don't have dead bodies."

"I agree," I reply. "Maybe we can go to the Cherry Patch next Thursday. Apparently, Astra is going to be working the pole."

Astra laughs and playfully slaps my arm. Rebekah looks at us with her head cocked, a curious expression on her face. I just grin and shake my head.

"It's nothing. Just part of the case we're working on," I say. "Anyway, what can you tell us about Mrs. Osweiler?"

I look down at the body and now that she's been stripped of her clothes, cleaned up, and had all the mud washed off, I can see deep purple bruises marring her skin. She's got a black eye, a split lip, and a host of bruises and abrasions on her body. This may not be the simple cold-blooded execution like we'd thought. This seems personal to me.

"As you can see, she was beaten pretty badly before she was killed. She put up a fight, though—you can see that her arms and hands are covered in defensive wounds," Rebekah starts. "Mrs.

Osweiler wears acrylics, and they were all broken off as you can see. I wouldn't be surprised if she got some licks in. It's a shame we don't have the nails. I'd bet my entire year's salary she's got some DNA under them."

"Good for her," Astra says. "So, somebody slapped her around before they shot her?"

Rebekah shakes her head. "No, it was with a blunt object. A bat maybe."

"How can you tell?" Astra asks.

"Fists leave a different bruise pattern," she explains and pulls back the sheet, pointing to a bruise across her torso. "As you can see, this long bruise isn't shaped like a fist. It's more like a stick or a bat—something hard and blunt."

We both nod and look at the collection of other bruises that litter her body. I frown as I think about the pain and torment she would have endured before she died. Mrs. Osweiler died a hard death. No question about it.

Rebekah grabs her clipboard and flips through the pages of her notes. "Mrs. Osweiler sustained internal injuries as a result of the beating she took. She also sustained a severe laceration and cranial fracture from a blow to the back of the head. Although it's the gunshots that killed her, it's very likely that without medical attention, she would have died of her wounds within a couple hours anyway."

"Jesus," I gasp.

"She took two shots to the chest. One of the bullets grazed her aorta, which was the kill shot," Rebekah reports.

Astra points to the wound in the side of her head. "What about this?"

"Superfluous," Rebekah says. "That shot was delivered postmortem."

"Wow," Astra mutters. "A little bit of overkill."

"A lot of overkill," I say.

"So, what are you guys thinking with this?" Rebekah asks.

"There are several different theories running around right now," I tell her. "We just can't get a grasp on what's happening yet. It's been dead end after dead end."

"One of those cases, huh?"

I nod. "One of those cases."

"This one seems even more incomprehensible than any of the others we've worked, though," Astra says. "We still don't have a solid suspect."

"I imagine being who she is, Mrs. Osweiler had a lot of enemies among organized crime," Rebekah offers.

"No doubt. But trying to connect any one of those scumbags to where she disappeared from has been an exercise in futility," I say. "The only verifiable lead we had was Conor Boyle, who was at the hotel at the same time as Mrs. Osweiler. But he was—otherwise occupied."

"She was having an affair but her side piece, so far, is a ghost," Astra adds. "We can't get a single whiff of who he is."

"Are you sure it's a he?" Rebekah asks.

I shrug. "We don't even know that either. It could have been a woman."

"That might explain the tension in her marriage," Astra offers. "Maybe she was realizing who she really was and was becoming resentful of having to live a life she knew was false."

"That sounds like a really plausible theory," Rebekah notes.

"That might also put her husband back in the suspect pool," Astra says with a look over to me.

I look down at Mrs. Osweiler's bruised and marked face and frown. It is a viable theory—as viable as anything else we have right now. And the fact that the beating she took was so savage that it feels personal might add a little credence to it.

"Great," I mutter. "Thanks for muddying the waters even more."

She shrugs. "Always happy to help."

"Well, It's a viable theory. It's something we're definitely going to have to check out."

"I haven't been able to process her personal effects yet," Rebekah says. "There are a few things I want to check out that I haven't had time to just yet."

"I appreciate that," I nod. "By the way, did you happen to find a burner phone with her things? A prepaid deal."

"There's a phone in with her effects but it doesn't seem like a prepaid phone. It's a nice iPhone. The latest model," she tells us.

"So, the phone is in the wind," Astra notes. "That tracks with how this case has been breaking for us."

"Right? All right, we appreciate the information, Beks," I say. "Call us if you come up with anything else."

"Will do," she nods.

We head out of the ME's office without much more information we walked in with. If anything, the issue is even more confused than before. But at the same time, I feel like we at least have a direction to point. Having seen Mrs. Osweiler's body and having Rebekah give us the details firmly establishes the fact that this was personal. That somebody she knew and took offense to something Mrs. Osweiler did is responsible for this. And judging by how badly she was beaten, whatever they took offense to was, in their mind, incredibly serious. At least to them.

It's not much but it's something.

CHAPTER TWENTY-THREE

Osweiler Residence; Windermere District, Seattle

"Do we really have to do this?" Astra asks.

"Unfortunately, we do."

"Can't we make the locals do it?"

A rueful laugh escapes me. "TJ Lee isn't in the mood to do us any favors," I reply. "So no, we're stuck doing it."

"Damn."

"Yeah, I feel the same way."

We get out of the car and walk across the street then up to the front door of the Osweiler home. Death notifications are the absolute worst part of the job. Usually, it would fall to the local officers or detectives to make the notification. But the SPD hasn't so much as lifted a finger to help us. It's no surprise, I guess. I just never expected that Lee would have the spiteful, vindictive streak he's currently showing off for us.

Paxton had mentioned he and Lee had a falling out. Not that there was all that much to fall out with, but Pax mentioned that Lee changed when he was named interim Deputy Chief. He said that somehow the stick up his rear end got shoved even farther up there.

Pax went on about how his ego had blown up with his new title, but that reeks of projection to me.

I don't think it's necessarily an ego thing. I personally think Lee is simply trying to work as hard as he can to do things right—to erase the stain his predecessor left behind—and to, of course, have that 'interim' label taken off the title. I can't blame him for any of that, even though it's annoying as hell to deal with.

We get to the front door and I take a deep breath. Astra glances at me as I ring the bell and gives me a small grin.

"You're doing all the talking," she whispers. "You realize that, right?"

"Why do I—"

"Because you're the one in charge. Remember?"

"I hate you so much right now."

I have to force my face into seriousness when I hear the door being unlocked. There would be nothing worse or more inappropriate than to have Mr. Osweiler open the door to find us there joking and laughing with each other. But when the door opens, I'm surprised to find that it's not Mr. Osweiler behind it.

"Ms. Keaton," I say.

She looks at us with those cold, green eyes. It's more than obvious that she's not happy to see us standing on the doorstep.

"Yes?" she asks. "What can I do for you?"

"We need to speak with Mr. Osweiler."

"I'm sorry, he's resting right now."

"We're going to have to insist on speaking with him, Wren," Astra says. "We have news he needs to hear from us."

"I can relay it to him—"

"No, Ms. Keaton, you can't," I reply. "Is there some reason you don't want to let us in?"

She sighs. "He's just a wreck. He's been inconsolable and he hasn't been resting," she says. "He hasn't been taking care of himself and I just want him to get a little rest."

"It's all right, Wren," Mr. Osweiler's voice echoes from the hallway. "I'm awake."

Behind him, I see him step into the foyer. He looks even rougher than the last time we saw him, and I can see why Ms. Keaton is so worried about him. He looks like he's withering and wasting away. She opens the door wider and steps back, allowing him to step into the doorway.

"What is it?" he asks.

"May we come in for a minute, Mr. Osweiler?"

He scrutinizes my face then turns to look at Astra and I watch as the realization dawns on him. His expression shifts and a shadow crosses his face. He knows why we're here. He swallows down his reply and simply nods as he turns and walks back into the house. Ms. Keaton gives us a look and I see the sadness etched into her features. She opens her mouth to speak but her words die on her lips, and she turns away. Astra and I follow her in, closing the door gently behind us.

As we step into the main room, the atmosphere is hushed, but pensive and mournful already. It is clean, though. Everything is absolutely immaculate and in its place. The sliders are all open and the miasma of body odor and alcohol has cleared out. Osweiler is still sleeping on the couch though. As I look around the place, I know it was Keaton who cleaned, tidied, and organized everything. She's bound and determined to see Osweiler through this, which is a good thing. I just don't know why she won't help bring him some peace by telling us who Mrs. Osweiler was seeing on the side.

He sits down on the couch and pulls his pillow into his lap as if it can help ward off the brutal blow we're about to deliver. Astra and I take the loveseat across from him and Keaton sits down next to him, her face pale and her lips quivering. I notice that she's gotten a manicure since the last time we saw her—which strikes me as a little callous. Who gets a fresh manicure while your best friend is missing?

Keaton fidgets on the sofa and looks scared, as if she knows what we're about to say and isn't prepared for it. Osweiler does know what we're about to say but is somehow managing to keep his composure, though it seems it's an iffy thing. But how can somebody really be prepared to find out their wife, or their best friend, was savagely beaten, tortured, and then murdered? You can't. It's that simple.

"Mr. Osweiler," I start softly. "I'm very sorry to have to tell you that we found your wife's body. She's been murdered."

He stares at me in silence as tears spill down his cheeks. An agonized wail erupts from Keaton, though, as she buries her face in her hands, her entire body shaking wildly with sobs. Mr. Osweiler puts a comforting hand on her back, never taking his eyes off me.

"Where was she found?" he asks.

"She was found behind a fishing club in East Hill," I tell him. "But that was a secondary location. She was killed elsewhere."

"You've never belonged to the East Hill Anglers Club or had any connection with it, have you, Mrs. Osweiler?" Astra asks.

He shakes his head. "I've never been fishing in my life. And I know Valerie hasn't either. It wasn't really our thing."

"I didn't think so, but we had to ask," I say.

I believe him when he tells me they have no connection to the club. But I make a mental note to check their financials anyway to see if they've paid dues to that fishing club before or not. No stone unturned.

Osweiler sniffs loudly. "Wh—what happened to her?"

"Mr. Osweiler, I don't think you want the specifics—"

"Tell me," he snaps, his voice forceful. "What happened to my wife?"

I hesitate. Whenever I've had to do a notification, I've always wavered when it comes to how much to tell them. On the one hand, I want to prepare them for what they're going to see when they have to go to the ME's office to make the formal identification. I don't want them to walk in and be shocked and traumatized by what they see. On the other hand, the last thing I want to do is distress them with details of the horrors visited upon their loved ones. It's a delicate line that's difficult to walk and I usually try to err on the side of caution and discretion.

"Agent Wilder, tell me what happened," he growls. "What did he do to my wife?"

I let out a long breath and look at Astra. She frowns and gives me a subtle shrug, telling me to do what I think is best. The trouble is, in this case, I don't know what's best. But he seems to want honesty.

"Mr. Osweiler, since you're going to have to make a formal identification, I want you to prepare yourself for what you're going to see. Your wife was beaten. Rather savagely," I start. "The ME concluded that the internal injuries she suffered would have likely led to her death on their own."

He sniffs loudly and scrubs at his eyes. Keaton's face is still buried in her hands and her body is convulsing. But he looks at me, his face as expressionless as a stone, and nods, telling me to continue.

"In addition to the injuries sustained in the beating, your wife was shot three times. The first two were to the chest," I tell him. "One of the bullets clipped her aorta, which was the shot that killed her. The killer also shot her once in the head, postmortem. Based on her examination, the ME determined she was most likely killed the day she was taken. There wasn't anything anybody could have done to save her."

"My God," he whispers. "Who would do that to her?"

"We're still trying to find out, Mr. Osweiler," I say. "Because this reads as a personal attack to me, it suggests it could be the person she was… seeing. Perhaps she tried breaking things off and this person didn't take it well. There are a lot of moving parts still, and the truth of the matter is, we don't have a solid suspect right now."

"How can you not know?" Keaton asks, her voice choked with emotion. "How can you have no idea who did this to her?"

"We're following every possible lead and angle, but unfortunately we didn't get the case until two days after she disappeared," I say honestly. "And if I could be frank, it hasn't helped us that we haven't had all the facts from the start. If we had the facts, we'd be able to coalesce around a single theory of this crime."

I didn't mean it to be such a sharp rebuke but both Osweiler and Keaton look down at their hands as if I'd slapped them. The emotion on their faces is more than clear. I could have probably handled that a little better, but the truth is, if either one of them had been honest with us from the jump, maybe we'd be on a better track. It obviously wouldn't have saved her life, but at least we could be closing in on a suspect.

"We are going to do our very best to find out who did this to your wife, Mr. Osweiler. And your best friend, Ms. Keaton," I say, my tone softer. "If nothing else, we hope we can at least bring you some semblance of closure. Some sense of peace."

"I'm not sure I'm ever going to feel peace ever again," he mutters.

"Do you think you can find the person who did this, Agents?" Keaton asks. "Do you think you can figure out who murdered her?"

"We're going to do our very best," I reply.

"But do you think you can? Do you think you can find them?" she asks again, her tone harder. "Do you have any leads whatsoever?"

"Nothing solid right now," I admit. "But we won't give up on this case. We won't give up on Mrs. Osweiler."

She glares at me. "I can't believe—"

"Wren, stop," Mr. Osweiler says. "Let them do their jobs."

"I'm sorry," she replies quietly. "I just—I want to know if they're going to bring the monster who took Val away from us to justice."

I look from Osweiler to Keaton and back again. They're both caught up in a tsunami of emotion, being pushed and pulled by the twin hands of grief and anger. I know what they're feeling because

I've been there too. I give Astra a nod and we get to our feet. I look down at the pair sitting side by side—their bodies are so close but at the same time they look like they're a thousand miles apart.

"I promise you we won't stop trying to solve this, Mr. Osweiler," I say.

He nods but won't meet my eyes. He's off in another dimension right now as he processes everything he's feeling. Everything that's happened. Astra and I walk out of the Osweiler home, and I can honestly say I've never felt so helpless in my entire career.

CHAPTER TWENTY-FOUR

Criminal Data Analysis Unit; Seattle Field Office

THE DOORS SLIDE ASIDE WITH THAT FAMILIAR HISS AS I WALK into the office. Mo and Rick are crowded around Astra's workstation and they're all whispering to one another excitedly. But when they catch sight of me, they all stand upright and look like I just walked in on them filching cookies out of the cookie jar.

"Where have you been?" Astra asks.

"I was over in Organized Crime," I reply.

I worked a brief stint over in OC at the beginning of my career in the Bureau. Jonas Hobbs is the Bureau Chief over there and was something of a mentor to me. He's a good man and knows more about Seattle's criminal underbelly than anybody else in the city. If something is brewing in the underworld, Jonas likely already knows about it.

"What did Jonas have to say?" Astra asks.

I shake my head and flash her a grin. "Other than a fairly lengthy monologue about your physical assets, not a whole lot."

"The man is like a hormone-riddled teenager in a middle-aged man's body," she rolls her eyes.

"You're not wrong. But he's never hurting for companionship," I reply.

"Well, he's definitely not bad looking."

"Yeah, that's a rabbit hole I have no desire going down with you," I say with a laugh. "He's like a father-ish figure to me and I really don't want to think of him that way."

"Speaking of personal trauma," Rick interjects.

"Oh, here we go," Astra says.

"I reviewed all the… footage… you sent me and unfortunately, Conor Boyle's alibi checks out," he says. "Boyle was… auditioning, I suppose we can say, from seven that morning until just after midnight—"

"My God," Astra says. "That man has got some stamina. I'm actually impressed."

"You can discuss it with him on open pole night," I crack, making her laugh.

"That's disturbing," Rick comments. "Anyway, after his last interview, there are receipts from the hotel bar that show he was drinking until just after two."

"That's corroborated by footage from his socials," Mo adds. "He was partying with the girls he hired."

I shake my head. "Wow. Some people really will do anything for their fifteen minutes."

"Hey, as long as it works?" Astra offers, sending out a cavalcade of laughter. "But anyway, that takes Boyle out of the suspect pool. Did Hobbs have anything?"

I shake my head. "He said he's heard nothing. No chatter about somebody taking Osweiler out," I tell them. "The Armenians, Japanese, Chinese, Russians, and Italians—nobody's taking credit for hitting Osweiler."

"That's unusual," Mo says.

I nod. "Somebody would be crowing about it. Osweiler cost them all a big chunk of change and made all their lives more difficult, which made her a big target," I say. "If one of them had hit her, Hobbs is sure they'd be throwing a party, loud and proud to have done so. But it's been radio silence from all the usual suspects."

"People do that?" Rick raises an eyebrow.

"More than you'd think," I reply. "If there's one thing these dirtbags are happy to do, it's sign their handiwork."

"Okay, so it looks like our organized crime angle is dead in the water. Her death has nothing to do with her work," Astra says. "Which is good because while you were over there flirting with Hobbs, the three of us developed an alternate theory. It's pretty good, I think."

"You did, did you?" I ask.

Astra nods. "We did. Something Beks said made me think of it. Then Mo and Rick helped add on and flesh it out."

"I wasn't over in OC that long," I say.

"We're just that good," Astra says.

"All right then, lay it on me."

I take my normal spot at the head of the room, folding my arms over my chest, and start pacing back and forth, my eyes fixed on the floor, listening intently.

"So, we started with the idea that Valerie wasn't involved with a man, but with a woman," Astra starts. "Now, who's a woman close to Valerie, somebody who'd trust her enough to go off with her without raising a fuss, and has an obvious secret she's not sharing with us?"

I look at her for a long moment. "You're not serious, are you?"

"Serious as a heart attack," she says.

"I went through Wren Keaton's socials," Mo adds, picking up the thread. "She's single and Valerie was all over her posting history. It's almost nothing but photos of them out together, status updates about something fun they're doing together, and words of appreciation about her friendship with Valerie. It's almost—obsessive."

"And building off what you said to Mr. Osweiler, we're thinking that maybe Valerie tried to break things off with Wren and she didn't take it too well," Astra goes on. "She's physically fit. She's strong. I have no problem seeing her swinging a bat like Barry Bonds. She could have gotten together with Valerie, taken her somewhere secluded, beat her, shot her, then dumped her out in East Hill."

The pieces all seem to fit but I'm still not convinced. I frown and keep pacing, turning their words over in my head again and again.

"Think about it," Astra presses. "You said our offender was going to be neat and organized. Almost obsessively so. What was the first thing you noticed out at Osweiler's place today?"

"That it was clean and organized," I say. "And I'm sure Wren was the one who cleaned it all. I assumed it was her effort to help take care of Mr. Osweiler out of a sense of loyalty to her best friend."

"Or alternately, out of a sense of guilt because she'd just brutally murdered his wife," Astra counters.

"But it doesn't completely track for me," I say. "If she was in love with Valerie, wouldn't she resent Scott for having what she wanted? Especially if Valerie was breaking things off with her? I'd think her resentment would be through the roof."

Astra shrugs. "I didn't say our theory was without holes," she admits. "But you have to admit, a lot of the pieces fit."

"Or it could be that she and Scott had a bond. I mean, you said they were friends, right? That she introduced Valerie to him?" Mo adds.

"Yeah, that's what she told me," I reply.

"So, they were friends," Mo says. "And they also shared a bond because they loved the same woman—even if he didn't know that. But it would give Wren some common ground with him. So, she clings to him, trying to get him to assuage her guilt, even if he doesn't know what she did to his wife."

I purse my lips as I pace. What she's saying makes a lot of sense actually. I can't say I'm one hundred percent sold on the theory yet. But I'm getting there. The pieces of this theory they're laying out for me are definitely intriguing. I just don't know if they all fit into one coherent picture just yet. I need more.

"This would be so much easier if we had that burner phone," I sigh.

"Any idea where we can find that?" Astra asks.

I shake my head. "Nope. Her bag was missing," I say. "I'm going to go back to the crime scene tomorrow to see if there's anything the techs missed."

"Good plan," Astra nods. "And as you do that, I'm going to start digging into Wren's life. We're going to do a deep dive and crawl right up in her delicate lady parts to see what else she might be hiding up there."

I nod. "Excellent. That's a plan," I say. "And when you figure out, she's not the one, see if you can't develop a couple more theories, huh? Keep checking the registered guests at the Churchill and cross-reference them with her case files and everything else. We really need to catch a break here."

"We really do," Astra says.

"Rick, go through Mrs. Osweiler's socials again. I want you to put together a list of her closest friends," I say. "We're going to start interviewing them and rattling some cages to see if they can tell us who this mystery boyfriend—or girlfriend—was."

"On it, boss," he says.

"All right. Good," I reply.

Orders given, I turn and head back out, bound for East Hill. Not really where I want to go, but desperate times call for desperate measures, I suppose.

CHAPTER TWENTY-FIVE

East Hill Anglers Club; East Hill, Seattle, WA

All the emergency vehicles and first responders are long gone when I pull into the former clubhouse lot and turn off the engine. Now that the cops have all filtered out, the area has returned to its natural state—which means a few rough-looking guys are hanging out near the dilapidated old building. Ribbons of yellow crime scene tape flutter in the breeze. They turn as I get out of the car and look at me the way a predator eyes its prey.

They're standing near the corner of the clubhouse that leads to the field behind it, which means I'm going to have to pass right by them to get there. I'm not real thrilled about that. They look like a group of guys who are just spoiling for a little trouble. But there's nothing I can do except roll with it and hope this doesn't turn ugly. Steeling my nerves, I start for the field. The three men are eyeing me up and down as I approach so I square my shoulders and walk on, drawing whistles and catcalls from the men.

I'm trying to ignore them but one man jumps in my way. He's tall and lanky with limp brown hair that hangs to his shoulders and dark eyes. His smile is cold and reptilian and the teeth he has left in his mouth are yellow and decaying. The several days' worth of stubble on his face hides some of the pockmarking but he's got an unhealthy patina about him. There's no hiding the open sores around his mouth though, which are likely from the meth he's obviously smoking.

"Hey baby, you lookin' for a good time?" he sneers. "Lookin' to score? I can hook you up. Maybe we can make a little trade, y'know?"

I slide my weapon out of its holster and hold up my badge for him to see. "You lookin' to get arrested or shot today? Your choice."

The two men who were standing behind him, sneering and snickering, take off running at the sight of my badge. But the man in front of me just laughs. He shrugs and gives me the elevator eyes, but he takes a step back all the same.

"Damn shame," he mutters. "Could've been fun."

"You better catch up with your friends."

He turns and saunters away like he's not the least bit intimidated and doesn't have a care in the world. I watch him until he disappears down a side street, then holster my weapon and slip my badge back into the pocket of my overcoat. Confident they won't be back, I continue on to the field where Mrs. Osweiler was found beside the pond. A thick layer of algae rests on the surface of the water, already climbing up to claim the shell of the old boat in the middle of the pond. There's just something sad about it.

It really is unfortunate that a place as nice as East Hill used to be has fallen so low. The economy took a tumble in this area and never really recovered, even as the rest of Seattle seemed to boom. And now it's a cycle: the only people who can escape are the ones with enough means to move to neighborhoods that are already growing and thriving. Meanwhile back in East Hill, social services crumble, the roads and streets are no longer maintained, property values plummet, and everyone who's been left behind suddenly becomes too poor to leave. So they remain trapped here as crime rises. It still astounds me that only a few minutes away are the glassy high-rises and opulent playgrounds of downtown Seattle.

I suppose it's the same as a lot of places these days. The rich get richer and the poor get poorer, and half the time on the very same block you'll see families in the process of getting evicted from their homes while millionaires brush past them rudely to get to whatever nightclub they're partying at that night. It seems like basic kindness and decency are in all too short supply these days.

But that's all philosophical and political navel-gazing that's probably best left for somebody more qualified to do it than me. I step over to the spot where Mrs. Osweiler's body was found and look down. We might have more clues to go on if we knew where she'd been killed. Knowing where she was dumped only tells us so much. Of course, other physical clues might be nice to have as well. But as the old saying goes, a wish in one hand, crap in the other.

I promised Mr. Osweiler that we'd find her killer. That's something I normally don't do. I try to avoid making promises to any victim's loved ones because the truth is, some cases can't be solved. For reasons I don't understand though, this case has become personal to me. While I admire the good Mrs. Osweiler did for a great many people, the truth is, she was a flawed person. She had her dark side. The fact that she was cheating on her husband proves that. Maybe I'm too strict or too judgmental, but I typically don't sympathize with adulterers.

Nobody is perfect, though. Everybody has their flaws and shortcomings. I know I've done my fair share of things others might view with a disapproving eye. And shouldn't the good Mrs. Osweiler did in this world, for so many people, outweigh her own personal failings? Maybe. I know I shouldn't be weighing matters of her character and integrity. I shouldn't be judging her. It's not my place. My sole focus should not be on who she was as a person but on who snuffed out the fire of a woman who, whatever her personal failings, had done a lot of good in this world and who was poised to do even more.

Besides, the truth is, I don't know what it was like inside their marriage. I don't know what sort of husband Mr. Osweiler was to her. I don't truly know what sort of man he is. His grief seems genuine and the man seems authentically devastated. But his anguish doesn't mean he's a good person. Nor does it mean he was a good husband. I just don't believe he's involved with his wife's death.

None of that matters right now though. Like my earlier thoughts on the decline of East Hill, it's philosophical navel-gazing better left to others. My only job is to find the person who killed Mrs. Osweiler. I need to clear my head of all the extraneous noise and do my job. I give myself a shake then close my eyes and turn my face up to the clouds, a lighter shade of gray today than yesterday, and feel the faint drizzle falling on my skin.

When I open my eyes again, I look around me, already feeling more focused and locked in. I try to picture the scene as it happened that night. The techs found tire tracks in the dirt, meaning the killer drove back here and dispose of Mrs. Osweiler. They took impressions of the tracks, but unless our killer drove a car with very specific or unusual tires, I don't see anything coming of it. For one thing, I don't think they would have wanted to stand out by driving something exotic.

No, I'm sure they would have driven something common. Something we see a thousand times a day and is so ordinary that we'd forget seeing it five minutes after it drove off. I can't say for sure obviously, but if I were forced to hazard a guess, I'd say the killer probably drove something like a Toyota or maybe a Honda sedan. A neutral color, probably. Those are among the most popular make of cars in the U.S., so I think it stands to reason our killer drives something like that. Something that blends in and fades into the background.

Which doesn't make things any easier for me. Of the three

million or so people who own cars in the Seattle area, I'd bet at least one million of those own a neutral-colored Toyota or Honda sedan.

My eyes still taking in the scene around me, I start to walk around, searching the ground and looking for anything that stands out. Anything that doesn't belong. All the while, I'm playing out the scenario in my head.

"Okay, so I pull up back here. I've probably got the body in the trunk. That means I know the area and know I can dump a body here without an overwhelming fear of being seen. If any of the junkies are back here, I scare them off first or go somewhere else. But nobody's here so I can make the dump," I say to myself as I look around. "I back up to this spot, pop the trunk and haul Mrs. Osweiler's body out. That means I'm strong. Strong enough to lift a hundred and thirty pounds of dead weight, anyway."

I kick at a small stone near the toe of my boot and watch it skitter away as my mind continues to spin out my theory. I go back to what Lou Glass had told me. She'd been partially covered—her face and chest. The techs had bagged an old sheet that looked like it was part of the collection of detritus that choked the field back here.

"After I dump her body, I take the time to find a sheet and cover her. Why?" I ask as I circle the spot where she'd been dumped. "Remorse. Guilt. There's still a small part of me that cares about this woman and I feel bad for killing her."

That all makes sense to me as I try to fill in the gaps in the profile. If I can build a strong profile, we might be able to narrow down the list of suspects, since we've all but eliminated Mrs. Osweiler's murder having anything to do with her work. It's going to be complicated since we don't know a whole lot about her personal life. We don't know who she spent time with, let alone who she was seeing on the side. We're just going to have to find a way to dig even deeper into her social life. There are bound to be clues that we haven't seen yet.

"Excuse me?"

My heart lurches when I hear the voice behind me. I wheel

around, my hand going to my weapon automatically. Standing behind me is a girl. She's no more than seventeen or eighteen and slight of build. I'd put her about five-four, with long strawberry blonde hair, blue eyes, and cold, pale skin. She's wearing black skinny jeans, a blue flannel, and black Chucks. The girl is definitely not a gangster, and she doesn't look like she's gotten into meth. Not yet anyway. She's got an innocent look to her and I just hope she gets out of this place before the bad stuff finds her and corrupts her life.

I stand up straight and pull my coat over my weapon again. The girl is staring at me with wide eyes, looking at me like she's a frightened rabbit and I'm the big, bad wolf who's about to devour her. I can tell she's teetering on the edge of scampering away, so I hold my hands up to show her I'm not a threat.

"I'm Blake and I'm with the FBI," I tell her, hoping it puts her more at ease. "What's your name?"

"I—I'm Coral," she says, her voice shaking. "Coral Allen."

"Hi, Coral. You live around here?"

She nods and gestures vaguely behind her. "Over there."

"Okay. All right. But you know, you should be careful about sneaking up on people," I say with a smile, trying to get her to loosen up.

"I—I didn't mean to. I just—you looked like you were concentrating, and I didn't want to disturb you. Not at first," she explains.

As I study the girl's delicate features, I can see she's got something to say. But she's jumpy and scared. Not only of me. It just seems to be her default setting and I suppose I can't blame her. Growing up in a place like this, surrounded by drugs, gangs, violence, and death is bound to leave a mark on some people. I find myself hoping she'll use that fear to propel her out of this place.

"What's on your mind, Coral?"

She swallows hard and licks her lips nervously. "You're—you're with the FBI?"

I nod and move slowly to avoid spooking her as I pull out my credentials to show her. She takes it from me gingerly and studies it closely, handling it like a bomb she expects to go off in her face. Coral finally looks up and hands my creds back to me.

"This is about the woman who was found here?" she asks.

I nod. "It is," I tell her. "Do you know something? Or did you see something?"

She shakes her head and looks away. I can see she's really fighting the urge to turn and run. The urge to avoid mixing herself up in this mess. I can't blame her for that either. In this sort of neighborhood, snitches don't get stitches—they usually get a pair of bullets in the back of the head. But I can also see that Coral is a good person who wants to do the right thing. She's simply afraid to.

"It's all right, Coral. We're alone here, and whatever you have to say, I'll keep a secret," I reply. "I'll do everything I can to avoid bringing your name into anything. Nobody will ever know you spoke to me."

She looks around, perhaps looking for anybody who might be watching us. That look of fear on her face grows deeper, but so too does the determination I see in her eyes.

"No, I didn't see it happen. But I was out here and saw her the next day," she says, her eyes shimmering with tears. "I've never seen a dead body before."

"I know it can be shocking," I say, my curiosity piqued. "What were you doing out here?"

"I—I was looking for stuff I can use in my art. There's always junk people throw out that I can repurpose for my sculptures," she tells me.

"So, you're an artist," I say. "That's really good. That can take you out of here and on to a better place."

She nods. "Yeah. I'm a good student. Get good grades," she tells me. "I'm hoping between that and my art, I'll be able to get a scholarship to a good school. Maybe back east somewhere. Anywhere but here."

"That's really admirable, Coral," I tell her. "I want that for you. I want you to get out of East Hill and find a better place."

A faint smile flickers across her lips and I watch as she takes a breath and holds it for a count of five. She's building up to what she came out here to tell me and I want to give her the time and space to say it. I don't want to spook her.

"Anyway," she finally says. "When I was out here looking for material, I found something. It was only later I realized it belongs—belonged—to the dead woman. I saw her on the news."

I feel an electric surge shoot through my veins. This might be the missing piece of the puzzle I desperately need. I'm doing my best to manage my expectations and temper my optimism. though. This very well might be nothing more than another false lead that takes to another dead end—which most everything has in this case so far.

"What did you find, Coral?" I ask after taking a beat to calm myself down.

"I would have come forward sooner but..." she lets her voice trail off and looks away, an expression of shame touching her features.

"That's all right, Coral. I know this has to be scary for you," I tell her. "It's scary for anybody. Believe me.

She offers me a small smile, though I can see that blend of guilt and fear warring on her face. She just needs a little push in the right direction.

"The important thing is that you're here talking to me now," I say encouragingly. "You're doing the right thing. So tell me, what did you find?"

She pulls her backpack off and I hold my breath as she opens it. Coral pulls out a handbag—an extremely expensive-looking handbag—and lets her backpack fall to the ground. She reaches in and fishes out a wallet, then trapping the handbag between her body and her arm, she opens it up and points to the driver's license tucked behind the plastic window.

"Valerie Osweiler," she says. "That's the dead woman, right?"

I nod, that electricity surging through me turning into liquid fire. My stomach churns and I feel my pulse begin to race as I pull a pair of black nitrile gloves out of my pocket and snap them on. I gently take the wallet from Coral and look at Mrs. Osweiler's photo.

"I—I'm sorry. I handled the purse without gloves," she says. "I didn't know it was important until—until after. And I made sure to put everything I took out back in. I didn't keep anything for myself at all."

I shake my head. "It's all right. You didn't do anything wrong," I tell her. "In fact, you did something very, very right. We owe you big time for this."

Her face lights up as if she's unaccustomed to hearing praise. "I did? You do?"

I nod eagerly. "Yes. Very much so. I can't begin to thank you enough for this, Coral. You may have put us on a path that lets us catch a killer."

Her smile is warm and sweet—and something she doesn't look very used to. I have to imagine there's not much to smile about in her life. But I respect the hell out of her for having a plan and trying to get out of this place. That takes strength and courage.

I paw through the wallet but don't see much of interest just yet. We'll have to do a deeper dive on this when I get back. I'm less interested in the wallet, though, than everything else that's waiting in Mrs. Osweiler's handbag. But it can wait. In the meantime, I dig the cash out of the wallet and see she was carrying a few hundred bucks. I know I should be vouchering this as evidence. But I also know the money is irrelevant. It's not part of any crime. I also know Mr. Osweiler isn't going to miss it—and Mrs. Osweiler has no use for it now. Nobody's going to miss it if they never knew it was there in the first place.

After I get Coral's information and give her my word to not just show up at her house randomly, but to call first, I hand her the cash. She looks at it then up at me.

"Are you serious?" she gasps.

I nod. "That's for you, Coral. Do something good for yourself with it," I tell her. "Don't give it to anybody else. Just do something nice for you. Be selfish. It's all right."

"Thank you. Thank you so much," she whispers.

I watch her run off, smiling at her unexpected windfall, hoping she does something nice for herself. She seems like a good kid who deserves to have something good happen in her life. That sort of thing is rare in East Hill. I walk back to my car, keeping watch for any of the creeps who were standing around when I pulled up. But the lot is empty and I let out a breath of relief. I'm glad I won't have to deal with them again. I just hope nobody saw me talking to Coral. If something happens to her, I don't know that I'll forgive myself.

I use my key fob to pop the trunk. I reach in and pull a large plastic evidence bag from a box of supplies I keep with me. As I slip the purse into it, my cellphone rings. I drop the bag into the trunk and slam the lid, then fish my phone out of my pocket. I connect the call and press the phone to my ear.

"Wilder."

"Blake, it's Rebekah," she says.

"Hey, what's up?"

"Can you come down to my office? It's important."

There's a tension in her voice I can't immediately identify. But it doesn't seem like she's worried about something. If anything, it almost seems like she's excited, which I find odd. But she is never one to call me down to her office for anything frivolous. Whatever she found has to be important. Inspecting Mrs. Osweiler's bag is going to have to wait for now.

"On my way," I say and disconnect the call.

CHAPTER TWENTY-SIX

King County Medical Examiner's Office; Downtown Seattle

I FOLLOW REBEKAH THROUGH THE WINDING CORRIDORS OF THE ME's office trying to ignore the cloying stench of bleach and antiseptics. She takes me to her personal office rather than to an autopsy suite, silent the whole way. If I'm not mistaken, Rebekah's got a spring in her step and seems excited rather than somber. It piques my curiosity.

She closes the door behind me and as I drop into the seat in front of her desk, she walks around to her own chair and sits down. Rebekah has a small grin on her lips and a definite cat that ate the canary expression on her face, which makes me laugh.

"You know, I thought you said we were going to start hanging out in places *without* dead bodies," I start.

"And we should!" she chirps. "But I just couldn't wait. I have something exciting for you."

I sit back in my seat, about to explode with curiosity. But she seems so excited, I don't want to rain on her parade. Rebekah opens a small box that's sitting on her desk and fishes out a plastic bag. She hands it over to me and I hold it up, looking at the necklace inside.

There's a lacquered charm that's got some kind of soft purple and pink flower painted on it. It's obviously hand crafted, and it's gorgeous. I turn it over and look at the inscription on the back of it. "Forever yours," it reads.

I raise my eyebrows. "Um. Thank you? But I didn't know you, um…"

She tosses her head back and laughs. "Oh my god, not like that."

"Then what am I looking at exactly?"

"That, my friend, is what's known in the common parlance as a smoking gun," she says.

"A smoking gun?"

She nods. "Yep. Valerie Osweiler was wearing that necklace when she was killed," she says. "I just had a hunch, so I had the lab dust it for prints."

I sit up again, my heart skipping a beat in my chest. "Please tell me you're going to say what I think you're going to say."

She can't contain her smile. "There is a pristine thumbprint on the back of the charm," she says. "And it does not belong to Mrs. Osweiler."

"You're kidding me."

Rebekah shakes her head. "One hundred percent serious."

I sit back in my seat again, feeling a profound sense of relief at the bit of luck that just fell in my lap. It's the second bit of luck we've had since Rosie handed us this file, which seems like it was about a million years ago. But for the first time since we started working this case, thanks to Rebekah's foresight and Coral's honesty, I'm starting to feel like we may actually close this case after all. And if we do, it's going to be thanks to them.

I'm squirming in my seat and doing my best to manage my expectations and temper my excitement. The contents of the purse may amount to nothing, and the thumbprint may not necessarily belong to our killer, but these are our first viable leads. Rather than flailing around in the dark, we're actually going to be pointed in one direction that could possibly lead us to Mrs. Osweiler's murderer.

"Have you run the print through AFIS yet?" I ask.

"I did but didn't get a hit," she replied.

I immediately feel my heart sink into my stomach. If the print doesn't belong to somebody who's in AFIS, it means they don't have a record, and our odds of identifying and catching them diminish to almost nothing. Unless of course, they are eventually caught committing a crime and get themselves printed. Either way, it doesn't give us a name right now when we need it most. Suddenly, that bit of good luck tastes sour in my mouth. And yet, Rebekah is still grinning at me like an idiot, which keeps that small guttering flame of hope inside of me alive.

"All right, you're still smiling," I observe. "That means you haven't told me something yet."

She nods. "Of course. A storyteller doesn't skip to the end. No, they draw the story out and pull the audience in before dropping the big reveal."

I laugh. "Okay, I'm ready for you to drop the big reveal. Please."

"Well, you're no fun."

"Sorry, I'm just anxious here," I say. "We've been beating our heads against the wall for days now and haven't gotten anywhere. You're offering me the first bit of fresh air we've had."

"All right, all right. I'll put you out of your misery," she says, laughing to herself. "I expanded the search into other databases, hoping that maybe, this guy got printed for a job or something."

"And I'm assuming he did."

She nods. "Yes, he did. And you are not going to believe this."

"Lay it on me."

Rebekah smiles wide and picks up her tablet. She logs into it and calls up the information she wants me to see then hands it over to me. I read what she's pulled up once and then read it again just to make sure I'm not misunderstanding what I'm reading. I scroll through the three pages of her reports and absorb everything. And when I'm done, I set the tablet back down and lean back in my chair, my eyes locked onto Rebekah's.

"You did some fantastic work, Rebekah," I say. "This is incredible."

"Think they'll give me a badge?"

I laugh. "If they don't, I will," I tell her. "Thank you, Rebekah. You went above and beyond. And if we solve this case, it's going to be because of you."

"Just doing my part," she replies with a grin.

"Well, since we're playing show and tell, I have something for you," I say.

She arches an eyebrow at me. "Oh? And what have you brought me?"

"Can we go into one of your suites?"

"Lead the way."

I pick up my bag and we walk through a door and into the autopsy suite that adjoins her office. I move over to the table and set my bag down, then grab a pair of gloves and snap them on. Curiosity on her face, Rebekah gloves up and joins me at the table as I pull the evidence bag out of my own then open it up and take the purse out.

She whistles. "Now who's the one giving surprise gifts? Prada? You shouldn't have."

I laugh. "Funny girl," I reply. "This is Valerie Osweiler's bag."

"And where did you come across this treasure trove?"

I relate the story of meeting Coral and everything that happened. As I speak, I start taking everything out of the purse and set it on the table in front of us. When I finish the story, I have the contents all laid out. Rebekah smiles.

"It's nice to know there are still good, honest people in the world," she says.

"Right? I want to help this girl get out of that place."

"She's an artist, huh?"

"Yep," I nod.

"Guess it's true what they say: inspiration can come from any corner."

We rifle through the contents of the bag and my eyes are immediately drawn to the cellphone. It's not her usual phone, which means this has got to be her burner. My heart beats a little faster and I feel a faint pulse of optimism coursing through me. I drop the phone into a smaller plastic bag.

"I'm going to take this," I tell her. "I need to have my tech guy crack it. I have a feeling we're going to get the motherlode from it."

"No sweat. I'll voucher it," she says.

"Think you can work your magic on the rest of this?" I ask.

"I'll do what I can. I doubt we're going to find much of anything on this—it's all personal stuff," she says. "But I'll give it a shot."

"I appreciate it."

Rebekah picks up the purse and starts to examine it. She turns it over and looks through the pockets, inspecting everything closely.

"Hold the phone," she says softly. "What is this?"

She swivels the overhead light and turns it on, casting the bag in a fluorescent halo. Rebekah grabs a pair of forceps off a tray beside the table and I watch as she slips them into one of the small pockets on the front of the bag. She extracts what looks like a fingernail. Setting the bag down, she stares at it closely, a small grin curling the corners of her mouth upward. I lean in and stare at it with her. As I do, I feel that familiar sense of excitement burning in my belly.

"Acrylic fingernail. Broken," she announces. "But I can see what looks like it could be tissue stuck to it. Looks like maybe Mrs. Osweiler got a good swipe in before she was killed."

"How did she get her fingernail into her purse though?" I ask. "For that matter, how do we even know it's hers?"

"One way to find out."

Rebekah sets the forceps down then walks over to the wall of refrigerated drawers and pulls one open. She slides the tray containing

Mrs. Osweiler's body out and folds the sheet up on both sides, exposing hands so pale they're almost blue. They're crisscrossed with abrasions and bruises, evidence of the fact that Mrs. Osweiler put up a hellacious fight. She comes back to the autopsy table and grabs the forceps. I walk back with her and watch as she holds the broken nail up to her fingers.

"And there it is," I note. "Right ring finger is a match."

Rebekah drops the nail into a small specimen jar and seals it. I stare at it for a moment, realizing that can be the key to breaking open the entire case.

"How soon can you get DNA off that?" I ask.

"It's going to take me a couple of days, and then I'll obviously run it against the database," she says. "But if the DNA isn't in CODIS or the NDIS, we're going to need a sample to compare it to."

"Leave that to me," I say. "I'll be sure to get one."

For the first time since Rosie handed me that file, I feel wide awake with energy, charged with anticipation bubbling up inside of me. The case is beginning to take shape and have a trajectory, and though it's still moving at a snail's pace, the fact that it's moving it all is heartening. Now it's on us to get this train moving.

CHAPTER TWENTY-SEVEN

Criminal Data Analysis Unit; Seattle Field Office

"We can forget about the Wren Keaton was her lover theory. Mrs. Osweiler was a more traditional cheater after all," I say and point to the picture on the screens behind me. "Allow me to introduce Samuel Ethan Ballard."

"And who is Samuel Ethan Ballard?" Astra asks.

"This is, more than likely, Valerie Osweiler's secret boyfriend," I tell her.

I grin as all three members of my team fall silent and their mouths fall open. They stare at Ballard's Seattle Police Department identification photo. He's handsome. Ballard is blonde with cornflower blue eyes, a square jawline, high cheekbones and bears a striking resemblance to Chris Evans, Captain America himself. Ballard definitely looks like the poster boy for everything stereotypically American.

"And how do we know this was Mrs. Osweiler's side piece?" Mo asks.

"We don't. Not for sure just yet," I say. "But that's on us to nail down."

"Then what put you onto this?" Astra asks.

"Rebekah down at the ME's office dusted a necklace charm for prints—a charm that was inscribed with the words 'forever yours', mind you," I explain. "And his thumbprint was on it. "I don't know about you all but that smacks of romance to me."

"Are we sure they weren't just friends or something? Maybe there's a logical reason for the print," Rick offers.

"It's possible, of course," I reply. "But if they were friends, did you happen to see Samuel anywhere on her social media accounts? Was she friends with him?"

Rick purses his lips then shakes his head. "No. I never ran across him."

"Me either," Mo adds.

"That's still not definitive proof that Ballard was boinking Mrs. Osweiler," Astra notes.

"No, it's not. But it's definitely intriguing," I say. "And it's on us to fill in those blanks."

"So, are we going to drag him in here and lean on him?" Astra asks.

I shake my head. "No, not yet. We need to handle this a bit more delicately."

"Delicate? When did we start doing that?"

"We don't have much right now and we don't want to spook this guy. I'd rather not tip our hand until we absolutely have to," I tell her.

"I've never known you to tread lightly," Mo says. "What aren't you saying?"

"Rebekah and I found a broken acrylic nail. One of Mrs. Osweiler's," I say. "There's possible tissue underneath—"

"We have DNA," Astra interrupts, that light in her eyes flaring.

"Maybe."

"Okay, so obviously a lot has happened," Astra responds. "Mind filling us in?"

"I was getting there."

"Well, get there faster."

I fill them in on everything that's happened. I tell them about Coral, about the purse, and about the phone. They listen and I feel a building sense of excitement in the room. I know though, that I need to temper their enthusiasm as I have to keep my own in check.

"Right now, we have a lot of disparate parts, guys," I tell them. "Even if we prove Officer Ballard was having an affair with Mrs. Osweiler, we can't prove that he killed her. Not yet. And I'd rather not tip him off to the fact that we're looking at him until we have to."

"That's smart," Astra says. "I get it."

They all nod in unison. Though I'm trying to throw some water on the flames of their excitement, I can feel it continuing to build. We've gone from a dog of a case that didn't look like it was going to end with an arrest, to having an undeniable forward motion. One look at my team and I can tell they can smell the blood in the water. As can I. But I meant it when I said all we have are disparate parts. We don't know yet if they all fit together. We're likely only going to get one bite at this apple so I don't want to screw it up.

I walk over to Rick's workstation and hand him the bag with the phone in it. He looks at it for a moment and nods.

"It's a burner," he says.

"It's already been dusted for prints, so you don't have to worry about taking it out of the bag," I tell him. "Crack the phone and find out what she's been hiding. Let's see if this phone really was for work or not."

"Got it, boss."

He plugs it in and starts banging away at his keyboard, his brow furrowed in concentration. I turn back to Mo.

"Did Ballard have a room at the Churchill that morning?" I ask.

She types away on her computer, going through the guest registry, then looks up at me and gives me a wolfish smile.

"He certainly did," she says. "He booked a one-night stay."

The pieces are starting to fall into place, but the picture is far from complete. Still, it's an encouraging start. The momentum is starting to build, and I can feel that train starting to pick up some speed.

"Mo, can you pull up Ballard's service records?" I ask.

"Right away."

She pecks at her keyboard and on the screens behind me, Ballard's file pops onto the screen. I take a moment to scan the file.

"Officer Ballard has a pile of commendations and citations for bravery in the line of duty," Mo reads off. "Oh, look here though. He also has a couple of marks on his permanent record. Seems he was accused of excessive force. Looks like Officer Ballard has a problem with his temper. He's been through anger management counseling. Twice."

"So, not exactly the kind of guy who'd take rejection very well," Astra offers.

"Sounds like he's got a temper, that's for sure," I reply.

"Ballard is thirty-seven and has been on the job for fifteen years," Mo continues. "He's consistently received high marks on his evals despite the issue with his temper. Looks like the department swept those under the rug."

"Big surprise," I mutter. "What about his personal life? Can you dig into his socials?"

Mo taps away at her keyboard again and the screens go from his records with the SPD to his Facebook page. Mo scrolls through it, giving us a glimpse into his personal life.

"Single, never married, no children. But his relationship status says, 'it's complicated'," Mo narrates for us.

"That's one way to put it," Astra says.

"Some of Ballard's favorite groups include Recreational

Shooting, Seattle Bow Hunters, AR-15 Enthusiasts, an MMA Appreciation group, and get this, the PNW Potterheads," Mo says with a laugh.

"This guy is a Potterhead?" Rick asks, looking up from his keyboard, sounding genuinely offended. "I call bullcrap. I bet the closest he ever got to a Harry Potter book was knocking one off the shelf at the bookstore."

"I agree with Rick here," Mo says. "There's no way this guy is a Potterhead."

I laugh. "You two seem pretty upset about that."

"We take our fandom very seriously," Rick says. "You don't disrespect Potter."

"Damn straight," Mo concurs.

"And this is why I don't hang out with you guys outside of work," Astra quips.

"Mrs. Osweiler belonged to a few Potterhead groups. She was a legit fan," Mo says. "I'm sure Ballard pretended to be one trying to impress her."

"The things we do for love," I say.

"I'm not seeing any declarations of love here," Mo says. "Though, he definitely does some vaguebooking about a woman."

"Vaguebooking?" I raise an eyebrow.

"It's when somebody doesn't want to come right out and say something, so they post a cryptic message that only they—and the person they're vaguebooking about—know what's really being said," Astra explains. "It's the height of being petty and passive-aggressive."

"And how do you know all this?" I ask.

She shrugs. "Do you even know me? I'm the queen of petty and passive-aggressive."

"She's not wrong there," Rick says.

We all share a laugh together as I look at some of the messages Mo is pointing out as being vaguebooking. By the things he's saying, it's clear he's got strong feelings for somebody but obviously can't name them.

"Is he really quoting that Rupert Holmes song when talking about this mysterious lady love of his?" Astra asks.

"Apparently so," I reply. "And look at the number of likes it has."

"It's as depressing as it is nauseating," she says.

"You're not wrong."

I look at the post in question and shake my head. I can't count the number of people I know who think singing about pina coladas and getting caught in the rain is the height of romance. None of them seem to know the entire premise of the song is built around adultery. It's about a guy who answers a personal ad to meet another woman only to find out he's meeting up with his wife. Yeah, all that cheating. So romantic.

"I've always hated that song," I groan.

"When we get him in the box, we need to explain to him what that song is really about," Astra tells me.

"You know, given the current situation, that song is kind of fitting," Mo offers.

I laugh. "That's true, I suppose."

"I don't think he's self-aware enough to realize that though," Astra replies.

"Yeah, there's that too," Mo admits with a chuckle.

Astra looks at me and her smile fades. "We can prove he's Mrs. Osweiler's boyfriend, but how are we going to prove he killed her?" she asks. "Even if we do get him in the box and sweat him, his lawyer is never going to let him give up a DNA sample."

"And unfortunately, we don't have enough to get a warrant to compel him," Mo says.

"We have his fingerprint on that necklace," Rick says.

"Which could have been left at any time, not necessarily the day she died," I reply. "Mo's right, we don't have enough for a warrant."

"So, what are we going to do?" Astra asks.

"How about this?" Rick says.

On the screens behind me the image shifts to the text messages from Mrs. Osweiler's phone. Rick cracked it even faster than I thought and what it reveals is frightening. Ballard is obviously an angry, controlling man.

"I told you it's over," Mrs. Osweiler wrote.

"I'm going to tell your husband everything," was the reply from Ballard.

"Leave me alone."

"You are a horrible slut who deserves every bad thing that happens to you."

It goes on for a while like that until eventually, Mrs. Osweiler stopped responding. Ballard apparently didn't appreciate being ignored, because it prompted a lengthy list of awful names and threats.

"You have to appreciate the idiot who digs his own hole," Astra says.

"I know I do," Mo offers.

Knowing I need to temper their expectations and keep them focused, I step into the breach and throw a wet blanket over them.

"All of this is nice, but it proves nothing," I tell them. "The first thing we need to do is prove it's Ballard on the other end of that phone. We need to establish the other phone belongs to her spurned lover. Rick, can you work on figuring out where the phone was purchased?"

"I'm not sure. I'll follow up with the serial number, but it could have been from practically any corner store in town. Places that aren't typically too organized with their record-keeping."

"Do what you can," I tell him. "And see what else you can get off that phone. The more information we have, the better."

"On it, boss."

"Mo, keep digging into Ballard. I want to know everything about his life. I want to know what he eats for breakfast. His shoe size. His favorite food," I tell her. "I want to know anything and everything about this guy."

"Copy that," she replies.

Astra looks at me. "And what are we going to be doing?

"We're going to get his DNA," I tell her.

"Oh, just when I thought today was going to be boring," she chirps. "This is shaping up to be an interesting day after all."

CHAPTER TWENTY-EIGHT

Emerald City Burgers; Belltown District, Seattle

"THE GUY JUST CHEWS ARROGANTLY," ASTRA SAYS.

I laugh softly. "How does somebody chew arrogantly?"

"It's the look on his face. It annoys me."

I glance through the window and watch Ballard and his partner sitting out on the patio, talking and laughing with each other as they eat. We've been following them for just about his entire shift, watching and waiting. They eventually stopped off for their lunch hour, giving us a chance to grab what we need to make our case.

There is no denying that as we've watched Ballard all day, that he's got a swagger to him. He holds himself with a very cocky, arrogant air. She's not wrong. Watching the interactions he's had with people, it's difficult for me to see what Mrs. Osweiler saw in him. It's equally as difficult to see why he's racked so many commendations in the department.

But then, I have to remember the SPD ran differently under Torres. Maybe with Lee in charge now, things will be better.

Maybe officers who abuse their authority will actually suffer consequences for their actions. It would be nice to see some of these cops who commit crimes under the color of authority be punished rather than see them continue to be able to hide behind their badges. Cops like that who do things the wrong way make me sick. It paints a bad light on those of us who do things the right way.

"I don't get it. Mrs. Osweiler was a strong, confident woman," Astra wonders. "What could she see in a blockhead like that with the personality of a goose?"

I shake my head. "I was just wondering that myself. I have no idea," I reply. "All I can think is that maybe he's the polar opposite of her husband. Maybe she was just looking for something different in her life."

"Yeah, maybe," she says. "But if you're unhappy with somebody, why would you not just divorce them? Why would you put somebody you love through something like this?"

"Because not everybody has the scruples you do," I say. "Or maybe she liked her life and just wanted a little fun on the side."

I look outside again and watch Ballard. He pops a fry into his mouth and laughs at something his partner said. The rain finally moved on and there are only a few fat, fluffy clouds drifting across the sky letting the sunshine rain down on the world beyond the glass. It's a really nice day. It'd be nice to spend a day as beautiful as this taking a walk through the woods or doing something outdoors. Almost anything would beat tailing Ballard around, that's for sure.

Ballard rolls up his uniform sleeves and my eyes zero in on the bandage on his arm. I feel that electric jolt of adrenaline shoot through me as I look at that stark white bandage would around his arm.

"Do you see that?" I point.

Astra nods, on the same page as me. "Looks like Ballard got an owie."

"One more nail in the coffin we're building," I note. "I bet you anything we'll find scratch marks under that bandage."

"You think we could get that lucky?"

I shrug and give her a rueful laugh. "I don't know. Things seem to be falling into place."

"A little too well if you ask me. I'm waiting for the part where the rug gets pulled out from under us, dropping us on our asses."

"Is it terrible that I'm wondering the same thing?"

"I'd say that just makes you realistic," she tells me. "Especially when it comes to this case."

We sit back and munch on our food. It doesn't seem like either one of us has much of an appetite as we're basically just picking at it. But we had to buy something to take this table and since we hadn't had lunch yet, we grabbed a couple of burgers and fries. It's been forty-five minutes of sheer torture watching Ballard leisurely eating his food. All we need is to get the straw from his cup. If we get that, we'll turn it over to Rebekah for testing then drag him in for questioning.

"So? How are we going to get what we need?" Astra asks. "We can't let it get into the trash can or it's going to be contaminated."

"I'm hoping he's the kind of guy who doesn't bus his own table," I say. "Honestly? Kind of seems the type."

"Yeah, I can see that."

Outside the window, I see Ballard grab his radio. He says a few words into it then says something to his partner which gets them both on their feet.

"It's showtime," I say.

Ballard and his partner walk off the patio and into the dining room. His eyes fall on mine and I see his face twist into an expression of outrage. So much for being able to go unnoticed. I roll my eyes at Astra, who laughs softly.

"I know you," he sneers.

"Pretty sure you don't," I reply coolly. "We've never met."

"No, you're the fed skank who got Torres thrown in the can," he growls.

I feel the eyes of the people in the dining room turning to me. I ignore it and keep my attention on him.

"No, Deputy Chief Torres is the idiot who broke the law and ended up getting himself thrown in the can," I shrug. "If you're looking to blame somebody for him being arrested, start with him."

"You took a good man off the streets—"

"Except he wasn't a good man," I cut him off. "And he hadn't been on the streets in what, twenty years or so?"

"Shut your mouth, bit—"

His partner grabs him by the arm, saying something quietly and cutting him off before he can really get going. Ballard glowers at me and I have little trouble believing if we were alone somewhere, he wouldn't have any compunction about putting his fist in my face to 'send a message'. It's going to make taking him down that much more satisfying. I didn't like him already. But knowing he's a Torres loyalist makes me dislike him that much more.

Ballard storms out of the burger joint, his partner hot on his heels. I jump to my feet and glove up, then pull a plastic evidence bag out of my pocket as I walk out to the patio. I grab hold of the cup Ballard left behind and pull the plastic lid off. The straw is still stuck through it, so I drop the whole thing into the bag then seal it. That done, I take both trays over to the trash can and bus the table they didn't. Lazy pigs.

Astra is grinning. "We got it?"

"We've got it."

"I'm going to love putting the bracelets on that guy."

"That makes two of us."

We walk out of the burger joint and I feel the momentum building faster. That train is starting to rocket along its tracks. I try to throttle it back though and remind myself: the faster the train, the more horrific the crash. We don't know anything yet. But I'm feeling good about the direction we're headed in. Really good. Which also sets the red flags waving in my head. Nothing ever comes easy for us. I just hope this is the exception to that rule.

CHAPTER TWENTY-NINE

Interrogation Suite Delta-2; Seattle Field Office

"YOU AREN'T HIS UNION REP, YOU'RE NOT HIS LAWYER. You have no right to be here, Deputy Chief Lee," I say. "SAC Espinoza has allowed you to be here as a professional courtesy."

He scoffs. "Professional courtesy?" he spits. "Professional courtesy would have been telling me you were looking at one of my officers, to begin with."

The following morning, we talked to Rosie and decided that since the DNA sample is at the lab, it was a good time to bring Ballard in for a few questions. It doesn't matter if we tip our hand now. The ball is rolling on the DNA comparison and it can't be stopped. We're going to give him a chance to get out in front of this.

"You made it very clear that you had no desire to work with us. Therefore, I was under no obligation to share the status of our investigation with you," I fire back. "And he's not under arrest. Officer Ballard is simply here to answer a few questions."

"If you're at the point where you're hauling him in for questioning, you must think you have a strong case already," he sneers.

"Otherwise, I'm sure you wouldn't have tipped your hand to your potential suspect. I know how this game works, SSA Wilder."

We're standing in the observation pod and Interim Deputy Chief Lee looks absolutely apoplectic. I shrug, neither confirming nor denying his statement. Lee turns and looks through the window into the interrogation suite beyond the glass. Ballard is sitting at the table, slumped back in his seat casually. As if he doesn't have a care in the world. Yeah, well, we're going to give him something to be concerned about.

It's not hard to understand why Lee is so worked up about this. A scandal on his watch is going to reflect poorly on him and jeopardize his promotion. All Lee is focused on is having that interim tag removed from his title. I get it. But I'm not going to soft-shoe anything for the sake of somebody's promotion. Nor will I apologize to him for doing my job.

"What evidence do you have?" Lee asks.

"You know I can't give that to you," I say, then hold up my hand when he begins to protest. "What I can tell you is that Officer Ballard was having an affair with Mrs. Osweiler."

Lee looks at me. "So, he was having an affair," he growls. "That doesn't prove he murdered her."

"Look, Deputy Chief—"

"Interim."

"Look, Lee, you know very well how we build cases. I understand why you're so upset but frankly, that's not my problem. I have a job to do. And I'm not in the business of covering up for killers," I say, then belatedly add, "Allegedly."

"Sounds like you've already made up your minds about his guilt," Lee says.

"We haven't made up our minds about anything. If Ballard didn't do it, we'll kick him loose," I shrug. "If he did, well, he's going to be sharing a cell with his hero, former Deputy Chief Torres. And here I thought you'd thank me for helping root out Torres loyalists."

"Part of my job is protecting the department," he tells me. "And believe me, this is going to be a massive black eye. You are going to cause a PR nightmare."

"Again, that's not my problem. Managing the optics and SPD politics is part of your job description, not mine," I say. "Now, if you'll excuse me, I have an interview to conduct. And you'd do well to remember that you are not allowed in that room."

Astra and I turn and walk through the door and into the interrogation suite, shutting it firmly behind us. Even in here, I can practically feel the rage coming off Lee. Ballard sits up and looks at us with that smug smirk on his lips. I set my folders down on the table then take a seat across from him. Astra drops into the chair beside mine.

"I want to remind you that you're not under arrest, Office Ballard. You're here to answer a couple of questions for us," I start. "But you're welcome to have a lawyer present if you wish."

He shrugs. "I've got nothing to hide. Ask your questions," he says. "But how about we start with you telling me what this is about?"

"Well, as to what this is about," Astra starts, "It's about your affair with Valerie Osweiler."

Ballard's face darkens and his expression grows tight. He folds his hand on the table in front of him and takes a moment to smooth out his face, stuffing his anger back down.

"I don't know what you're talking about," he says.

"Lying to us isn't a great way to start this interview," I tell him. "Gives us a bad impression and makes us think you're going to lie to us again."

"I don't care what you think about me," he spits.

"How'd you get hurt?" I ask, pointing to the bandage wrapped around his forearm.

"Transient with a knife got me," he tells me. "Not very deep but it bleeds a lot."

"A transient with a knife, huh?"

"That's what I said."

"Okay. No problem," I say.

I open the file and pull out a picture of an email Rick had been able to retrieve from the secret email address she kept. I turn it around and show it to him. Ballard looks at it and I see his jaw tighten.

"Steamy stuff," I say.

"Reads like an erotica novel," Astra adds. "Though, a little less well written."

"I don't know what that is. That's not mine," he says.

"Really? That's funny," I counter. "Our tech team traced the recipient address and strangely enough, it originated from your IP address."

"Even stranger is the fact that this email address is completely secret. Mrs. Osweiler set it up to speak with only one person," Astra adds. "You."

"We have the emails that started when you two first got together about two years ago," I continue. "And we also saw the emails where she was breaking up with you."

"Being broken up with in an email is pretty rough," Astra tags in. "Second only to being broken up with via text."

Ballard simply sits there staring at us as we speak. His face is a mask of neutrality. He has absolutely zero emotion on his face. He clears his throat and runs a hand through his hair.

"Let me save you some trouble, Agents," he finally says. "I didn't kill Val."

"No?"

"No, I didn't," he growls. "Why would I kill her? I loved her."

"You killed her because you have anger and impulse control issues," I say. "And you couldn't stand the thought of her breaking up with you."

"That's total crap," he scoffs. "Do I look like a guy who has trouble getting chicks? So she broke up with me. It's not like I couldn't get another."

"Yeah see, except for the fact that we know how much she meant to you," I say.

Astra holds up the bag that contains the necklace Rebekah had pulled the print from. Ballard stares at it and for a moment, I see a flash of emotion cross his face. Maybe seeing it again drives the realization that she's dead home for him again. But Ballard is good at controlling his emotions. He pushes them all down aside again and does his best to keep his face blank and emotionless.

"Forever yours," Astra reads. "Seems like she kind of meant something to you."

"Just because I gave her a necklace doesn't mean I killed her."

"No, of course not," I tell him. "That's not what I was getting at."

"Then what were you trying to get at?" he snaps.

"Just what I said—that she meant something to you," I say. "And these emails only bolster that belief. Why, I have one here where you told her you loved her for the first time."

"That's sweet," Astra says.

"We have your fingerprint on the necklace," I go on.

"Which could have been left the day I gave it to her for all we know."

I shrug. "Sure. That's possible."

"So, is that all you have?" he asks. "Some emails and a fingerprint on a gift I gave her?"

"We want to give you a chance to get out in front of this, Officer Ballard," Astra says.

"There's nothing to get out in front of," he responds tersely.

"You were at the Churchill the morning Valerie went missing—from the Churchill," I say. "That's quite a coincidence, don't you think?"

"No, I saw her. We had one last fling—for old time's sake," he says. "And when we were done, she was left. The next time I saw her, it was on the news after she'd been murdered."

"So, for the record, you're telling us you saw her at the hotel—"

"And we had sex. Then she left. That's it," he cuts me off. "She broke things off. Said she wanted to give things with that loser husband of hers another chance."

"That didn't sit well with you, did it?" I ask.

He shrugs "Whatever. I was upset, sure," he says. "But I didn't hurt her."

I pull the screenshots of some of the threats from her burner phone out of the file and drop them in front of Ballard. He thumbs through them, an inscrutable expression on his face.

"What's this?" he frowns.

"That's you sending threats from your burner to hers," I say.

He looks at me with a strange look on his face. "Those aren't mine. I didn't send those."

"No?" I ask. "That's strange because Valerie's burner had one phone number programmed into it. Yours."

"I'm telling you, this isn't my number," he says, a quiver of fear in his tone.

Ballard reaches into his pocket and pulls out a pair of cellphones and holds them up for us to see. Then sets them back down on the table. He taps the first one.

"This is my regular phone," he says and unlocks it. "Look at my messages to her. Feel free to read them all."

Ballard turns on the second one and unlocked it as well. He slides that one over to Astra, who picks it up.

"Look through those messages too," he says. "You'll see she stopped texting me weeks ago—when she first started talking about breaking things off. She would only communicate with me by email."

Astra and I exchange glances and I can see by the look on her face that she's not seeing the threatening messages Rick pulled off the burner. But that's still not incontrovertible proof. I set the phone down then turn to him.

"You could have easily erased those texts," I say.

"Or got another phone you were sending those messages from,

knowing that after you killed her, we'd eventually circle around to you," Astra adds.

"This is utter bullcrap," he says. "You're not listening."

"Oh, we're listening. But we're waiting to hear the truth," I tell him. "Now's the time to get out in front of this, Officer Ballard."

"I didn't do anything. I never hurt her. I wouldn't. I loved her," he says. "I loved her with my entire heart."

"It must hurt that she didn't love you back that way," Astra says.

"That must have angered you, huh?" I add.

"Screw you guys," he hisses. "You guys have nothing on me, or I'd be in cuffs right now. But you have nothing on me because I didn't do it!"

"All the arrows point to you," I say.

"This interview is over," he spits and gets to his feet. "I didn't do it. I loved her. But you go ahead and try to frame me for it anyway."

He heads for the door, and I judge it's the right time to deliver my final salvo.

"We'll be having a much more formal interview with you very soon. One you will definitely want to bring your lawyer to," I say. "Just as soon as we get the DNA results back."

"DNA?" he asks, a flash of concern on his face.

I nod and give him a predatory grin. "Yes, DNA," I tell him. "See, I swiped your cup from that burger joint the other day and submitted your straw for a comparison. We should have those results back here very soon. And when we do…"

I let my voice trail off, the unspoken threat hanging thick in the air around us. He pauses with his hand on the door and I can see him trembling. Whether it's from fear or anger, I don't know. But, he doesn't take the bait. Instead, he opens the door and walks out, leaving Astra and me staring after him. She turns to me and smiles.

"I think that went well," she says.

I shrug. "Could've been worse, I guess."

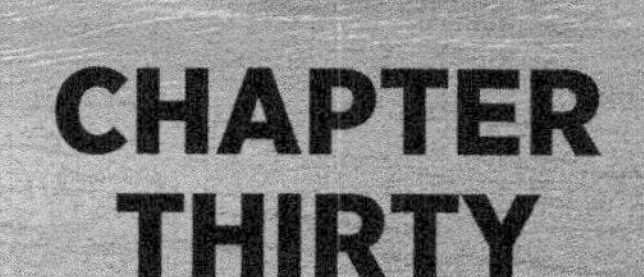

CHAPTER THIRTY

Criminal Data Analysis Unit; Seattle Field Office.

"I can't believe Deputy Chief Lee didn't say goodbye before he left," Astra says. "Rude. Bad manners."

"Interim," I counter in a stiff approximation of his voice. Astra laughs as we step into the CDAU. Rick is busy clacking away at his workstation, but Mo is nowhere to be found.

"Where's Mo?" I ask.

"She's running down a lead," Rick says.

"A lead?"

He nods. "Yeah, I was finally able to get the information I needed to determine where that cellphone came from," he says. "Mo ran out there to get footage if she can, or at least a description of the person who bought it."

"That's good," I say. "Because Ballard is saying it's not his."

"Showed us the burner he used for Mrs. Osweiler and his regular phone," Astra adds.

"Why wouldn't he use his regular phone to contact her?" Rick asks.

I shrug. "No idea. Maybe he was afraid it would get out if

somebody used his phone. Could be an abundance of caution out of respect for her since Mrs. Osweiler was obviously being very careful."

"Not careful enough," Astra points out. "Not when a couple of people, including her husband, saw her using her burner."

"True," I say.

Astra takes a seat at her workstation, but something is bothering me. Crossing my arms, I pace the front of the room, letting my mind work out the knot in my brain.

"What is it?" Astra asks.

"Not sure yet," I reply and then it hits me. "Rick, can you pull up SPD incident reports?"

"Yeah, I think so. What do you need?"

"I need you to pull up an incident report for Officer Ballard," I say. "He says he was attacked by a transient with a knife. If it's an on-the-job injury, it's going to be well documented I'd think."

"What's bothering you about it?" Astra asks.

"I don't know for sure. He was just so confident when he told us what happened," I reply. "And it's easily verifiable, so if he lied, he'd be screwing himself."

"Maybe he thought we wouldn't follow up."

"If that's true, then he's a bigger idiot than we thought," I say. "But I actually think the guy is smarter than that."

"Let's hope he's not," she says.

"Here we go," Rick announces. "On the screens."

I turn and look at the screens behind me as the incident reports come up. According to the reports, he's telling the truth. He was attacked by a man at a homeless encampment and suffered a gash along his forearm.

"Are there photos?" I ask.

"Coming up," he says.

The image on the screen changes to a photo of Ballard's forearm. And when I see it, my heart sinks into my gut. The slice along his arm is a neat, clean line. The sort of injury you'd get if you were sliced with a knife—not ripped with a fingernail.

"He was telling the truth," I sigh.

"About that," Astra offers. "He could have gotten scratched anywhere. If we had him strip down, I'm sure we'd find scratch marks."

"Yeah. Maybe," I say, suddenly feeling less certain.

"Can we not have guys stripping down again?" Rick asks. "I've filled my quota of naked dudes for the year."

I continue staring at the photo of Ballard's injury. Astra is right. Mrs. Osweiler could have scratched him anywhere. The upper arm. The back. The leg. There is a host of places she could have scratched him under the clothing, in a place we can't see. The cut on his arm has to be a coincidence. That just has to be it. There's nothing else it could be. Right?

"You look worried," Astra says.

I nod. "I am. I'll be honest, the fact that it's not a fingernail scratch under that bandage has me feeling a bit shook. I was so sure he was lying that finding out he wasn't rattled me."

"Don't let it," she says. "We probably can't see the wound. And besides, when the DNA comes back, we're going to have him cold."

"Yeah. I'm really hoping the DNA matches. If it doesn't and Ballard didn't do it, we're going to be so screwed," I sigh. "Unless she can find the DNA in CODIS or the NDIS database."

"Relax, Blake," Astra says. "It's going to turn out all right."

I just wish I believed that. We've already been taken for so many twists and turns on this case, I feel like I'm just waiting for the next one. I know it's because this one has really gotten under my skin, and I want so badly to close it. Now that we could be nearing the end, I'm sure it's just nerves making me feel so doubtful and uncertain. It's taken some time to get to this point, but everything lines up and it all points to Ballard.

But then, as I think about the facts as we know them, that worm of doubt crawls into my mind again. He put himself with her the day she went missing. Would he really do that if he was guilty? Would somebody who murdered their lover tell us he was with her, possibly the last person to see her alive? A cop of all people would know how big of a spotlight that would cast on them. So why would he willingly offer up that information?

"I see that big brain of yours working," Astra says. "You're spooking me."

I shake my head. "There are just some things I can't get out of my head," I reply. "I'm sure you're right, that I'm just overthinking it all and freaking myself out. But there are a few things that just aren't lining up for me."

"Like what?"

"Like him putting himself at the hotel with her the day she vanished," I say. "How many guilty people do you know who'd do that?"

"He may have known the security cameras were down—from my understanding, that's kind of status quo at the Churchill. It helps protect their guests' anonymity," she says. "So, knowing that, he can put himself with her and then say she left—just like he told us—knowing there's no way we can prove that she didn't actually leave. It's reverse psychology."

"Maybe. I mean, that's as plausible as anything I've got," I say.

"Relax, my friend," she says. "This is all going to work out."

"One way or another," Rick mutters.

"Stow it, hipster boy," Astra barks at him.

The doors slide open and Mo comes bustling through. She's wearing an expression that tells me my worst fears are about to come to fruition.

"Houston, we have a problem," she starts.

"I knew it," I grumble. "I knew it wasn't going to be that simple."

Astra sighs. "It never is," she says. "Talk to us, Mo. Tell us about how you are going to shatter yet another theory and ruin our entire day."

"Well, I spoke with the guy who runs the bodega over in First

Hill where the phone was purchased," she says. "He doesn't have a working security system at the moment so there is no footage, but he did say he remembered when the phone was bought. Said they don't sell a whole lot of phones so it tends to stick out when they do sell one."

"Wow. Guy must have a mind like a steel trap," Astra says.

"He is very sharp, that's for sure," Mo replies.

"What does he remember?" I ask, trying to keep them on track.

"Says he remembers it was a woman who bought the phone," Mo says. "I checked the serial number Rick dug up against his logs and he had the day and time spot on. Makes me pretty sure he remembers the sex of the person who bought it too."

A woman. It makes no sense. What in the hell is going on here?

"Ballard must have made her buy it for him," I say. "Maybe to protect himself, maybe to throw anybody investigating off the scent. But I'm sure whoever this person was who bought the phone was put up to it by Ballard. That's the only explanation that makes sense to me."

Astra nods. "That tracks. The guy is slick and he's smart," she says. "And being a cop, he's going to know how we work and the countermeasures we'd employ to catch him. So yeah, I think that checks out."

"Or," Mo offers. "It could really be a woman Mrs. Osweiler was involved with who bought the phone."

"Are we really circling back to that again?" Astra raises an eyebrow. "All the facts we have line up and point to Ballard."

My cellphone rings, and when I glance at the caller ID I see it's coming from Rebekah. I know when I answer this call, I'm going to have my answer one way or the other. I connect the call and press the phone to my ear.

"Hey, Beks," I start. "Thanks for calling."

"Not a problem," she replies. "I got the DNA comparisons back and the skin I found under the nail—it's not your guy. The boyfriend didn't kill her."

"Damn," I mutter.

I feel like the world is crashing down around me in fiery heaps right now and silently scold myself. I know better than to let myself get too close and too personally involved with a case. And yet, here I am. Waist deep and sinking.

"Here's the interesting thing though," Rebekah goes on. "The DNA profile came from a woman. A woman is likely your killer. You have any idea who she might be?"

I nod. "Yeah. I think I do. Thanks, Beks."

CHAPTER THIRTY-ONE

Osweiler Residence; Windermere District, Seattle

AFTER GETTING THE NEWS FROM REBEKAH, I HAD RICK crack into Wren's email accounts. It didn't take long at all to find what we were looking for. What we should have seen from the start. Well, what I should have seen from the start. Astra, Rick, and Mo had floated the theory, but I shut it down because I thought it was too farfetched. I was wrong.

"She's here," Astra says. "You were right."

"Where else would she be?" I reply soberly. "This is her big moment. Her time to shine and show Mr. Osweiler what he's been missing."

"You sound like you're kicking yourself."

"I am. I should have seen this. I should have listened to you guys."

She shrugs. "Yeah, you should have," Astra says with a grin. "But to be fair, we were mostly having a goof because we had no other viable leads at the time."

"But she fit with the profile I'd been piecing together. She checked all the boxes," I reply. "And I still couldn't see it."

"Yeah well, we're here now. Doesn't matter how we got here, but we're going to close this case," she says. "That's all that matters. Nothing we could have done would have changed the outcome for Valerie but maybe now, we can give Scott a little peace."

"Yeah, maybe."

I park the car at the curb across the street from the Osweiler home and we climb out. We cross the street and start up the walk to the front door. All the while I stare at the late model, black Toyota Avalon in the driveway. It belongs to Wren Keaton, and I am absolutely positive that when we have the techs go over it, they're going to find blood stains in the trunk. Wren would have had to transport Mrs. Osweiler's body in it and unless she replaced all the carpets, there is going to be some residue that will be picked up with the luminol and a blacklight.

I don't think Wren is smart enough to replace the carpeting, and I think she's arrogant enough to think she's gotten away with it. I'm going to kick myself for this for a long, long time. Wren fits the profile, but I flailed around for days, trying to find a viable male suspect. And all the while she was right under my nose. It's not that I haven't been wrong or failed before. I have. Many times in my life. It's the simple fact that was wrong because of my own blind spot. One I didn't even know I had. That's what pisses me off the most. I truly bought into the grieving best friend act.

We ring the doorbell and a couple of moments later, Mr. Osweiler opens the door. Wearing black sweatpants and a t-shirt, he's still disheveled and rumpled, but he looks like he's at least gotten a little bit of sleep since we last saw him. There's slightly more color in his cheeks and the circles beneath his eyes aren't as dark as they were before.

"Agents," he starts. "What can I do for you?"

"Actually, we wanted to give you a status update on our investigation," I say. "Is Ms. Keaton here with you?"

He nods. "Yeah, she's in the living room."

Mr. Osweiler holds the door open and allows us in. He closes it then leads us back to the living room. It's still clean as a whistle and Wren is sitting on the couch with a blanket over her lap watching TV. She turns as we come into the room, and I see a shadow cross her face. She licks her lips nervously then puts on a smile for our benefit.

"Agents Wilder and Russo. It's nice to see you again," she greets us. "How are you?"

"We're well, thank you," I say.

Mr. Osweiler sits down next to her while Astra and I take the loveseat. I'm not sure what to expect just yet, not sure how this situation is going to play out. But I know we need to be on our guard. She already murdered one person.

"So, you said you had a status update?" he asks.

"Yeah, we've had some developments we wanted to talk to you about," I say.

"Developments?" Wren asks with a slight quaver in her voice.

I nod. "What we can tell you right now is that we learned the identity of the man your wife was having an affair with," I say. "His name is Samuel Ballard. He's an officer with the SPD."

Mr. Osweiler looks down at his hands, a deep frown crossing his face. I give him a moment to process the information. Wren leans over and puts a comforting hand on his shoulder, murmuring a few words of sympathy to him. She turns back to us, her face sober.

"I need some water. May I get you two anything?"

"No, I'm fine," I say.

"I'm good," Astra replies.

Mr. Osweiler takes another moment then looks up at me. His face is stony and expressionless for the moment, and he seems ready for me to continue.

"Your wife was ending things with Mr. Ballard," I say. "She told him that she wanted to give things with you another shot. So she broke up with him."

I'd hoped that would soften the blow a little bit. Knowing that his wife wanted to give their marriage another go, I'd hoped, would lift his spirits if only a little. I don't see that this information has the slightest bit of impact on him though.

"We found a secret email she'd set up where she corresponded with him," I go on.

"I want those emails," he tells us. "I want to read them."

"We can make copies for you if you'd like," I say. "But given their content, maybe—"

"No. I want to read them."

"As you wish," I say.

Wren returns with a bottle of water. Standing behind the sofa where Mr. Osweiler is sitting, she takes off her sweatshirt and I notice the bandage on her forearm, just below the elbow. I hadn't noticed it before because until now, we'd only seen her in long-sleeved shirts or sweaters. This was the first time we got a look at her bare arms, and I can see where Mrs. Osweiler tried to take her pound of flesh from her supposed best friend.

"How'd you hurt yourself?" I frown.

"A workplace accident, I'm afraid," she says.

I nod. "Yeah, I imagine you get yourself dinged up, bruised and bloodied, all the time."

She shrugs. "Not all the time. Just when I'm not paying attention."

I nod and give her a smile, but Wren has a strange look on her face. One I can't quite interpret. It seems caught somewhere between fear and rage. She seems to be a bit unstable at the moment and I'm suddenly worried this is going to get out of hand. She's too close to Mr. Osweiler and needs to step back. That crazed gleam in her eye has me worried that she's going to do something rash. She must sense we're here for her or something because she seems to be putting herself in a prime location to strike out at him.

I have no idea if she's armed or not, but I'm concerned that she could do real harm to Mr. Osweiler, if not kill him outright, if we don't find a way to get ourselves between the two of them. Perhaps sensing what I am, Astra stands up. She walks around the living room, pretending to be staring through the sliding glass doors, and manages to get behind her. Wren casts a side-eye over at her as if realizing she's caught between us. Her cheeks flush and she clenches her jaw. I can see her mind working, trying to figure out her next move. I just need to head her off to keep this from getting out of hand.

"Do you have a suspect, Agent Wilder?" Mr. Osweiler asks.

My eyes cut to Wren instinctively, but I try to cover it by turning back to him as if I'm trying to include them both. I silently kick myself for such a stupid move. I can't tell if she bought it or not. But she tenses up and I'm getting a strong cornered animal vibe from her.

"We have a couple of very strong leads we need to follow up on, yes," I say. "But nothing in stone just yet, I'm afraid."

He sighs heavily and I give them both my best sympathy face. But then Wren acts. She reaches under her shirt and pulls out a Glock.

"Whoa!" shouts Mr. Osweiler, who tries to scramble back away. Astra and I try to step forward, but she aims it at me, then Astra, then finally presses the barrel of the gun to Mr. Osweiler's head. His body grows stiff, his eyes wide, and he looks up at her.

"Wren, what—I—what in the hell are you doing?" he stammers.

"They're here to arrest me," she says. "And all I wanted to do, all I ever wanted to do was take care of you."

He swallows hard. "Wren—"

"Stand up!" she screeches.

Astra and I have both drawn our weapons and have them trained on her. But we can't shoot her simply because even if we manage a clean headshot, her death reflex will likely pull the trigger on her gun, resulting in Mr. Osweiler's head splattering all over the floor.

"Get up, Scott. Get up now!" she screams. "We're leaving."

"I don't understand what's going on," he screams back at her.

"You do, Mr. Osweiler," I say. "You know exactly what's happening here. Wren is in love with you. Always has been. She murdered your wife hoping to build a life with you in the aftermath."

"Wren? Is that true?" he asks, his voice wavering.

She hesitates but nods after a moment. "Everything I did, I did for us."

"Wren, there is no us. There never has been."

"Don't say that. Don't ever say that, Scott," she snaps. "If you say that again, I'm going to kill you."

"Just like you killed his wife?" I ask.

"Shut up!" she screams. "If not for you people, my life would be blissful. He would have fallen in love with me, and I would be happy! You've ruined it all!"

Mr. Osweiler looks down at his hands again, Wren's pistol still flush against his head. I can see he wants to deny what I'd say but he knows this is something he can't outrun. For the last six months or so, she'd been emailing him, telling him that his wife was cheating. She said the most heinous things about her best friend just to try and split them up. And it wasn't hard to see that she was setting herself up to take her place by his side. Everything she did was to further her chances of snagging him on the rebound.

"Get up, Scott. I'm not going to tell you again!" Wren yells.

"Wren, where are you going to go?" I ask, staring at her down the barrel of my weapon. "There's nowhere for you to go."

Scott numbly stands and Wren slips in behind him, pressing her body to his, trying to make herself as small a target as she can. Astra is on the far side of the room, and I glance at her, silently asking if she has a shot. She shakes her head.

"You two need to back off. Now," Wren growls. "Scott and I are leaving."

"You know we can't let you do that," I say.

"If you don't, then you're going to be cleaning up Scott's brains off the flooring for weeks," Wren shouts at us.

"You're not going to do that, Wren," Astra calls.

Wren wheels and fires at Astra. She ducks to try to avoid the shot, but it's too late. The slug slams into her shoulder. It spins her around like a top and she falls backward, cracking the glass door and sending a spiderweb of fractures up the glass.

"Astra!"

Wren turns and fires at me just as I dive out of the way. The bullet tears into the wall I was standing in front of a moment ago, tearing out chunks of plaster.

"Move, Scott!" Wren demands.

"No."

"Don't make me shoot you, baby. I don't want to shoot you," she pleads. "But you're mine now."

Crawling across the floor, I come around the couch and look at Astra. She's staring back at me and gives me a weak thumbs up. There is a lot of blood pooling on the floor behind her and her face is a mask of sheer agony, but she'll live. I need to get her some help. But I need to stop this woman too.

"Wren. Stop this!" I scream at her. "It's over. You're not going to have the fairytale ending you've been hoping for."

"Shut up. Just shut up!" she screeches.

All at once, a bunch of different things happens. Mr. Osweiler pitches forward, throwing himself to the ground as I get to my feet. Wren spins and fires at me. The bullets whiz by so close, I can feel them, but they hit the TV behind me, sending a shower of sparks and guttering flames. My heart thundering, I squeeze off a shot, but Wren is already in motion and I miss by a country mile.

She's running for the front door, and I give chase. Wren is just ahead of me and slips through the doorway that leads to the foyer and just as I round the corner, I throw myself forward onto the ground. Lucky I did, because she's already in a shooter's stance and squeezing the trigger. I crash hard against the hard tile and grunt as the air is knocked out of me. My gun falls from my grip and the walls vibrate with the shockingly loud concussion of her squeezing off three shots. They all slam into the wall but as she brings the pistol to bear on me.

My body feels like it's been filled with electricity and fire, and I scramble to my feet. Wren fires off another pair of shots that miss badly and I scoop up my weapon. I drop to a knee and train it on her. She stops moving and stares at me. Tears stream down her face and her cheeks flush scarlet. Her arms hang limply at her sides, the gun loose in her grip.

"Drop it, Wren."

"You ruined everything. He was going to be mine," she screams. "He was mine and you screwed it up for me!"

She raises her arm, bringing her weapon to bear, so I squeeze my trigger and fire off three rounds. I watch her body twitch and jerk as the bullets tear through her. Wren falls backward, hitting the ground with a sound like wet meat slapping concrete. Blood pools out from beneath her and I stare at the tight grouping center mass. Textbook.

Wren's green eyes are wide open and are staring off at nothing with that glassy sheen only death can provide. And a thin rivulet of blood spills from her mouth.

Holstering my weapon, I pull my phone out of my pocket and sprint back to the other room to find that Mr. Osweiler is already putting pressure on Astra's wound and calling 9-1-1 at the same time. He looks at me, his face still stony, his expression one of hurt, rage, and something else I can't put my finger on. But he reminds me of somebody who's just shut down completely and has successfully packed away their emotions.

"Thank you," he says. "You and Agent Russo have given me the truth. I think it's going to take a while to make peace with it. If ever, really. But at least I know. At least I don't have to pretend anymore.

So, thank you for what you've done. Truly. I thank you for finding Val's killer. Maybe now, she can rest in peace."

The air outside is shattered with the sound of sirens and a moment later, first responders are flooding the house. I lose track of Mr. Osweiler and go with the EMTs, who have Astra on a stretcher. The scene is sheer chaos and as we pass through the foyer, I look down at Wren's wide, sightless eyes and all I can think is that she got what she deserved. Valerie Osweiler wasn't perfect, but she didn't deserve a death sentence. What Wren did earned her one, though.

I know I should feel something—regret, pity, remorse—anything. But as I step around the woman's body, following Astra's stretcher, I feel nothing. And I'm not sure what that says about me. I don't want to grow cold, but I don't know that I can stop it.

CHAPTER THIRTY-TWO

Office of SSA Wilder, Criminal Data Analysis Unit; Seattle Field Office

I LEAN BACK IN MY CHAIR AND TAKE A LONG SWALLOW FROM THE glass of bourbon I just poured. I close my eyes and relish the feeling of the amber liquid leaving a trail of fire as it slides down my throat and into my belly. It's late and the bullpen is dark. I sent everybody home hours ago. I need to stay and catch up on some paperwork.

I take another drink and set the glass down, then turn back to my computer and continue writing my after-action report. I'm going to have to meet with the Office of Professional Responsibility tomorrow to go over the shooting. It's all perfunctory and I'm sure I'll be cleared by tomorrow evening. It was a good shoot. No doubt they'll insist that I get some counseling though to help me cope with the fact that I took a life.

I'm not opposed to counseling. Not in the least, obviously, given the fact that I've been seeing Doctor Reinhart, off and on for years. And as I sit and think about it, I figure it's probably a good time to go in for a mental tune-up.

My mind drifts back to the case. It took me a while, but I think I've finally figured out why this one got under my skin as deep as it did. And I think the problem I'm having is that just about everyone I encountered here—Wren Keaton, Officer Ballard, Conor Boyle, even Valerie herself—treated love so cavalierly. Whether it was in manipulating others for their own ends, sneaking around behind their backs, or constructing a complex web of lies and secret resentments against the people they made commitments to, it was like none of them saw just how good they had it. They were all so busy treating each other selfishly they forgot to actually remember what it feels like to be in love.

My mind drifts over to Patrick and Beth Foles. I'm not going to lie, there's more than a twinge of jealousy that washes over me as I remember the way they look at each other. I know I may be a cynic, but I want to believe real love exists. It's out there. I'm not so naïve to believe that it's all sunshine and rainbows every waking moment, but even that would be better than... well, this.

What this case has made me realize is that deep down, I'm lonely. Deep down, I want to have feelings for somebody. I want to be in love. And I want somebody who will love me every bit as fiercely as I love them. What I don't want is somebody who treats love lightly. Somebody who doesn't take it for granted.

I just don't know that it's in the cards for me. More than that, I don't know that I have the courage to take that leap. Not after Mark. What he did caused me more damage than I've ever let on. It's made me stop trusting most people on a fundamental level. Especially if they show interest in me. That sets off my warning bells immediately. It's why I pushed Charles away the way I did. He seems like a really good guy. He seems sweet, compassionate, and considerate. Yet, I blew him off anyway.

And why? Because Mark Walton poisoned the waters around my heart.

I like to think that maybe one day, I can get back to the place where I trust people enough to open up to them. There are so very few I trust that much. I want to get there, but the truth is, that may be out of my reach. Just how cold I felt when looking at Wren's body—a woman I'd just killed—and yet felt so oddly indifferent to it tells me I'm changing. I'm shutting down. And I don't know how to open myself back up again.

As I ponder those thoughts, a news alert pops up on my computer screen. I click it and take a sip of my bourbon—and very nearly spit it out immediately when I see the headline: ***Seattle ADA, SPD Officer Involved in Murder/Suicide.*** I scan the article wrapped in disbelief and astonishment. I can't believe this just happened. I shake my head and try to wrap my mind around it—and am unable to.

"Jesus," I whisper.

Scott Osweiler confronted Samuel Ballard and shot him five times in the head and chest before turning the gun on himself. So many lives snuffed out because of a callous disregard for love.

I don't understand this world. I really don't. And maybe because I don't, I need to learn to grow cold just to survive.

CHAPTER THIRTY-THREE

Wilder Residence, The Emerald Pines Luxury Apartments; Downtown Seattle

After a long soak in the tub, I put on my warmest, fluffiest robe, pour myself a glass of wine, light a few candles—and make sure they're far away from anything flammable—turn on some Coltrane, and stretch out on the couch. I turn my head and look through the windows, watching the world light up as lightning flashes behind the screen of slate-gray clouds. Thunder rumbles, making the windows vibrate. It's a perfect night to lay back and relax after a case as trying as Mrs. Osweiler's was. And of course, how the whole sordid affair ended with Scott Osweiler's unconscionable actions. It's been one hell of a rough week. The worst I can remember having recently.

I take a sip of my wine—a merlot Kit had picked out for me before she vanished again. I really wish I could call her but that would entail knowing where she is and how to reach her. But I've got no clue where she is or how to reach her. It would just be nice to hear her voice. I want to tell her about my case. I want to hear about where she is and what she's doing. But more than that, I just want to know that she's all right. I worry about her. I'm scared for her.

The flame on the candles flickers, casting writhing shadows across the walls. As I stare at the flame on the candle closest to me, I feel my mind drifting away. It feels as though something is shifting inside me or a dense fog is lifting, making visible all that was obscured. I suddenly remember that I haven't yet remembered what happened the night of the fire, and with that memory, it's like a door has been unlocked and pushed open, allowing my memories to come rushing back in. My body taut, my mind whirling, I sit up and let it all play out in my mind...

"Well, I should get out of here. I've got a few things to do," she says. "But I'll check in with you in a couple of days."

I nod. "You better."

"I will. Love you, Sis," she says.

"Love you back."

I set my computer down on the coffee table and hold a hand out to steady myself. I've had more wine than I usually do and feel a bit woozy as a result. That's all right though. I don't have to be in too early tomorrow so I can go for a run, get some coffee, and do what I need to do to take the edge off in the morning.

All I want is to lay down and sleep for a bit. I should probably crawl to my bedroom, brush my teeth, and get into my pajamas, but lying here for a minute sounds like a better idea. I move to lay down when the sound of glass breaking from the back of my apartment sends a current of white-hot adrenaline coursing through my veins. The fuzzy feeling quickly evaporates and I'm suddenly awake and aware.

I hear a soft thump on the floor back there, almost as if somebody had just crawled in through the open window and leaped from the sill to the ground. I shoot to my feet and go to the small table in the corner, yanking open the drawer. I reach in to grab my weapon and freeze. It's gone. I always keep a spare weapon in that drawer for emergencies and now it's not there.

"What the hell?" I whisper.

My first thought is that it's an assassin sent by the Thirteen to finish me off. I know Kit and I dismantled a large part of their organization. We devastated them. But I also know we didn't destroy them completely. I know there are remnants still out there and that they're not forgiving. It's why Kit left. To protect me as well as to protect herself. My heart lurches and my stomach churns as I look at the darkened hallway that leads to the rooms in the back.

I strain my ears and listen but don't hear a thing. My apartment is silent. The only thing I hear is my heartbeat roaring in my ears. But then a peal of thunder crashes, louder than it should be, which tells me I'm not imagining any of this. There is somebody in my apartment. They must have rappelled down from the roof to get to my windows, which only scares me more. It means they're a professional. And they're here to kill me.

My service weapon is on my nightstand. I don't know which room the breaking glass came from but if I'm going to defend myself, I need to get to my weapon. I look at the front door and know the smart thing would be to run out and call for backup. But I'm not going to let them run me out of my home. I'm not going to give that to them. I've beaten their assassins before, and I can do it again.

The only way to get clear of this, to protect me and my sister and force them to leave us alone, is to show them the cost of continually coming after us. To make the price too high. This is a war of attrition, and we are going to win. What's left of the Thirteen is not going to beat us. We will keep taking the fight to them.

Steeling myself, I grit my teeth and make a break for it, darting down the hallway. As I pass my war room though, a figure in black hurtles out of the darkness and body checks me into the wall. The breath is driven from my lungs as a man that seems more hard muscle than anything slams me into the wall, pinning me with his body. He delivers a couple of solid blows to my kidneys and leaves me gasping for air.

I manage to pull away from him and stagger back out of his reach.

I grope through the darkness and pain and flip the light switch, suddenly flooding the hallway with light. I find myself squaring off with a man dressed in black from head to toe. He's got a balaclava over his head and goggles over that, keeping me from even seeing his eyes.

He launches himself at me and I spin to the side, throwing a hard elbow behind me. I connect with the man's head and hear him grunt, the impact jolting me all the way to my shoulder. Knowing I have scant seconds to move, I drop to the ground as the man's fist slices through the air where my face had been a moment before. I drive my hand upward and deliver a hard blow to the man's groin. He doubles over with a loud "oomph."

I use the moment to scramble backward and get out of his range and get back to my feet. The man has mostly recovered, though he's moving a little more gingerly. We square off again and my body tenses, readying for the attack. But then I feel somebody behind me a moment before I hear the footstep on the hardwood floor. My eyes widen and my stomach clenches as I start to turn.

It's too late, though. Something blunt comes crashing down on the back of my head. There's a blinding flash of pain and I'm driven to my knees. Points of light burst in the darkness behind my eyes and the room starts spinning around me. Waves of dizziness wash over me and then the ground is rushing up to meet me…

"Hurry up," a gruff male voice says. "Let's go, let's go."

My eyes flutter open and I find myself laying on the floor of my war room. Fragments of green glass from a wine bottle are arrayed on the ground around me, glittering in the light. My head is throbbing, and I feel like I'm going to be sick. I lie there, my cheek pressed to the floor, unable to think straight. Unable to move. Every inch of my body hurts. It's as if after they knocked me out, they worked me over.

"She's awake," one of the men in black growls.

"Doesn't matter. She'll be dead soon enough," the second one says.

I watch helplessly as they begin setting things on fire around my room, staging it to look like an accident. The smell of smoke fills my nose, and I can already feel the heat from the flames that are taking hold. I watch as bits of charred and flaming paper drift to the ground, igniting piles of other papers the men had laid out.

They take off their balaclavas and goggles then stare down at me with smug smiles on their faces.

"You take care of yourself now, sweetheart," the first man says, his voice colored with what sounds like an Australian accent.

"Let's go," says the other.

They rush out of the room and all I can do is helplessly watch the room around me burning. The smoke is thick and fills my nose, making me cough—an action that makes me cry out in pain. Darkness creeps in at the edges of my vision. I try to fight it, but I'm not strong enough and it's not long before it claims me…

I jump to my feet. My body is trembling and I'm gripped by the icy fist of fear my memories wrought. Nothing about the night of the fire is what I thought it was. It wasn't some drunken accident. It wasn't my fault. The Thirteen sent men here to kill me. And they almost succeeded. Jesus, they almost succeeded.

I lean back and take a long swallow of wine, replaying the events of that night over and over again, letting it sink in. I'm overwhelmed by a wave of fear, but more than that, of anger. This is never going to end. They'll keep sending men. Keep trying to kill me. They will never stop coming.

The realization hits me hard enough to take my breath away. And I'm not sure what I'm going to do about it.

EPILOGUE

Undisclosed location; Washington DC

"YOUR MEN FAILED," HE SAYS.

"I'm aware of that."

"The Wilder women are harder to kill than you thought."

"It would appear so."

I sit back in my chair and cross one leg over the other, doing my best to keep my temper in check. I fold my hands and rest them on top of my knee simply to keep myself from clenching them into fists. The man sitting behind his desk across from me is comfortable in his own power and believes everybody answers to him. He believes he's a king and everybody sitting in the chairs I am now are his servants.

I would love nothing more than to pull the pistol in my shoulder holster and put two rounds in his face. But I know if I did that, I would bring hell down on my head. I would be on the run and looking over my shoulder for the rest of my life, and to be frank, I've grown very comfortable with the life I've built for myself here. I have a solid reputation, more money than I can possibly spend in my life, and all I want is more. More money. More women. More power. I want more. And the only way I'm going to keep accruing all those things is to work with people like the man across from me. Or rather, work for them. As detestable as it is.

But I want an office just like this. Not the obviously expensive hand-crafted bookcases, the Persian rugs, or the massive and intricately carved cherry wood desk. The desk was carved out of one solid piece of wood. It wasn't put together with screws and bolts. It's a beautiful piece that seems to radiate with authority. I don't need the photos of myself with celebrities and politicians that line the walls. Nor do I need the expensive and elaborate gifts from foreign dignitaries that cover nearly every surface in his office.

No, what I want is the power this office conveys. You step through the door, and you can feel the power. You can smell it. When you walk into his office, you immediately know you're in the presence of a man who wields tremendous power and influence. A man who's so very well connected that he somehow survived the purge in the wake of the Wilder women dropping a daisy cutter on his organization.

"What are you going to do to rectify the situation?" he asks.

I frown and consider my next words carefully. He's not going to like hearing them, but he needs to hear them anyway. He pays me in part to counsel him. The other part is for strategic planning and wet work, but he also wants my advice.

"If you want my advice, you'd be wise to let it go," I tell him. "You'd be better off leaving the Wilder women be. Stop pursuing Kit and stop trying to murder Blake."

"And why would I do that?"

"Because the more you antagonize them, the more attention you draw to yourself," I tell him. "And you know Blake Wilder is the type who does not give up. If she decides she's had enough and sets her sights on finding you, she will. Look what she and her sister did to your organization. If you keep pushing her, it may come back to bite you."

"I wouldn't have to worry about it if your men could do their jobs properly," he replies, his tone cold.

"Sir, I have to say—"

He slams his fist down on his desk so hard it rattles everything on top of his desk. He turns his face to me, his lips curled back in a sneer. I figured this was going to be his reaction, but he needed to hear the truth anyway.

"Shut up. I won't hear your counsel right now," he snaps. "Those women cost me more than you can even calculate. They delivered a blow to my organization that will take years to rebuild. If it can be rebuilt at all. They've cost me a fortune, ruined plans I had in the works, and destroyed everything I have been working toward. They have to die."

"I hear you. But maybe you can take a step back—just for now. Give things a chance to cool down. Give them a chance to let their guard down," I tell him. "Eventually, if they're not running for their lives, they'll get comfortable. Complacent. Eventually, Kit will come back to Seattle to be with her sister. That's when you should strike. Kill two birds with one stone."

"That could take years."

"Play the long game, sir. A little immediate gratification might feel good in the moment. But it could lead to bigger problems down the line," I point out. "If you wait until there are fewer eyes on Blake Wilder, it will feel just as good to take her out. And it will help keep you out of harm's way and your hands clean."

"We wouldn't be here right now if you and your men were something close to competent," he growls. "If you and your men were competent, the Wilder woman would be dead now and we would be able to operate as normal."

"Sir, I—"

He waves me off and I fall silent. He's not in the mood to be contradicted. The man is impulsive, full of himself, and when he's in a bad mood, prone to do stupid things. Like now. I'm sure he's going to order me to plan another op. I don't think it's a good idea so soon after our last attempt on Blake's life. But the man wants what he wants, and I am merely a slave to his whims and wishes.

He stares at me in a contemptuous silence for a long moment. I'm half-convinced he's going to tell me to plan it now. But he takes a deep breath and lets it out slowly and I can see some small bit of anger draining from his face.

"These two women will need to be dealt with," he says.

"I agree. But it's a matter of time and place, sir," I reply. "This is neither the time nor the place. We need to be smart about this, sir."

"Get out," he says. "I'm tired of looking at you."

I give him a nod as I stand, then leave his office. I consider the fact that he didn't order another hit on Blake Wilder a win. He obviously didn't want to. He wants them dead sooner, rather than later. After everything that went down and the resulting difficulties the organization has faced, he's become obsessed with the Wilder women. They're all he seems to talk or think about. They are taking over his entire life. His obsession with them is understandable in some ways, but it's also frightening and reckless in others.

But I was able to calm him down and head him off this time. I just wonder how long I'm going to be able to do that.

AUTHOR'S NOTE

I hope you're enjoying the second season of Blake Wilder FBI Mystery Thriller. My intention is to give you a thrilling adventure and an entertaining escape with each and every book.

Being a new indie writer is tough. However, your support has helped tremendously. I don't have a large budget, huge following, or any of the cutting edge marketing techniques. So, all I kindly ask is that if you enjoyed this book, please take a moment of your time and leave me a review and maybe recommend the book to a fellow book lover or two. This way I can continue to write all day and night and bring you more books in the Blake Wilder FBI Mystery Thriller.

Also, don't forget to check out my Pax Arrington and Olivia Knight FBI Mystery Thriller. By the way, if you find any typos or want to reach out to me, feel free to email me at egray@ellegraybooks.com

Your writer friend,
Elle Gray

ALSO BY
ELLE GRAY

Olivia Knight FBI Mystery Thrillers

Book One - New Girl in Town

Blake Wilder FBI Mystery Thrillers

Book One - The 7 She Saw

Book Two - A Perfect Wife

Book Three - Her Perfect Crime

Book Four - The Chosen Girls

Book Five - The Secret She Kept

Book Six - The Lost Girls

Book Seven - The Lost Sister

A Pax Arrington Mystery

Free Prequel - Deadly Pursuit

Book One - I See You

Book Two - Her Last Call

Book Three - Woman In The Water

Book Four- A Wife's Secret